the art
of
escaping

the art
of
escaping

Erin Callahan

Amberjack Publishing
New York | Idaho

AMBERJACK
PUBLISHING

Amberjack Publishing
1472 E. Iron Eagle Dr.
Eagle, ID 83616

Names: Callahan, Erin, author.
Title: The art of escaping / Erin Callahan.
Description: New York : Amberjack Publishing, [2018] | Summary: When Mattie, seventeen, seeks out the reclusive Miyu, daughter of a famed escapologist, to indulge her secret desire to learn the craft, it leads to a friendship with classmate Will, who bears a huge secret of his own.
Identifiers: LCCN 2017057654 (print) | LCCN 2018005270 (ebook) | ISBN 9781944995669 (ebook) | ISBN 9781944995652 (paperback : alk. paper)
Subjects: | CYAC: Escapes (Amusements)--Fiction. | Magic tricks--Fiction. | Secrets--Fiction. | High schools--Fiction. | Schools--Fiction. | Recluses--Fiction. | Family life--Rhode Island--Fiction. | Rhode Island--Fiction.
Classification: LCC PZ7.1.C3153 (ebook) | LCC PZ7.1.C3153 Art 2018 (print) | DDC [Fic]--dc23
LC record available at https://lccn.loc.gov/2017057654

Cover Design: Faceout Studios & Stepheny Miller

Printed in the United States of America.

For Troyson.

*For talking me into this writer-gig in the first place,
and for making my senior year one of my favorite years.*

(Fri, Apr 13, 5:22 p.m.)

Will:

>Hey.

Mattie:

>Hey yourself. What's up?

Will:

>I just finished it.

Mattie:

>Ugh. And now you know exactly why you shouldn't have talked me into taking a Creative Nonfic class.

Will:

>Au contraire, Mattie-O. I quite enjoyed it.

Mattie:

>But???

Will:

>I didn't say but.

Mattie:

>I know you. There's a but coming. I can feel it.

>Hello????

Will:

>Ok ok. There's maybe some stuff you left out.

Mattie:

>Like what?

Will:

>It's not your fault. It was a while ago and you weren't there for ALL of it.

Mattie:
>Fear not, I'm going to write some foot-
notes for you.

Mattie:
>Footnotes? What the f
>Shit hang on Stella's calling.

Will:
>Groovy. I'll just be here. Writing my
footnotes.

(Fri, Apr 13, 5:31 p.m.)

Mattie:
>Sorry I'm back. She wanted to make sure
we're still on for dinner.

Will:
>Why doesn't she just text?

Mattie:
>Ha! I asked her that once and she said
something like "you never know what you'll
hear if you call instead"

Will:
>Oh my god.

Mattie:
>I know! Can you believe that?

Will:
>That girl is a hoot.

Mattie:
>We ARE still on for dinner right? You're
not going to spend the night writing footnotes or whatever?

Will:
>I suppose I can tear myself away for

sushi. *sigh*
>Plus Frankie borrowed Labyrinth and prom-
ised he would give it back tonight.

Mattie:

>Yay. Meet you outside Warner at 6:30?

Will:

>I'll be there.

(Fri, Apr 13, 5:39 p.m.)

Will:

>Hey Mattie-O?

Mattie:

>Yes Will?

Will:

>I heart you.

Mattie:

>I heart you too you big weirdo.

Cram school crawled by. I wanted to do well on my exams, but my mind was full of ropes and knots and chains and locks. I wondered how long it would take me to escape if someone chained me to the desk, or if I'd be doomed to listen to lectures for all of eternity. The thought made my fingers itch.

Yumiko passed me a note during the lecture, her eyes full of repressed giggles. "Naoki is the most beautiful boy I've ever seen. And so well-mannered, don't you think? I want him to ask me to the social on Friday. Do you think he will?" She'd drawn little hearts along the border.

Only one response came to mind. "I don't care."

— Akiko Miyake, Tokyo, April 3, 1973

Mattie vs. Tiny, Icky Things

I fought through a hangover on Saturday morning and forced myself into the shower. After washing bits of broken roofing shingle out of my hair, I downed two glasses of water, even though all I wanted to do was crawl back into bed and die. My important business of the day trumped nursing a hangover.

The drive to Grayton took less than twenty minutes. I parked on the street, right in front of the dilapidated villa that still managed to shine in a neighborhood full of McMansions. Fat drops of rain began to fall as I climbed out of the car, and I paused after a few steps down the stone footpath to take a deep breath.

Come on, Mattie. This is easy. The worst thing she can say is no.

The decrepit front door had shed black paint chips all over the porch, but it still boasted ornate woodcarvings of snakes and birds. I pressed the yellowed button and heard a deep *bing! bong!* echo through the house.

Then silence. I waited with my palms sweating and a headache throbbing above my eyebrows. More silence. I shut my eyes, massaged my temples, and rang the bell again. I turned and watched the rain fall on the tall grass in the front yard for a minute before ramming my determined index finger repeatedly against the yellowed button, sending a clamor of bells pealing beyond the door. Then I switched to rapping on the door, hoping an assertive knock would convey more urgency than my manic bell ringing.

Soft footfalls sounded inside the house and then abruptly stopped.

"Hello?" I asked.

A panel with a hummingbird carving flipped open and a pair of dark eyes peered out at me. "Hey, Girl Scout," said a throaty voice. "I don't want any cookies."

I blinked at the dark eyes. "Um, hello?"

"Beat it, Girl Scout."

The hummingbird panel snapped shut.

"Wait," I shouted as I resumed my frantic knocking. "Wait, Ms. Miyake. I'm a big fan of your mother. I just wanted to ask you a few questions."

The panel flipped back open. "If that's the case, I'm definitely not buying what you're selling. Get the fuck off my porch, Girl Scout."

The panel snapped shut again, and I stared at the hummingbird carving. Rain was pouring on the lawn now, and I couldn't bring myself to walk back down that stone path to Stella's car. I sank down onto a pile of paint chips and gazed through the tall grass.

I don't know how long I sat there. It could have

been hours, but it didn't feel like sitting on the roof drunk on bourbon. My mind didn't wander into unpleasant territory. It stayed focused on the rain and the buzz of the grasshoppers, the feel of paint chips as I rolled and cracked them between my fingers, and the soreness of my ass against the wooden slats of the porch. And then I thought about Akiko.

I pictured a seventeen-year-old girl, dressed in a quintessential school uniform with a sailor-style collar, pushing open the door of a magic shop in Tokyo and bullying the middle-aged magician behind the counter into making her his new assistant.

Then I pictured a twenty-year-old woman stepping onto American soil with sensible shoes and a visitor's visa, even though she planned to never go back home. I imagined her disembarking from a trans-Pacific ship, because it seemed more romantic than arriving by plane and landing in some dingy airport in California. But I suppose there was something poetic about that as well. An airplane brought her to the land where her career would truly begin, and another airplane would end it.

I didn't even notice when the hummingbird panel flipped open again. "I thought I told you to get off my porch."

"I believe your exact words were, 'Get the fuck off my porch, Girl Scout.'" I could have sworn I heard just a flicker of laughter behind the door.

"How long are you going to sit there?"

I shrugged. "I'm pretty comfortable."

"I don't really like cops," she huffed. "Don't make me call them."

"It's not like I'm bothering you. I'm just sitting here."

"You sitting there *is* bothering me."

"Then come out here and talk to me."

"I don't spend much time outside. And especially not on the porch."

"I can see why. You should really sweep up all these paint chips."

The hummingbird panel remained open, but I heard footsteps leaving and then returning. The door creaked open just long enough for her to toss a broom and dustpan onto the porch.

"If you clean up the porch, I'll invite you to tea." With that, the panel snapped shut.

I picked up the broom and dutifully swept the dirt, dust, and paint chips into the dustpan before returning to my seat. The rain stopped and started again, then the door slowly creaked open. I rose from my seat, but there was no sign of her. I pulled the door all the way open and peered into the house.

"Hello?" My voice echoed through the cavernous foyer. I glanced up at the cathedral ceiling and exposed wood beams as I stepped over the threshold. I heard rattling coming from the hallway to my right and headed in that direction.

"You're late," she said when I entered the dining room. Two teacups and a teapot sat on the table.

"What happened to my formal invitation?" I asked.

"It was implicit, not formal. Sit."

I took a seat in a stiff chair across from a thirty-something Asian woman. Her thin lips formed a perfect horizontal line, but her expression was far from blank. She glared at me like I was spoiled, soft. A marshmallow ready for roasting. I picked up my steaming teacup and burned my fingers.

"Ow," I mouthed.

One corner of her lips curled upward. "I don't use milk or sugar."

"It's fine. Thanks for the tea, Ms. Miyake."

She bristled. "Don't call me that."

"Then you should probably tell me your first name."

"Miyu," she said before taking a sip of scorching tea.

"And you're Akiko Miyake's daughter." I felt my face slip into a goofy expression of reverence before I burned my tongue on a tentative sip of tea. "I have so many questions, I don't even know where to start. I mean, what was she like?"

Her glare intensified. "I bet you think I'm so lucky. That I had such a wonwderful childhood, raised by nannies who never lasted more than six months because they couldn't possibly live up to my mother's impossible standards. I bet you think I enjoyed spending countless hours backstage with my only friend. His name was Game Boy, by the way."

"Oh. Sorry." She'd guessed that my childhood had been more standard than hers and she wasn't wrong. Apparently, I didn't look like the type who'd grown up on the road with my primary caregiver in the spotlight.

"Whatever, Girl Scout."

"It's Mattie, actually."

She waved my name away. "I was going to call you Girl Scout until you got fed up with it and left."

"I don't care what you call me as long as you're willing

to talk about escapology."

She took another sip of tea and didn't seem the least bit fazed by the blazing heat. "You're younger than most of them."

"Most of who?"

She cleared her throat with a forceful cough. "You mean whom, not who. And I'm referring to the fans who show up here. There haven't been many in the past few years, but they're usually middle-aged. And male."

"Huh. Well, isn't it refreshing I don't fit the usual profile?"

"I don't think refreshing is the right word."

"Did she teach you?" I asked.

Miyu laughed. "Teach me what? How to call for room service? How to hail a cab at the age of four? How to buy painkillers on the black market?"

I saw right through her game, but I wasn't even close to my breaking point.

"Your mom's entire life was wrapped up in escapology. You must have picked up something along the way." I thought about my dad and the many hours of *Star Trek* I'd watched with him. "You wanted to bond with her, didn't you?"

She studied me as she drained the rest of her tea. "What exactly are you looking for? A mentor?"

I nodded. "I know it's a long shot, but I also know I won't reach the level I want on my own. There's only so much you can learn from guidebooks and YouTube videos."

"Why?"

"Why what?"

"Why do you want to learn the art of escapology?"
Why, indeed?

"Mattie? Are you all right?"
I don't know. Am I?

I certainly hadn't expected to end up in the guidance counselor's office during the last few hours of my junior year at Vincent Cianci Jr. Regional High School, having *a moment*. It wasn't quite a panic attack because I didn't feel like I was going to die, but my palms were clammy and a stubborn little knot had tightened in my chest and one of my ears was ringing like someone had very rudely struck a tuning fork right next to my head.

If I were a nineteenth-century housewife, some well-meaning doctor would say, *Oh, fiddlesticks. You've caught the hysteria. Time to pluck out your wandering womb.*

This particular *moment* had been brought on by a confluence of tiny, icky things. First, the god awful Successories posters hanging behind Ms. Simmons's desk telling me to *make it happen* and *walk the talk*. Then there was the little smudge of lipstick by the corner of Ms. Simmons's mouth, the single flaw in her otherwise put-together persona. Finally, there was the almighty trigger word—well-rounded. I hated that word.

"Anyway, as I was saying. A college is going to want to know right off the bat that you're well-rounded. So in addition to bringing your GPA up just a few tenths, I'd really like you to think about participating more next year. Throw yourself into some extracurriculars. That sounds doable, right?"

Her glistening blue eyes made my face twitch.

"No, actually. Not doable."

She blinked at me. "What?"

"Higher grades I can handle, but there's no way I'm spending a second more of my day here at school. Especially when no one who joins extracurriculars really cares about extracurriculars. They join them so they can look good on paper."

"I sincerely don't believe that's the only reason."

"Regardless, *I* don't care about extracurriculars. Joining one now so I can impress a college admissions board is completely disingenuous."

She took a deep breath and started bending a paperclip. "It's not disingenuous if it's something you enjoy. There must be something, Mattie. What about French Club? You took three years of French, didn't you?"

"I took two years, and I hated it. Besides, who cares about French these days? Everyone knows Spanish is the second language you should be learning."

"Okay," she said softly, "then Spanish Club."

"I don't speak Spanish."

"Math Team?"

"I barely passed Geometry last year."

"Debate Team?"

"I hate confrontation."

The paperclip she'd been torturing finally gave way and snapped in two. "Chess Team?"

"I hate competition."

"Mock Trial Team?"

"Yawn."

"Newspaper?"

"Double yawn."

"Yearbook?"

I stared at her. "That's a joke, right?"

"Maybe you could propose a new extracurricular to the Student Activities Committee."

I tried to picture my own handpicked extracurricular. Jazz Appreciation Team? Historical Non-Fiction Book Club? Kitschy Knickknack Collectors Alliance? Then, of course, there was that *other thing*. That thing I hid from everyone. Whenever I thought of someone like me saying that sacred e-word aloud, I imagined Akiko Miyake rolling over in her grave at Swan Point Cemetery. *Thou art not worthy, suburban millennial.*

"Wow. I'm truly honored, Ms. Simmons. But that sounds rather overwhelming. I think I'll pass."

"Mattie, I don't like to say things like this to students, but I don't think I have a choice with you. Sometimes . . . you have to play the game unless you want to go to some godforsaken party school for nonstarters."

I crossed my arms. "No thanks. I'll see how far I can get with my integrity intact. Besides, a party school could be fun. Who doesn't like parties?"

That was the moment her blue eyes finally stopped glistening, and she shooed me out of her office with a hall pass and pamphlet for Bristol College. Once I got my bearings, I realized I'd instinctively headed toward Liam's classroom. But I didn't want to walk in there looking like I was on the verge of a panic attack, so I hooked a left into the ladies' room and shut myself in a stall.

Sweet, sweet solitude. The moment you close the door of a public bathroom stall almost never fails to blow my mind. There's something almost sacred about it. It's like a breath of fresh, serene air except it usually smells a little bit like toilet.

I washed my hands without glancing in the mirror. I hadn't bothered to tame my mousy brown hair with a blow-dryer that morning or put concealer on the dark under-eye circles I'd inherited from my mom. I probably looked like a frizzy zombie, but there was zilch I could do about it.

At least my outfit wouldn't make me a target. I had on jeans, clean white socks, a red t-shirt with no graphics or slogans, and a generic black hoodie. It's not that I wanted to dress like a nondescript extra from a teenage-problem-of-the-week movie, I just couldn't quite bring myself to wear anything from my collection of vintage dresses to school. The crown jewel of my collection was a blue and white party dress from the '50s with cap sleeves and a Peter Pan collar. I generally preferred the fashions of the Jazz Age to midcentury-modern, but I didn't have the cash to buy a dress from that era and refused to settle for a contemporary knockoff. I pictured myself wearing the party dress while trying to dig a fat chemistry textbook out of my locker and almost laughed out loud.

I took one last serene breath and forced myself back into the hall. I found Liam hunched over his desk, scowling and scribbling on a notepad. He had his closed fist pressed against his forehead, as if he planned to punch himself in the face once his frustration reached its peak.

"Your chicken scratch looks fascinating. But can I suggest a laptop?"

"Huh?" He looked up at me but kept his fist against his forehead. "Judas Priest, Mattie, I didn't even hear you come in," he said with just a hint of his New Zealand accent. "Well . . . One more grueling year almost over."

"Thank fucking god." I tried to come up with something more insightful, but the word *well-rounded* was ringing in my ears again.

He squinted at me. "What happened?"

"Ms. Simmons sat me down for a chat."

Liam leaned back in his chair and propped his feet up on his desk. "That woman is exhausting. She smells lovely and is strikingly pretty, but she's utterly exhausting."

I realize most students don't swear casually in front of their history teachers and most teachers don't disclose co-worker crushes to their students. But Liam and I have had this dynamic since the day I accosted him about a note he wrote on one of my exams. He claimed my sentimental hero worship of Sacajawea was clouding my critical thinking, and I informed him that he was a joyless misogynist. He laughed and upped my B to an A for "having the ovaries to call a forty-five-year-old man a misogynist to his face."

"What did she want?" he asked.

"I don't know. She rambled on for, like, ten minutes about liberal arts colleges, extracurriculars, and well-roundedness."

"She wants you to pad your resume?"

"I think that was the general idea."

"Hmmm. Can't you say you're the sole research assistant for a soon-to-be-famous historian?"

I snorted. "That's a well-rounded lie."

"If it makes you feel better, I think most colleges are just as impressed with independent interests. You've got history . . . what else?"

I shrugged.

"Mattie, what do you do when you're not at school?"

"Hang out with Stella?"

"Okay, we can work with that . . . call yourself a devoted sidekick to a vapid overachiever."

"Wow. So helpful. And Stella's not vapid."

"Kidding, kidding. What else?"

"I also collect quirky antiques and vintage clothing, watch *Star Trek*, listen to old jazz records . . ."

Liam looked at me with his lips all scrunched into the corner of his mouth.

"What?"

"This is off topic, but has it ever occurred to you that all of your interests involve consumption, rather than creation?"

"Et tu, Liam?" I whined. "You mean I don't make anything, right? You sound just like my mom."

Whenever I told her I was going to spend an evening dusting my jazz records or watching *Star Trek* with my dad, my mom would say, "When I was in high school, I started a band and we lugged all our equipment fifteen miles through the snow so we could play at some shitty rec center and then lugged it back home again. Uphill both ways."

"I really do need to meet your mum one of these days," Liam said with a dreamy look in his eyes. "She sounds like a positively fascinating woman."

"God, Liam. Ew. And I didn't come in here to talk about my mom."

"Sorry, sorry. Well . . ." He steepled his fingers under his scruffy chin and then shrugged. "I'm sure you'll figure it out."

I blinked at him. "'You'll figure it out?' That's all the teacherly advice you have for me?"

"Mattie, it's the last day of school. I dispensed the last of my teacherly advice back in December. You need to time your crises better."

My phone vibrated in my back pocket, letting me know that I needed to be back in homeroom in two minutes. "That's my cue. So help me god, Liam, you better come up with something better than 'have a nice summer.'"

He narrowed his eyes and tapped a pen against his desk. "Enjoy the solstice?"

"Ugh."

I stalked off to my last homeroom session of the year and found Stella sitting in her unofficially reserved seat. Her already sunny face, framed by two blonde pigtails, brightened a few more lumens when she spotted me. The effect was blinding.

I met Stella in sixth grade, the year she convinced her on-the-verge-of-divorce parents to stop home-schooling and send her to public school. Dressed in a sweater vest and knee socks, she was practically a swan among the slouchy, publicly educated riffraff. But she was also desperate for someone to guide her through the promised land of semi-normal kid-dom. I somehow talked her into hanging out with me that afternoon, and because she didn't own a TV, subjected her to a pedantic PowerPoint presentation on all the various *Star Trek* series. Whereas most eleven-year-old girls would have run home screaming, Stella had just smiled while she sat cross-legged on my bed and said, "Neat. This is fun." My head had pretty much exploded.

"We're almost there," she said. "I can see the light at the end of the tunnel, Ginger."

"Ugh," I moaned. "I can't handle nicknames right now. Especially nicknames derived from embarrassing hair-dye-related incidents."

Her million-dollar smile dropped to a cartoonish frown, like the blue sad face they use to teach preschoolers about emotions. "What happened?"

"Am I that much of an open book?" I whined. "I sicken myself. Anyway, Ms. Simmons pulled me out of seventh period."

"Oh my god. Ginge—I mean Mattie—please tell me you're still on track for graduation next year."

"Christ, Stella, I'm not even close to risking not graduating. As always, I'm solidly in the middle, where I belong."

"So what did she want?"

"I don't even know. It was all extracurriculars . . . blah blah blah . . . well-roundedness . . . blah blah blah."

Stella opened her mouth to say something but held back.

"What?"

She shook her head. "Nothing."

Meadow Winters breezed in and took her unofficially reserved seat in front of me. Today, she was sporting what Stella referred to as her "off-duty model hair," with her glossy locks piled on top of her head, like a delicate nest for a few cartoon songbirds.

"Hey, Mattie," she said as she pulled out her phone.

"Hey, Meadow."

"What are you guys up to this summer?"

"I'm working at Café Italiano and—"

She took a two-second break from scrolling, scrolling, scrolling to say, "Oh my god, they have ah-mazing gelato."

"Yeah, it's okay." The tiny state of Rhode Island didn't have much to offer the world besides hot wieners and rich people with yachts, but at least we had decent gelato. "Stella's abandoning me for St. Joe's," I added.

Yes, my best friend, the traitorous overachiever, had been accepted to the prestigious summer session at St. Joseph's Academy, a private high school that opened its hallowed halls each summer to motivated public high school seniors so they could experience a small taste of college-prep life. Only two other students from our class had been accepted—a guy from Stella's AP classes who I'd dubbed Marlon *Blando* because he shouted *Stellll-ahhhh* literally every goddamn time he saw her, and this fourteen-year-old genius named Frankie who'd skipped two grades and had zero friends.

"Oh, wow. Congrats, Stella," Meadow said as she finally looked up from her phone and turned to face us, and by us I mean Stella. "I could never waste a summer going to school, but good for you."

Though I agreed St. Joe's sounded about as much fun as a root canal, Meadow's backhanded compliment made me cringe. Stella must have seen me grimace because she flashed me a smile that said *play nice*.

"I was just telling Mattie that it's not like regular school," Stella cheerfully explained to Meadow. "We get to read books the teachers wouldn't dare cover in public school, and we work on independent projects . . ."

Stella trailed off as Meadow nodded and waved to Will Kane when he trotted into the classroom with his tousled brown hair and sinewy basketball player limbs. He took the seat next to Meadow and tossed his messenger bag on the desk.

"What's shakin', kids?"

Even though Will had said "kids," as in plural, Stella and I both knew he was really talking to Meadow. Will had been dating Meadow's best friend, Betsy Appleton, since middle school, which, for most people my age, was before the dawn of time. As Will typed out something on his phone with lightning speed, he and Meadow struck up a conversation about an end of the year party at some rich kid's beach house and ignored Stella and me.

Okay, here's where TV always gets it wrong. Meadow didn't need to flip her hair and sneer at me or sprinkle me with epithets or shove me into a locker to let me know that me and my BFF didn't matter to her, and that we didn't matter to anyone who matters. The dismissive little nod she gave Stella the second Will plopped down at his desk said it all, loud and clear.

You might even say this was worse, because this was nothing. Insults and epithets would at least be something. But this was all Meadow thought Stella and I deserved from her.

I'd become generally impervious to that kind of shit. Sometimes, though, I could see it wearing on Stella, grinding her down ever so slightly. I didn't think it would ever break her, but six years of it had dulled her shine. And that made me want to stick a big, wet wad of gum in Meadow's off-duty model hair. Maybe I expected more from Meadow because we shared pre-high school history. Will had grown up in Grayton, the town over from Tivergreene, and I doubted he even knew my name.

I took a deep breath and shoved my notebook into my backpack. Deep down I knew semi-invisibles like Stella and me had a better chance of escaping Cianci Regional unscathed and becoming reasonably well-adjusted adults. High school traumatized some people and spoiled others, like Meadow and Will. They took for granted an endless supply of sycophants and self-esteem boosters, and never learned the subtle art of not giving a shit.

Stella heaved a dreary little sigh, bringing another grimace to my face. I'd expected the last hours of my junior year to be a breeze at best and a tolerable bore at worst. But Ms. Simmons's command to sand down all my sharp edges plus Liam's completely unhelpful burnout multiplied by Meadow and Will had ruined it and left my palms sweaty, my chest full of sharp little icicles, and my ears all ringy.

And the worst was still to come. The Stella-less summer heading my way would drive me from the comforts of my jazz records and knickknacks and vintage dresses and into the dining room of a resentful stranger who insisted on calling me "Girl Scout."

The magician stared at me from across the counter of his magic shop in Shinjuku. "Assistant?" He scratched his balding head with his stubby sausage fingers. I wondered how he pulled off sleight-of-hand tricks with those monstrosities. "You're too young. Just a school girl."

I tugged at the sailor collar of my uniform and cursed the fact that I'd taken the metro straight from school. "I'm old enough," I croaked as I wiped a bead of sweat from my brow. "And I live with my family so you don't even have to pay me." I resisted scratching an itch below my nose and watched him squint at me. "I just want to get my feet wet. Soaking, in fact. I want to be knee deep in escapology."

– Akiko Miyake, Tokyo, January 24, 1974

Mattie and the All-Purpose Key

I'm not ashamed to admit that I'd never mowed a lawn before. Despite my mother's feminist leanings, our house followed a fairly traditional chore division. Besides, my dad loved mowing the lawn and then sitting on the back porch with a beer or a glass of expensive scotch to admire his work.

But now, my budding career as an escapologist hinged on my promise to mow Miyu's neglected lawn and her promise to at least *consider* training me. That was the best I could get out of her after she'd bristled at my offer to repaint the front door or power-wash the stone walkway.

"All these things," she'd explained, "send a clear message of *keep away*. But the lawn has been a point of contention between me and the neighbors. If shorter grass means I don't have to hear them bitch for a few weeks every time I go out to the mailbox, I might be open to it."

After my early shift at Café Italiano, I flew over to Miyu's in Stella's Bug and pulled the dusty push mower out of the garage. The home's expansive lawn seemed endless, but within a couple hours I'd managed to take most of it down, right up to the edges of a swampy swimming pool. It didn't look nearly as perfect as my dad's lawn, and my mowing lines curved and wobbled. I hoped Miyu wouldn't mind as long as the lawn looked like a lawn instead of a prairie.

Exhausted and drenched in sweat, I shuffled across the porch. Miyu opened the door before I even had a chance to ring the bell.

"Dining room," she barked.

I nodded and followed her. An epic spread of padlocks and boxes of all sizes covered the dining room table.

"We'll start small with one of the essentials."

"Lock picking," I said.

"Pick up the Westin four pin," she commanded.

I scanned the table for brand names, but saw only a few. None of them were Westin.

Miyu sighed and picked up an imposing hunk of stainless steel that looked like it weighed at least two pounds. She pulled a bobby pin from her pocket and handed it to me. "This is your all-purpose key. Keep it on you at all times. Now have a seat."

I sat in the same stiff chair I'd sat in during our awkward tea party. She passed me the lock, and I immediately shoved the bobby pin inside and began poking around.

"I don't care what you've seen on TV, Girl Scout.

That is never going to work."

"I just have to press the right pins, right?" I shoved the bobby pin further into the lock but succeeded only in producing some clicking and scraping noises.

Miyu snatched the Westin four-pin out of my hand and pulled a bobby pin from her own dark hair. She pried the pin apart, straightening the bend, and then snapped it in half. "When picking a lock, you will almost always need two tools—a pick and a torsion wrench. And if you hear anyone refer to it as a tension wrench, you should slap them straight across the face."

"Noted."

With her newly-made pick and torsion wrench, Miyu defeated the Westin four-pin in under six seconds.

"Awesome," I whispered. "You must've done that with your mom a million times, right? How fast could she do it? Did she pick locks just for fun? Or did she never carry keys so she could always get practice in?"

"No questions," she snapped.

I gulped. "Sorry."

Miyu explained the basics of lock picking and, after handing back the re-locked Westin four-pin, stared at me with crossed arms. Without a hint of humor, she said, "You will not leave until you've picked every single lock on this table."

I tried to hide my laughter but failed. "Wow. I get that you're trying to pull off the whole hard-as-nails mentor with a well-hidden heart of gold thing, but I have a family. And a summer job. If I don't show up at home or at work, someone will call the police. And I know you're not a fan of cops."

"Fine, I'll rephrase." Her lips curled into an unnerving smile. "If this truly is important to you, you will figure out a way to stay here until you've picked every lock."

I rolled my eyes. "Well, when you put it that way."

With occasional impatient instruction from Miyu, it took me almost an hour to pick the Westin four-pin. The sun was already beginning to set, so I texted my mom to let her know I was watching a movie marathon at Meadow Winters's house and wouldn't be home until late.

This, of course, was the first of many lies.

By 10:30 p.m., I'd cracked less than a quarter of the locks on the table. Blisters were rearing their ugly heads on my fingertips, and I had to pee.

"I need a bathroom break," I said to Miyu. "And I'm starving." With the exception of the two minutes it took her to retrieve a paperback from the living room, she hadn't left the table and had continued to give me exasperated pointers throughout the night.

"I will be very displeased if you relieve your bladder or bowels on that chair," she said. "Bathroom is down the hall to the left. And I'll throw a frozen pizza in the oven."

Feeling minimally refreshed after peeing and scarfing two slices of cardboard parading as pizza, I returned to the table. The night became a blur of locks and pins, picks and torsion wrenches. Sometime around midnight, I tackled the last piece on the table—a locked jewelry box with gold inlay. My fingers ached, and my brain was running on autopilot, but after some frustrated and sleepy picking, the box popped open with a satisfying click.

"Holy crap," I said as I gazed at my handiwork. A pair of hand-carved jade earrings rested on the silk cushion inside the box. The sight of them made my heart hiccup. I pictured Akiko in one of the few television interviews she'd given during her career. She smiled and tugged at one of those jade earrings when the reporter asked how she became interested in escapology. A very young Miyu had been flitting around, humming the *Pokémon* theme song and making silly faces at the camera.

Miyu, now the polar opposite of that energetic little kid, snored from the chair across from me, her head dipped back at an awkward angle.

"Miyu, wake up. I'm done."

She snapped to with a snort and studied the table. "Took long enough. I mean well done, Girl Scout. Now go home and get some sleep. And take a shower for god's sake. You reek."

I drove home on a rush of adrenaline.

All my victory adrenaline had faded by the time I cracked open the back door and tiptoed through the kitchen in the wee hours of the morning. But after giving Guinan, our ancient Shiba Inu, a good scratch behind the ears, I still had just enough energy left for a sad little ritual I like to call Mattie Pokes the Bear. The bear wasn't an actual bear with fur, claws, and picnic breath; it was a toxic trio of twenty-something dudes who I found sprawled over the couches in the living room watching late night TV. They'd probably gone to a bar for cheap beer and come back because my parents were tolerant, and because they didn't have anywhere cooler to be.

My brother Kyle, his best friend Connor, and their handpicked runt of the litter, Austin, were perfectly content to ignore me and keep their glazed eyes glued to the tube. But I would not stand for it.

Phase One of Sad Ritual: Say something obnoxious to ruffle the toxic trio.

"How was your evening, slackers? I'm sure you guys needed to unwind after a long day of being a burden to society."

"I have an actual job, man," Austin protested.

Kyle squinted at me. He was wearing the same pair of flannel pajama pants he had worn all day. And the day before. And the day before that. "You were out late."

Connor just glared at me from the couch, probably because he knew what was coming. My opening line stirred the bear from its hibernation cave, but now I was going to get all up in its snout.

Phase Two of Sad Ritual: Hone in on the real target.

I plopped down on the couch next to Connor, taking up almost two full cushions so he had to scrunch himself to one side to avoid spooning with me.

"Why do you smell like gasoline and sod?" he asked. "Do they have you doing landscaping at the café now?

"You had a morning shift," Kyle said slowly. "Where have you been?"

"Worked a double." *Lying liar-face.*

"But the café closes at nine."

I shrugged, and it probably came off as aloof, but I really just couldn't think of a good excuse and was secretly cursing myself for being such a dismal liar.

"Oh," Connor said. "Oh, I see what this is all about. She wants us to think she was out with a special someone, but if we asked who, she'd probably tell us we don't know him because he's from Canada or some bullshit."

That earned a laugh from both Kyle and Austin. In the background, the late-night host made a crack about politically correct hippie-Nazis.

"Give me the remote," I said. "This guy is an ass."

"You brought this on yourself, Mattie," Connor said. "You don't get to change the subject. So. Anyway. As I was saying, the only person you ever hang out with is that preppy weirdo with the nasally voice . . ."

"Stella's actually pretty cool," Austin chimed in.

Both Connor and Kyle told Austin to shut up before Connor continued. "She's at brainiac bootcamp for the summer, so I know exactly how your night played out. First, you picked out the perfect poem by Emily Dickinson or Sylvia Plath or some other depressive chick to post on LifeScape. After that, you walked around the mall but didn't buy anything. Then you picked up a pint of Ben & Jerry's, snuck it into a chick flick, and seasoned it with your sad, lonely-girl tears."

I smiled, not just because Connor would never in a million years guess that I'd spent the night learning to pick locks, but also because he'd left me a picture-perfect opening.

"It must be hard for you to imagine a satisfying night alone considering you and Kyle have been co-dependent since you were five."

"Yeah. It's such a burden having friends. You know, more than one."

This is the point at which I'd usually feign boredom and stalk off to my room to listen to jazz records with my giant headphones and dig into some fantastic piece of historical nonfiction. But my sore fingers and cramped shoulders and adrenaline hangover must've brought out something mischievous. And maybe even a little dark.

"Do you really have friends, Connor? You and Kyle are psychologically dependent on each other, but that's more like some sick symbiosis than friendship. And everyone else you hang out with tolerates you only because you're always in close proximity to Kyle."

Austin snickered from the armchair, and Kyle shook his head.

"You're on the rag right now, aren't you?" Connor said, still cool as a cucumber. "You can be such a little cun—"

"Connor, knock it off," Kyle said.

Phase Three of Sad Ritual: Let big bro do his big bro thing.

"Dude, she started it."

"She always starts it. And then you always feed into it."

I flashed Connor my best Disney Princess smile before heading upstairs to collapse on my bed. "'Kay, g'night."

It probably looks like this ritual is all about me. But honestly—I swear—I did it for their benefit. Austin got to point out he's the only one of the three who's gainfully employed, Connor got to be pissed off about something (which is the only thing that makes him happy), and Kyle got to feel like a classic big brother, straight out of a bad teen comedy.

And, yeah, fine. Maybe when you spend your schooldays being mostly ignored by your peers, this is the kind of fucked up attention you crave. I'm not a shrink, so I don't really know.

And, yeah, sometimes I probably took things too far with Connor. But it was like jumping into the deep end of the pool with water wings on. I knew he'd never say anything truly devastating to me because I still had a secret hanging over his head.

Many months ago, during a raging party my brother threw while my parents were in New Jersey, visiting my mom's favorite aunt, I heard a quick knock on my bedroom door. I looked up from my copy of *The Devil in the White City* just in time to see Connor slip into my room, his smirk dampened by one too many craft beers. Without a word, he pulled the book from my hands, extracted my giant headphones from my hair, and planted a soft kiss on my closed lips.

I probably should have pushed him away, stomped off, woken Kyle up from his drunken slumber on the bathroom floor, and told him his best friend had just made a pass at his kid sister. But the ugly truth is, I'd been wanting something like that to happen for a long while. So I leaned into him, and he wrapped his arms around me.

The making out part had been great. More than great, actually. Thrilling and safe and soothing and terrifying all at the same time. When I pulled his clothes off, I swear I forgot all about the time he'd said the Joan of Arc Halloween costume I'd slaved over for weeks made me look like a "faggy squire."

But the sex had been *meh* at best. Awkward enough to make me realize what a huge, irreversible mistake I'd made. When Connor asked me afterward if I was okay, I'd just smiled cryptically and the two of us tacitly agreed to never, ever speak of what had happened. No one, not even Stella, knew what had transpired between Connor and me, and I thanked the mystical forces of the universe that my brother never found out.

But none of the tiny, icky things, including Connor, were going to bother me on this particular night. Not when I'd mowed a prairie-like lawn to win over a recluse and then trounced a table full of tricky locks.

The magician and I stood backstage, ready for our inaugural performance at The Golden Pebble, a theater that sat an audience four times the size of the rinky-dink cabarets we were accustomed to. I wrapped my fingers around a lock of hair behind my ear and tugged. The sensation took the edge off my nerves, helping me to focus on the task ahead.

"What are you doing?" the magician whispered.

"Nothing," I snapped. "Just something I do when I'm nervous."

I tugged harder and prepared for the stage lights and a thousand pairs of eyes to bear down on me.

—Akiko Miyake, Tokyo, May 4, 1975

Mattie in Real LifeScape

I took a seat on an overturned crate in the storage-slash-break room at Café Italiano and pulled out my phone. As soon as I opened the LifeScape app, I was hit with a news feed that made my skin prickle. Everyone, including people I'm not even "friends" with, was asking about me. "Where's Mattie?" they wanted to know. "She hasn't posted anything in four days, six hours, and seventeen minutes. How are we supposed to keep tabs on her?" I powered off my phone and shakily exited the break room for the gelato counter.

"Marni had to leave to have a tooth pulled," my boss said. "I need you on the register for a bit."

I nodded and tried to rub the goose bumps off my arms. I attempted to ring up a customer, but found the screen at the register somehow displaying my LifeScape feed. "Did Mattie just shut off her phone?" people were asking. "Why would she do that?"

"Did you really shut off your phone?" the customer

33

erin callahan

asked. "How are your friends supposed to know what you ate for breakfast, or what your favorite memes are, or where you are on Friday night?"

I bolted from behind the counter and busted through the front door, scanning for places to hide as I scrambled down the cracked sidewalk. I half-ran, half-slid down an embankment on my worn-out sneakers and spotted Kyle's old tree house. I struggled up the rope ladder, beads of sweat dripping off my forehead and blurring my vision. I yanked the rope ladder up into the tree house, but it was no use. My LifeScape "friends" had found me and were poking their desperately curious claws through the hole in the floor and between the wooden slats of the fragile walls. I cowered in a corner, covering my face with my hands. "Why are you doing this?" I screamed. "Why do you even care? I have nothing to offer you, okay? There, I said it. I have nothing to offer, nothing even worth judging. My life is boring."

I awoke in a panic, realizing I'd had another of my recurring LifeScape nightmares. Still wearing my grubby clothes from the night before and now coated in sweat and a sheen of paranoia, I sat up and stared at my laptop screen. I resisted the urge to double check whether I'd logged out of my account as I climbed out of bed and headed for the bathroom to take a shower.

As we've already discussed, I'm not a shrink. But I possessed enough self-awareness to glean some insights from my LifeScape nightmares. The details of each dream might change from night to night, but two things were always the same. One, I was terrified of being looked at, scrutinized, put on display. And two, I was even more terrified that if someone took a good, hard look—like, got all up in my nooks and crannies and crevices—there'd be nothing to see, aside from some meticulously alphabetized jazz records and a collection of antique knickknacks in need of a good dusting.

I shuddered under the shower's scalding water. I'd officially crossed the line from consumption to creation, and now there *was* actually something to see. But my something wasn't playing co-ed volleyball or volunteering in Ecuador for spring break. My thing was weird. Dangerous. My thing required an explanation. My new hobby wouldn't earn me a flood of hearts and two thumbs up. It would earn me a blistering comment blast full of whys and GIFs of shocked faces.

"Mattie, I have laundry," my mom shouted through my bedroom door as I was getting dressed.

"Just a sec." I buttoned my jeans, adjusted my t-shirt, and opened the door.

She stormed in with a basket full of folded clothes, like a frowny cloud of disapproval dressed in a sweater set. "You realize it takes two seconds to pop your own dirty clothes in the washer, right?"

"But then I have to fold it," I whined.

Instead of dignifying my whining with a response, she changed the subject. "You look tired. Up late at Meadow's?"

Oh fuck, that's right. "Yeah. We started a horror movie

marathon around midnight."

"Ah. Watch anything interesting?"

"Not really. Just schlocky standards like *Nightmare on Elm Street* and one of the *Child's Play* sequels. I tried to get Meadow to watch *Vertigo*, but she didn't go for it."

I'm pretty sure I managed to say this without batting an eye, but inside I was tearing my own hair out and screaming *The lies! Dear god, the lies!*

"You know, I haven't seen Meadow around since you were in middle school."

Double fuck. I didn't want to reveal any fabricated details that might come back to haunt me later, so I just played the aloof teenager card and said, "Hm."

"I hope she's still a good influence."

"Ugh. Mom." This conversation clearly needed to be steered into new territory. "Dad home?"

"Had to do some emergency rewiring for one of his customers in Grayton. A power surge blew up a TV or microwave or something."

"Sounds exciting."

"Working at the café today?"

"Yeah. I have an afternoon to evening shift, and then I'll probably go out again. Or, you know, hang out at Meadow's."

"That's fine," she said. "But promise me that this week—yes, this week—you'll pick out a few colleges and line up some tours. The fall will be here before you know it."

"Hm. Hey, can I pull a Dad and go to trade school instead of college?"

She scowled at me. "I'm not having this conversation with you again. I'll be in my office."

My mom referred to her nook off the kitchen as her home office, but she spent most of her time in there listening to obscure post-punk records and reading back issues of *Bitch* magazine. My brother and I had dubbed it *the mom-cave*.

After narrowly avoiding another iteration of the College-Is-Not-An-Option Argument I'd had with my mom at least a dozen times, I drove Stella's Bug to Tivergreene's small center and took my post behind the gelato counter at Café Italiano. I stretched and cracked my wrists in preparation for a long shift of scooping.

"You need to refill the stracciatella," my boss remarked as she emerged from the walk-in freezer.

"It's still got one scoop left. I don't like to mix fresh stracciatella with the old stuff."

"Then clean it out. What if someone comes in here and wants two scoops."

"Then he or she should acquire some patience."

My boss rolled her eyes but dropped it. She didn't seem to mind my attitude as long as I kept it in check in front of customers.

The bell at the door jingled and Meadow Winters's best friend, Betsy Appleton, trotted into the café with the effortlessly cool Will Kane in tow. I tried not to flinch. Though I preferred scooping gelato to most of the summer job alternatives—junior camp counselor, lifeguard, photocopy slave, french fry bitch—the downside of working at Café Italiano was the occasional frequenting by students from Cianci Regional.

"Oh, hey." Betsy smiled at me as she approached the counter. "How's it going?"

Instead of answering, I asked, "Would you like to try our new strawberry basil gelato?"

Betsy laughed, and it sounded the way sunlight looks when it glitters on a golden lake. I suppressed a grimace.

"Um, sure. That sounds great," she said.

I handed sample spoons to both Betsy and Will. They mmmm'ed and nodded at me politely and then revealed themselves to be painfully boring by ordering vanilla and chocolate, respectively.

"I'm going to order an iced tea, too," Betsy said to Will. "You want a cappuccino or something?"

Will shook his head and lingered by the gelato counter for a few seconds, squinting at me. I raised my eyebrows, waiting for him to say something. He remained silent and finally waltzed off to join Betsy at the barista counter. At the time, I didn't give our brief staring contest a second thought. But in hindsight, I wonder if it was a moment of recognition. I wonder if, somehow, the two of us could sense what was coming.

After my mother said goodnight, I sprang out of bed, fully dressed, and pushed open my window. I shimmied out onto the fire escape, trying my best not to rattle it and wake the angry widow who lived on the second floor.

A cool breeze ruffled my hair. In less than an hour, I'd be onstage at a theater in Shimokitazawa. As I closed the window and stared back into my empty bedroom through the smudged glass, I wondered how many more times I'd have to sneak out of my own house to do what I loved most in the world.

— Akiko Miyake, Tokyo, September 18, 1975

A Footnote by Will With Two Ls

Moments of recognition. Entangled lives. Destiny!

What a beautiful, Mattie-esque sentiment. That's how her romantic historian's brain works. If a chance encounter precedes a full-scale invasion, it's a cosmic spark. The first trail marker on the path toward a life-changing destination. The first line of an epic poem. The first tinkling piano note of a jazz standard.

And maybe she's right about all those romantic notions. But I can tell you exactly what I was thinking as I stared at her just long enough to make it awkward.

Two things:

One: that gal needs to use more conditioner.

Two: more importantly, she doesn't care about her frizzy hair or my opinion because she doesn't give a muskrat's ass about what anyone thinks of her.

Turns out I was mostly wrong about the second one.

After I left Café Italiano with Betsy Appleton, my main squeeze, she drove us to Providence Place. She was the Bonnie to my Clyde, but the poor girl had no idea our relationship was a fraudulent criminal enterprise.

For the record, I fucking hate malls. All those candy-colored displays under blue fluorescent lighting make me yearn for black and white films and the golden glow of energy-sucking incandescent light bulbs. I don't want to contribute to the destruction of the planet, but some things, like lighting that doesn't give you a splitting headache, are sacred.

Betsy parked in the garage, expertly sliding into a compact car spot. She always drove with quiet sophistication, never too fast or too slow. Something about her driving posture was almost debonair—arms relaxed but still diligently at ten and two, shoulders back, neck elongated to swan-like proportions. Sometimes I wanted to buy her driving gloves and a headscarf and some of those big *Thelma & Louise* sunglasses and take glamour shots in my dad's prized '65 Shelby Cobra. But she'd end up making that toothy, I-ate-sunshine-for-breakfast face she makes in all her photos and ruin the mystique.

Betsy is the kind of good-but-not-too-good, pretty-but-not-too-pretty, smart-but-not-too-smart girl that other girls wish they could hate. They can't hate her because she might be the nicest person on the planet.

She reached over and clasped my hand, giving me a toned down version of the I-ate-sunshine-for-breakfast smile.

"You're quiet today. What are you thinking about?" she asked.

"Still thinking about that gelato," I said without skipping a beat. "So refreshing." Of course this was a lie. I was still thinking about Mattie and her frizzy hair and the zero muskrats' asses that she gave. And, as I always did in Betsy's car, I was picturing Betsy behind the wheel of a black Shelby Cobra, her cherry-red lips like a fresh scratch against her alabaster complexion. It killed me that she never wore cherry-red lipstick. Just pinkish gloss that smelled like grapefruit. The only girls at our school who wore real lipstick cut their hair like Bettie Paige, rolled their eyes when they got paired up with me for group assignments, and called me a "jock strap casualty" behind my back.

Betsy laughed. "I love that they use real vanilla. When I see all those little black flecks I feel like I'm eating real food instead of something gross and synthetic, you know?"

"Ab-so-tive-ly."

"Your coach wouldn't be mad about all the sugar and saturated fat?"

"Ha! He'd probably make me do a full hour of suicides and a thousand free throws just to compensate. But it's summer, so what he doesn't know won't kill him."

We rode the escalator up to the food court and took a seat at the Johnny Rockets counter. I dig nostalgia more than the average bear, but the fact that Johnny Rockets was in the mall basically negated the retro diner vibe.

Betsy's best friend, Meadow Winters, floated over to our stools with a pencil tucked stylishly behind one

43

ear, ready to take our order. For the record, Meadow floated everywhere she went, her size sevens always just whispering along the ground. Meadow and I remained on good terms because I was her BFF's arm candy, but, even now, I'd sooner jump off the Atwells Ave overpass into I-95 traffic than cross her. It must be her eyes. She has these intense hazel beauties rimmed with subtle black liner that I'm convinced could stop your ticker dead in its tracks if she looked at you the wrong way. Also, not many gals could put on a Johnny Rockets uniform and still look dressed to kill. Meadow rocked that bowtie and silly hat like they'd been handpicked by a personal stylist.

"What can I get you guys? Milkshakes?" Meadow asked.

"We already had dessert," Betsy explained. "Gelato at Café Italiano."

This prompted an ooohhh-aaahhh-OMG-fest that lasted, I shit you not, at least three full minutes. I like gelato as much as the next cat, but it hardly deserves three minutes' worth of vocal fry.

Again, I thought of Mattie. Despite being a gelato peddler, she clearly had more interesting things on her mind. Unreadable gals who gave zero muskrats' asses had no use for vocal fry or three-minute odes to dairy products.

While Betsy and Meadow moved on to discuss the evening's plans (a brief appearance at a weed dealer's party followed by breakfast-for-dinner at IHOP), I allowed myself to fantasize about skipping the shindig and hanging out with Mattie instead. I imagined the two of us speeding down I-95 to the seacoast in my dad's Shelby while she taught me how to stop being such a chickenshit pansy.

Here's where you might think Mattie was right. Me fantasizing about becoming her bosom buddy and trusted confidante could be a cosmic sign that the two of us somehow knew we were about to find ourselves in a cat's cradle. But the sad truth is this wasn't even close to the first time I'd daydreamed about a mythical friendship with someone I didn't even know.

It happened all the time. With the hipster girl who delivered pizza to my house. With the lady who sat in the last row of the crosstown trolley with an empty cat carrier. With the chubby guy who worked at the city library and wore suspenders to hitch up his ill-fitting skinny jeans. Every time I sat behind the kid with the green mohawk in Physics—and we're talking genuine *mo*hawk, not some half-hearted fauxhawk—I pictured the two of us getting splifficated on Kool Aid spiked with cheap vodka and TP-ing our teacher's house. Sometimes I even brought my semi-imaginary friends together in my mind. I figured the catless trolley rider would probably get a big ol' kick out of green mohawk kid. The three of us could take the trolley to Fox Point, enjoy the sea breeze, then steal a Chihuahua from the dog park for the lady's empty cat carrier.

On days when I wanted to tear off my own skin and wave it around like a wacky flag of desperation, my imaginary friends and I time traveled to imaginary places. Hipster pizza girl (I'd nicknamed her Val), chubby librarian (a.k.a. Schmitty) and I donned our finest, gunned the Delorean to eighty-eight and got our drink on at a charming little juice joint full of bootleggers and cats hip enough to know the password (the password, by-the-by, was "horsefeathers").

Val would sit on her perch at the bar, wrapped in a red cocoon coat with an ermine fur collar and threads of gold lamé that sparkled under the chandeliers. "You're on the up and up, bub," she'd say to me between sips of bathtub gin. "Stick with me and everything'll be Jake."

Schmitty would bob around on the dance floor, soft shoeing for hours before collapsing on a barstool, his straw boater cockeyed and his plaid suit dotted with sweat. When he got tipsy on too many sidecars, he'd make eyes at me, and Val would laugh and tell him to stop trying to play the drugstore cowboy. Tucked away in that speakeasy, we could be cool kids and never have to worry about free throws or fluorescent lighting.

Betsy ran her warm hand through my hair, settling her fingertips at the nape of my neck. "Are you okay?" she asked through a laugh. "You disappeared on me again. Where do you go?"

I flashed Betsy my best grin. "Still thinking about that silky-smooth gelato."

Betsy giggled and put her lips to my ear. "Can I tell you a secret? I have the most adorbs boyfriend in the world."

I let that grin crystallize on my face and bit my tongue even though I wanted to tell her that wasn't a secret. Real secrets weren't sweet nothings you whispered in your arm candy's ear. Real secrets are snarly little beasts that feast on your insides and poop out paranoia. They don't fill you with warm fuzzies. They make you itch like a patient stuffed to the gills with morphine and leave you feeling like a phone dangling off the hook.

Meadow shot me a blink-and-you'll-miss-it eye roll. She couldn't have known I was thinking about cruising down the interstate with Mattie McKenna, but she knew me well enough to know I'd just sold poor Betsy a loaf of baloney.

I told Betsy the burger from Johnny Rockets didn't sit well in the old breadbasket so I could bail on the weed dealer's party. I decided I'd rather lie on my bed and drown myself in the *Cabaret* soundtrack than rub elbows with a bunch of zozzled kids yapping over each other. None of the guys from the basketball team would smoke because we were all subject to random drug tests, but they weren't afraid to drink themselves into a frenzy. The more shitfaced they got, the louder they got. Ryder, our starting point guard, had no sense of personal space after three or four shots. He'd shout right in everyone's faces, sprinkling them with vodka-tinged spittle. I'd back away, trying to reestablish that customary one-foot bubble, but he'd always follow me, tilting his vast forehead toward mine.

Most of the time I could handle that sort of thing, but tonight, just thinking about it made my head throb. I didn't want to shrink into a ratty, vomit-stained couch while Ryder close-talked me to death about which broads he wanted to bang. I wanted to dance with Sally

Bowles at the Kit Kat Klub. Instead, I pulled a pillow over my face and massaged my temples.

"Willem, sweetie. You look positively consumed with teenage ennui."

My mother was the only person on earth who used my full first name. She was also the only person I knew who could throw a word like *ennui* into a mundane conversation and make it sound natural. If I threw around a word like that, I'd sound like a pretentious douchebag.

"I'm just tired."

I felt her take a seat on the bed, the mattress sinking below my right leg. "I don't believe you. Why aren't you with the Stepford-wife-in-training and her pinched-face little friend?"

"Please don't call them that. I know you know their names."

She sighed. "Yes, I know their names. I'm trying to make you laugh, sweetie."

"You're failing."

"You didn't answer my question. Did you finally tire of Betsy's heroic devotion to All-American feminine ideals?"

I threw the pillow at her, and she laughed. I would never tell her this, but I loved my mom's cackle. When it rang through our house, it reminded me of traipsing through museum after museum with her as a kid, not even in grade school yet. I was probably happier back then. Little kids have nothing to hide.

"She's at some party. I didn't feel like going."

"Well, good. You should spend time with your

father and me tonight."

I exhaled a sarcastic "woo-hoo."

My mom cackled again. "Don't play coy with me, Willem. A night out on the town with us is, hands down, more fun than lying on your bed in a pool of angst."

I sat up. "You're going out?"

"Of course we're going out. Do you think when you're not here we just sit around and twiddle our thumbs, worrying about whether our precious babe is facedown on the floor at some godforsaken frat party?"

"Where are you going?"

"To Providence." She winked at me the same way she used to wink at me when I was a little kid ready for adventure.

"Is it some obnoxious coffeehouse thing? Because if it is I'm not going."

"Only one way to find out. Come on, Willem. Live a little."

The bored, lonely guy buried beneath my aloof-teen-ager-shell screamed at me to choose life. I ignored him and let my head plop back down the mattress. "Not worth the risk. You're going to some awful poetry reading, I just know it."

"Suit yourself." She left me to my ennui and headed downstairs.

I put the pillow back over my face and fell asleep.

A few hours later, I awoke when my phone buzzed on my nightstand—a text from Betsy.

>Feeling better? Party is cray cray. You should check out the pics on LifeScape. Miss u oodles. XOXO

For a million reasons, this little digital love note made me wish desperately that I'd gone with my parents to Providence. Any sort of distraction would've been better than lying in the dark reading clipped dispatches from a girl who thought she was in love with me when, in fact, she didn't have any idea who I really was.

And though I didn't know it at the time, Mattie was already secretly living the dream. At that very moment, she was halfway through cracking a table of locks while her mentor withheld Thai food.

So maybe there's a tiny bit of truth to Mattie's romantic notion of historical destiny. Because instead of planting that pillow back on my face, I restarted the *Cabaret* soundtrack and told myself this was the last night I'd spend wallowing in *weltschmerz*.

I'll never forget the first time I saw it. It wasn't on TV or in a movie, it was right in front of my face. I was seven and my father had brought me to a traveling circus. I munched on roasted peanuts and greasy popcorn while I watched a parade of elephants. I giggled at the clowns and clapped for the trapeze artists as they swung from the top of the tent. And then a diminutive man took the center of the ring.

He performed a classic water torture cell escape, which had been done many times and with more grace by a great many other performers. But I didn't know that. All I knew was that time stopped in my child-mind when I watched him escape. Everything but him became a dull shadow. For three protracted minutes, he was the only thing that was real.

— Akiko Miyake, Tokyo, January 31, 1976

Mattie vs. Wil Wheaton

The second my boss at the café told me to skedaddle, I headed to Grayton for day two of training.

Miyu opened the door wearing striped pajamas. "I just woke up, and I need food. Go pick us up takeout." She shoved two twenties into my hands.

"I just came from Café Italiano," I whined. "You couldn't have called me?"

"I don't have your number, Girl Scout."

"Oh, right. Get me a pen."

Miyu returned with a pen and a takeout menu for a Thai restaurant. "I'll call in the order so you don't screw it up," she said as I wrote down my cell number for her.

"Gee, thanks."

The restaurant looked like a total dive, but I was so hungry by the time I got back to Miyu's, I didn't care if I was about to scarf something that a few cockroaches had crawled through. Miyu snatched the brown paper bag from my hand as soon as I stepped into the dining room.

"Sit," she commanded. I took a seat and realized that every padlock and box on the table had been re-locked. "You don't eat until you've unlocked everything here," she said as she handed me a fresh bobby pin.

"You've gotta be freaking kidding me," I whined. "It'll take me all night."

"Then you better get started." She pried open a box of garlic chicken, and the scent made my mouth water.

"Was your mom this mean when she trained you?"

"No questions," she barked.

I huffed and broke the bobby pin in two. I went after the Westin four-pin first. My empty stomach growled, and my sweaty fingers kept slipping against the bobby pin. I wanted to throw the padlock across the room, but I didn't have very good aim, and I was afraid I might damage the exquisite antique hutch in the corner.

"Focus, Girl Scout," Miyu said before shoving a piece of chicken into her mouth. "Take a deep breath. Your life isn't hanging in the balance. Yet."

I dried my sweaty hands on my jeans and took her advice. My stomach growled again, and I was about to give up when the lock popped open. The sound of it startled me, but Miyu didn't look surprised. "Don't stop now, Girl Scout. You've got a whole table to crack."

Despite my hunger and exhaustion—or perhaps because of it—I somehow found a rhythm. Something must have sunk in during the Night of Epic Lock Picking, because I conquered everything on the table in just under an hour.

"Holy crap! I am amazing," I shouted as I got up

to do a victory dance. "I feel like I finally cracked the code."

"Congratulations," Miyu deadpanned. "Though you've shown no natural aptitude for the art of lock picking, you've now got a grasp on the basics."

"I think I'm allowed to be a little impressed with myself."

"If you say so. But you're not even close to proficient. Each day that you come here to train, picking every lock on this table will be your first task."

I huffed again. "Whatever. Can I please eat now?"

When I was halfway through scarfing a pile of Pad Thai, I took a moment to reflect on how I ended up in the dining room of a resentful stranger, picking my way through a spread of locks armed with just a bobby bin.

The truth is, it's at least sixty-two percent Wil Wheaton's fault and fifteen percent my dad's fault.

By the time I was eleven, my poor father had exhausted a great deal of effort trying to interest me in Westerns.

"You like old things, right Mattie?" he'd say. "Well, these are old movies about how life was a long time ago."

I did like old movies, just not Westerns. With the exception of *True Grit*, which I probably appreciated only because of my plucky namesake, I just couldn't get into the outlandish machismo, the damsels in distress, and the cheesy-twangy tough-guy dialogue.

"It's not like the real Old West," I'd try to explain to my dad. "It's like a glorified fantasy version of the Old West. In the real Old West, all the prostitutes had STDs."

My dad did not appreciate explanations involving prostitutes and STDs coming from his eleven-year-old daughter. He would just sigh and shake his head and mumble something about the American education system.

Besides Westerns, my dad's interests included golf, expensive scotch, mowing our perfectly-maintained lawn, and washing and vacuuming his car. Though many of my peculiar interests had come and gone over the years (serenading my parents from the back seat with off-key renditions of patriotic songs, birding with a pair of binoculars the size of my head, needle pointing nonsensical wall hangings), the constants included history and, like most children of the aughts, television.

Seeing as I had no interest in cars or competitive sports, and I wasn't old enough to drink, TV was going to be my only viable shot at a common interest with my dad.

He didn't watch a lot of TV, but *Star Trek*, in all of its various incarnations, was something he could sink his teeth into. On some level, it made perfect sense. By boldly going where no one had gone before, what were the crew of the Enterprise if not a bunch of highly organized space cowboys in matching unitards? Like my dad, I enjoyed the predictable but well-constructed plotlines and the retro-futuristic technology installed on the Enterprise. I'm also not ashamed to admit now that, at the tender age of eleven, I'd developed a rather unhealthy infatuation with everyone's favorite Mary Sue, Wesley Crusher.

Oh, Wesley Crusher. The precocious teenage son that

Captain Picard never had. The poor guy didn't even get that much screen time, but I basked in every second of it, soaking it up like cosmic radiation. I wanted to live on the Enterprise so I could be his girlfriend. I wanted to hang out with him on the Ten-Forward deck and sip classy interplanetary cocktails as I stared into his warm, brown eyes. And I wanted an elaborate, but tasteful, holodeck wedding, perhaps with a nineteenth century garden party theme.

My dad was, of course, oblivious to my crush until Kyle pointed it out. He saw the way my face lit up every time Wesley appeared on the fifty-inch plasma screen in our living room and perpetually mocked the thoughts he imagined were flitting through my pubescent head.

"Oh, Wesley," he'd moan breathlessly in an over-the-top falsetto. "Fly me away in your spaceship."

"Only *Star Trek* fans are allowed in the living room when we're watching *Star Trek*," I'd scream as I kicked his shins and sent my skinny fists flying toward his chest.

Kyle would laugh and then ride off on his bike to hang out with his friends or engage in some form of semi-acceptable troublemaking. Even at eleven, I was well aware that good-looking boys who played sports and got decent grades could get away with murder.

I recovered from my desperate puppy-love for Wesley within a year, but not before Wil Wheaton managed to suck me into a secret obsession that I kept entirely to myself. On a lazy Sunday afternoon in my thirteenth year, while I was dusting my knickknack collection, my dad shouted up the stairs from the living room.

"Mattie! Come check out this movie on the Disney Channel. It's got what's his name in it. Your buddy, Wesley Crusher."

"What movie?" I asked when I breezed into the living room, trying to look casual and failing miserably.

"Not sure what it's called, but it's about Harry Houdini."

"The escape artist?"

Dad nodded and I took a seat on the couch. Even at the impressionable age of twelve, I could acknowledge that the movie, made in the mid-1980s, was kind of a hot mess. Yet it sparked an interest in me I couldn't fully explain.

Why did this specific thing worm its way into my DNA like a virus? Maybe I stumbled on it at the right age at the right time. Maybe it was the incandescent glow of an era gone by. Maybe it was the gritty mystique of the performers.

Or maybe it was the act itself. The hubris and the palpable fear. The staggering contrast between the carefully crafted showmanship and the raw unpredictability of physically fighting your way out of a deathtrap.

Maybe it was none of these things. Or all of them at once. I can only say for certain that I got more jazzed about the art of escapology than anything else I could remember—even the first time I read *The Diary of a Young Girl*, after which I refused to leave my room for a week, claiming—like a misguided and pretentious ten-year-old—that I was trying to experience some level of solidarity with poor Anne.

Despite my new and unparalleled level of excitement for all things Houdini, I didn't say, *Holy willikers, Dad! That just blew my mind, and I'm going to go upstairs right now and look up everything I possibly can on Harry Houdini.* Instead, I said, "That movie was wicked cheesy," and then went upstairs and conducted extensive Houdini research in secret.

I immersed myself in the life of Erik Weisz, the mysterious immigrant whose stage name became synonymous with escapology. A few months later, I wanted to learn everything I could about Dorothy Dietrich, the girl-next-door who escaped a troubled past to become the first woman to perform a straitjacket escape while suspended hundreds of feet above an amusement park. Finally, my focus shifted to Akiko Miyake, our local hero, who emigrated from Tokyo in the '70s and perfected a dramatic aquarium escape before her tragic death in a plane crash on December 3, 1999.

After each feverish research session, I would delete my browser history to eliminate the possibility that anyone snooping on my computer might find out what I was up to. Perhaps my newfound obsession was too much for my twelve-year-old mind.

Or perhaps I realized that anyone who encountered a twelve-year-old girl preoccupied with escapology and early twentieth century magicians would surely give her *the look* and feel compelled to ask *Why?* It was always more of an accusation than an actual question. I simply couldn't handle that kind of scrutiny.

The travel agent gawked at me. *"Just a one-way ticket? But you only have a visitor's visa."*

"I know. I need to be back to get settled before I start at the university," I lied through my teeth. "But I don't want to get locked into a time-frame. I want to take this trip at my own pace." I smiled and glanced at the framed photos on her desk. She had posed in each of them with the same man and young boy, probably her husband and son. In one of the photos, her little nuclear family had encircled someone dressed in a Mickey Mouse costume.

"The United States is a big country," she said with a nod. "Much bigger than Japan. You could stay a year and not see it all."

"Oh, I know. But Disneyland is at the top of my list. I've heard it's wonderful."

"It is!" she squealed.

I smiled again, knowing I had no plans to visit Disneyland or any other tourist destinations. I also had no intention of returning to Japan.

— *Akiko Miyake, Tokyo, June 22, 1976*

Mattie, Monologues, and Mayhem

The next two weeks flew by in a haze of gelato scooping, lock picking, sleep deprivation, and endless texts from Miyu.

>Yr time on the Westin four-pin is still
unacceptable. Visualize it throughout the
day.

She followed that with:

>If you can still focus on scooping
gelato, yr not visualizing hard enough.

And later that day:

>Girl Scout, I won't let you in unless
you bring tacos from Tres Amigos. Corn
tortillas, not flour!

My phone buzzed again a minute later.

>Pick me up a book from the library.
Something smart but not too serious.

Giving her my number might have been the poorest call I'd made in my entire life, but I considered it part of paying my dues as a young escapologist in training.

Then there was the whole lying to my parents and sneaking around thing. I honestly thought it would be fun. Whenever I pictured Akiko sneaking out of her parents' flat in Tokyo to go perform, it gave me a thrill. There's something romantic about a young girl sneaking out in the middle of the night to fulfill a lifelong dream. Unless you're the girl. Then it's just a giant, anxiety-provoking pain in the ass that turns you into a lying liar-face. I'd never been a bad kid, and now I knew why.

After tiptoeing down the stairs in the dark and almost tripping over Guinan asleep in the kitchen doorway, I arrived at Miyu's at 12:01 the night we started working on straitjacket escapes. I picked my way through every lock on the dining room table in twenty-one minutes and eighteen seconds.

"That'll do, Girl Scout," Miyu said. "Now stand up so I can strap your arms behind your back."

I winced as she tightened each of the three buckles against my back, pinching my skin. "I can't breathe in this thing."

Miyu scoffed. "You think this is bad? Wait until I try to cure you of your claustrophobia."

"I don't have claustrophobia."

"That's what you think."

As soon as we started claustrophobia training, which involved Miyu locking me in a trunk the size of a child's coffin, I panicked.

"My legs are going numb in here. And I can't breathe," I whined.

"If you can talk, you can breathe," she barked.

"Seriously though, Miyu. I can't stay in here."

"You can, and you will. At first, your fear will increase. Then, it will plateau. Eventually, you'll learn how to deal with it."

I heard her footsteps as she walked away. "You bitch," I screamed as I slammed my fists against the lid of the trunk. My heart pounded in my ears, and I felt every scratchy piece of wood in that trunk wrapping itself around me, suffocating me.

Once I accepted the fact that she wasn't going to let me out, I shut my eyes, took a few deep breaths, and tried to relax my muscles. At some point I must have fallen asleep, because I woke abruptly when Miyu threw the lid of the trunk open.

"Oh, good. When you stopped squawking and whining, I thought maybe you'd died in here. Not a mess I'd like to clean up." With that, she locked the trunk back up, and I stewed in my own panic until I learned to push through it.

Once again, it's time to talk about how I ended up locked in a trunk by a resentful stranger. Well, there was that soul sucking last day of school. But long before that there was my dad introducing me to *Star Trek*, and also Wil Wheaton being adorable and then introducing me to Houdini.

The final nudge that drove me right over the edge? Twelve measly Stella-less hours.

The day before I drove to Grayton for the first time, and, quite literally, put my life in the hands of a thirty-something recluse, Stella and I had a last supper at Bollywood Palace to "celebrate" her abandoning me for a whole goddamn summer. I very graciously let Stella pick the restaurant since she'd be eating cafeteria food for two months, and she chose a totally mediocre greasy spoon without actual waiters because the place was wallpapered with flatscreens playing Bollywood classics. This is what happens when you grow up without a TV. I suppose I should've been thankful she hadn't dragged me to a sports bar or Chuck E. Cheese's.

"Oh my god, I love this one," Stella said the second we sat down. "I think I've seen almost the whole thing, just not in chronological order."

I rolled my eyes and headed toward the counter where Naveen, the owner's nephew and my favorite reluctant restaurateur, was flipping through a comic book.

"Hey, Mattie. The usual?" he asked without looking up.

"Yup. Chicken tikka masala for me and lentils for my hippie friend."

He shouted something into the kitchen in Hindi and went back to his comic book.

I was already headed back to our table when I heard a *psst*.

"Huh?"

"What are you guys doing tonight?" Naveen asked.

For a brutal second or two I panicked over the possibility that he was trying to ask one of us out, and, if necessary, drag the other one along as an awkward third wheel. Naveen practically oozed with quirky, smoldering adorableness, but he was well into his twenties. More importantly, with a Stella-less summer looming before me, I couldn't handle being a third wheel.

Naveen glanced behind his shoulder and pulled a flyer out from behind the counter. "When my uncle comes out here with your food, do not tell him I gave this to you."

"Um, 'kay."

"My band is playing tonight, and we really need an audience. You guys seem like you're into, you know, weird stuff." He handed me the flyer, which featured a little girl in Victorian clothing having a very serious tea party with an octopus wearing a top hat. A bloodied letter opener lay ominously on the table between them.

"Mollusk Brigade? Where's . . . Say-loan Pos-tail?" I knew I'd probably butchered the pronunciation of "Salone Postale" and waited for Naveen to correct me.

"Salon-eh Post-all. It's a semi-secret venue up in Federal Hill. Right on the border of Olneyville."

"Oh, great," I muttered. "I'll be sure to get mugged while I'm there."

He ignored my concerns. "It's in the basement of the old post office. The bar upstairs is legit, but the salon doesn't officially have a liquor license. That's why they keep it on the down low."

"If I go will I learn how this tea party plays out?" I asked, pointing at the flyer.

"You can ask the artist. She's in my band."

Naveen's uncle emerged from the kitchen, and I pocketed the flyer and zipped back to my table. *Yup. Playin' it cool.*

By the time our food was ready, Stella had been fully hypnotized by a Bollywood dance sequence, so we scarfed mostly in silence. It was probably for the best because, behind all my sarcasm, eyerolls, and cross-armed proclamations that Stella was going to ruin her summer by going to a snooty prep school for two months, I was terrified. I couldn't even enjoy my mediocre masala because a grisly little knot had bound itself up at the bottom of my ribcage.

I would never tell Stella this, but I needed her more than she needed me. Back in middle school, she'd needed someone to clue her in on all the strange little rituals and arbitrary rules of public school. Why she picked me, with all my weirdo red flags blazing like the freaking sun, I'll never understand. Seriously, the *Star Trek* PowerPoint alone should have sent her running for the hills, but there was also me dragging her to a gazillion antique stores and estate sales, me forcing her to listen to hours of Gilberto & Getz, me yapping incessantly about the key differences between The Gilded Age and La Belle Époque.

I might've survived until sixth grade with just a few come-and-go associates, but now that I had a true compadre, I didn't know if I could go back. Stella, on the other hand, no longer needed me to point out that a handshake is a greeting best reserved for school principals and your parents' co-workers. She was fine on her own, and two months with a bunch of other smartypants overachievers would probably help her figure that out. Even if we survived a summer apart, I knew what was going to happen without my tether to the outside world. I'd hole up in my room and emerge only for shifts at the café and occasional bear poking.

"I have something for you," Stella said as we neared the end of our meal.

I scowled at her. "Please don't make this awkward."

She laughed. "Oh, Ginge. I mean Mattie. Okay, it took a little while for me to talk my parents into this, but it's just silly to let my car sit in my mom's driveway for two months." She jingled her keys with a bright-eyed smile, like she was about to give a yippy little dog a treat.

I had not seen this coming. "Wow. Um . . . Wow."

She laughed again. "Yes, you're welcome. You'll take good care of her, right?"

I nodded, though I honestly had no idea how to take good care of a car other than to avoid speeding and driving head-on into big, stationary things. Like trees.

We headed to Red's Cream Hut after that for scoops of Hangover Helper (coffee ice cream embedded with massive Oreo-chunks), and then Stella called it a night.

"Sorry, Ginge. I need a good night's sleep. Tomorrow's a big day, and I'm trying not to be nervous, but you know me. Now get out of the car so I can hug you. It'll make me feel better."

We hugged in the driveway with the driver's side door of the Bug still open and the ignition going *ding-ding ding-ding*.

Another thing I'd never tell Stella—even with what are possibly the world's scrawniest arms, she gives really great hugs. More than anyone I've ever known, Stella hugs like she means it.

I drove home after that because where else was I going to go? It wasn't until I reached into the pocket of my hoodie for my house keys that I remembered the flyer for Salone Postale. Being hastily shoved into my pocket had crumpled the poor thing, but the little girl and the octopus with the top hat still made me giggle.

And then something weird happened.

You look troubled, child, I imagined the octopus saying as he adjusted his monocle.

Of course she's troubled, the little girl said. *It's Friday night and she's got a car, but she's about to go bug her brother and his friends and then hide in her room.*

Where would I go? I asked them.

The little girl huffed and stomped her tiny foot and pointed to the letters spelling out Salone Postale. *Here, obviously!*

I don't go to places like that.

The octopus steepled two of his tentacles under his chin. *That's no reason not to start now.*

What if I run into someone from school?

He squinted at me with his monocled eye. *The likelihood that any of your cohorts will make an appearance at a secret playhouse in Federal Hill is . . .* He rubbed his tentacles together, presumably calculating the odds. *Well, I don't have the exact figure, but it's very, very slim. Infinitesimally slim.*

Start. The. Car. the little girl growled.

Ugh. Fine.

Half an hour later, I parked Stella's Bug in some sketchy alley, ducked through a dark, narrow bar, and found myself face to face with a purplish-red door, like an ornate slab of cough syrup, at the bottom of a stairwell.

I took a deep breath, pushed the door open, and made my way into a windowless little theater full of café tables. The primary source of light appeared to be a gazillion flickering votive candles, so I figured that even if I ran into someone from school, it'd be fine because we'd surely both die in a theater fire.

"Can I get you something?" the woman behind the bar at the back asked. Tattoos dotted her bare arms, and her lipstick matched her cherry-red hair.

"She'll have a Long Island iced tea," Naveen said as he came up behind me and slung his arm around my shoulders.

I shook my head at the tattooed bartender. "I have to drive home. Also, I'm—"

She interrupted me before I could explain I was underage. "If you're planning on staying for an hour or two, you'll be fine."

"Um, 'kay."

"I'm so glad you came," Naveen said. "Almost all of my other so-called friends bailed for the night. We go on in ten, so I'll come find you after the set."

I nodded as he made his way through the small crowd hovering around the bar.

The bartender handed me a tall glass that smelled like way too much booze for my taste. "How much do I owe you?"

She shook her head. "I put it on Naveen's tab."

"Oh. Thanks." I raised my glass and wandered to an

empty table. Just a small sip of the "tea" puckered my face. I set the glass down on the table to let the melting ice dilute some of the alcohol, and pulled my phone out of my shoulder bag to make myself look occupied. A few minutes later, a middle-aged man with a handlebar mustache took the stage and cleared his throat into the microphone. He wore a battered black tux with coattails and a red lapel. The noisy patrons at a table up front whistled and then raised their glasses.

"Good evening, ladies, gents, in-betweeners, thieves, poets, politicians, lonely souls. Welcome to Salone Postale. We have a fabulous night planned for you that will include music, monologues, and mayhem."

"Mayhem! Hell yeah!" one of the noisy patrons shouted.

The man in the tux grinned at him. "Most of you already know me, but for those of you who don't, my name is Monty the Magician. I will be your master of ceremonies, here to provide a little lubrication between acts."

The crowd laughed, and I swallowed another boozy sip of my drink.

"Before we subject you to the strange stylings of the Mollusk Brigade, how about a little foreplay?"

"That's what I said to your mom last night," the noisy patron by the stage shouted.

Monty didn't seem to mind, and I wondered if heckling was par for the course at Salone Postale. He pulled a deck of cards from his pocket. I'd seen the trick before at a few birthday parties, but Monty performed it with such cheeky panache that I couldn't help but find it amusing. He almost came off as a parody of a birthday party magician, like he knew the golden era of stage magic had long passed, but he didn't give a shit and would continue to milk that old song and dance for all it was worth.

"Ta-da," he shouted with a flourish of his hand. He poked his head between the plum-colored curtains and then re-emerged with a toothy smile.

"Without further ado, the Salone Postale proudly presents . . . the Mollusk Brigade!"

A nearly deafening cacophony of brass instruments busted through curtains, gyrated on the stage for a moment, and then shimmied onto the floor, snaking between the café tables like a caterpillar on drugs.

The band wore dark blue marching band uniforms, like the color of a stormy ocean, with pink and white nautilus shells embroidered on the shoulders and lapels. Once the initial cacophony ceased, they launched into a catchy instrumental cover of Television's "See No Evil." Most kids my age wouldn't have recognized the tune, but my mom had spent a chunk of my childhood trying to educate me on "good" music. I preferred jazz to all of her guitar-heavy punk, though, in moments like this, I appreciated the knowledge she'd handed down.

A juggling act came on after Mollusk Brigade, and then a guy in waders delivered a monologue about the solitude of deep-sea fishing. By that time I'd finished three quarters of my drink and realized that the kindly octopus and little girl in puffy sleeves had led me down a rabbit hole and into some sort of vaudevillian parallel universe.

Naveen finally emerged from backstage during the intermission. "What did you think?" he asked as he brought me another Long Island.

"I'm not drinking that. But your band is great. Fun . . . kitschy in a good way."

He pursed his lips. "I guess I can live with that."

"Can I meet the girl who designed the poster?"

"Yeah, I'll see if I can track her down."

Monty the Magician wandered toward the bar as Naveen ran off to find the artist. He ordered a drink, took it from the bartender without paying, and then eyed me for a moment. I scrunched into my chair as he made his way to my table, praying that if I made myself small enough I'd disappear.

"Hey there, noob," he said as he pulled out the chair next to mine and took a seat. "How'd you find your way in here?"

"I'm friends with Naveen. Sort of."

His thick lips curled into an unnerving smirk as he rattled the ice in his glass. "Does that mean you're sleeping with him?"

"No. I'm, like, underage."

"Oh. Of course. Good to know we're now serving minors." He shook his head. "Really classy establishment we're running here."

"It's just tea," I said with a smirk of my own.

"Yeah, right. I'll let it slide this time. What did you think of the first half of the show?"

I paused for a moment, debating whether I should continue down the trail of idle chit chat, or give him an honest answer. Part of my brain was screaming for me to say something bland, like *good* or *interesting*, when my honest answer somehow popped out of my mouth. "I'm not saying this to flatter you, but you were the best part. I've always been kind of fascinated by magicians."

He raised his greasy eyebrows. "Really?"

My whole brain was firing on all cylinders at that point, screaming for me to abort, but my mouth, well lubricated with alcohol, must have responded with *Fuck off, cerebral cortex, I got this.* "Yeah. Magicians are like kindred spirits of escapologists. I've been obsessed with escapology for . . . I don't even know. Like, forever."

Monty's dark eyes lit up. "Did you know Akiko Miyake used to perform here?"

I nearly spat out a swig of my second drink. "She did?"

Monty nodded reverently. "She developed her aquarium escape here. We still have the tank in the back. Would you like to see it?"

My mouth finally gave up, and I just stared at him.

"Okay. I'll take that awkward silence as a yes."

I followed Monty toward the side of the stage and through a series of doorways and curtains that blurred together in my tipsy state. I stumbled after him into a storage closet and squinted when he flicked on the overhead light. As my eyes began to adjust, I could make out the silhouette of a massive box, like the industrial coffin of an unlucky giant. So much dust had collected on the glass panels they'd become opaque, almost matching the tarnished brass running down the corners of the tank. On the left-side panel, some clever soul had dragged his finger through the dust to draw a cartoonish representation of male genitalia.

"It obviously hasn't been cleaned in a while." I punctuated my statement with a painful hiccup.

Monty shook his head. "I know. It's terrible. We haven't had a props master in years, so no one takes care of all the stuff in storage."

I walked around the tank, examining the ladder to the top. I tried to picture myself climbing it, but the thought sent a boozy laugh rumbling through my chest.

"What was she like?" I asked.

"Alas, her heyday was before my time. I only know her through second-hand anecdotes passed around by some of the older patrons. But I'm friends with her daughter. Sort of."

I grinned again. "Does that mean you're sleeping with her?"

Monty chuckled. "You don't miss a beat, do you? When I say we're friends, I mean I've met her a handful of times. She doesn't get out much so the salon volunteers are the closest thing she has to friends." Monty rocked forward and back on the toes of his wingtip shoes. "I've gotta be onstage again in a minute, but you can hang out here as long as you want."

"'Kay," I said between hiccups. Once Monty left, I planted myself on the concrete floor. Even if I knew the most exciting thing in the history of the universe was about to take place on the salon's small stage, I wouldn't have been able to tear myself away from that dusty tank. Instead of returning to my seat, I sat on that floor until I sobered up, then snuck out a back exit and drove home to Tivergreene.

Guinan clacked over to me on the kitchen tile when I pushed open the back door. "Hey, girl."

I found Kyle in the living room without the usual suspects. He looked at me with bleary eyes and took another swig of something that smelled like drunk old man.

"Where're Mom and Dad?"

"Went to visit Aunt Millie in Jersey. Remember?"

"Oh. Right." In the midst of my losing my BFF for the summer, I'd apparently turned into the kind of self-centered kid who can't keep track of her own parents.

I took a seat next my brother and tried to relax. I cracked my wrists, kicked off my shoes, stretched my toes. None of it helped. I still felt like I wanted to jump out of my own skin.

"What the fuck is wrong with you?" Kyle asked.

"Ugh. I don't know. I had a weird night."

"Where were you?"

I eyed the bottle as he took another swig. "Can I have some?"

"Since when do you drink bourbon?"

"Is there bourbon in a Long Island iced tea?"

His eyes popped open.

"I can have secrets," I said. "No one needs to know everything about me."

He handed me the bottle, and I took a deep swig. It tasted nothing like the drink I'd had at the salon and burned my throat on the way down. Once we'd polished off half the bottle, everything seemed to move faster and slower at the same time.

I glanced over at Kyle. My eyes paused on his three-day-old stubble and his droopy eyelids. I swear he hadn't always been a drunk bum who wore pajamas more often than actual clothes. He'd practically been a rock star from grades K through 12—starter spot on the basketball team, honor roll, a gazillion friends and girlfriends, the whole deal. And then college happened.

Everyone thought Kyle was destined for great things. What they didn't realize is that his golden boy life had turned him into a relentless praise-whore. Seriously, the guy was addicted to "attaboys." But no one throws "attaboys" your way when you fuck up your knee three days into the first semester of college. And the attention you get after multiple surgeries isn't the same as the attention you get when you win the big game with a three-point buzzer shot.

That's all it took to drive my brother down into a gloom spiral. I'll forever be haunted by the image of him limping around the house, all smelly from not showering, his eyes glassy and bloodshot from pain-killers topped off with stolen sips of whiskey and vodka from my parents' liquor cabinet. He came home one weekend and never went back.

He tried at least half-heartedly to get a job, but the recession was in full swing, and no one wanted to hire a perpetually mopey college dropout who they assumed would go back to school once he snapped out of it. But a year later, he still hadn't snapped out of it.

Connor, his best friend, dropped out at the end of freshman year. Even with his fierce dark eyes that stared through everyone and everything, he'd never been charming enough to get the kind of attention he craved unless he was standing in the glow of Kyle's halo. And when the halo crumbled, so did Connor's plan to bask in that glow for another four years while he attended college with my brother.

Sometimes my heart kinda broke for the two of them. Sometimes I wanted to scream at Kyle for being such a mopey wuss-face. *Aw, boo hoo, you got hurt and now you can't play basketball. Meanwhile, children in third-world countries are starving and have probably never even seen a basketball. Grow some freaking perspective.* And sometimes a rotten little part of me, a slimly kernel full of maggots, was glad my rock star brother had crashed and burned because it made me look good by comparison. And an even more rotten part of me was glad Connor had gotten a raw deal because, you know, screw him.

But as I stared at my brother, I realized I only looked good by comparison because no one really expected anything from me. I guess I was a little bit like Austin, Connor and Kyle's third wheel, who never even applied to college and went straight into some low-wage cubicle gig. We weren't fuckups because we'd never really tried at anything. We just skated by under the radar. At least I could say that instead of befriending a couple cool kids who treated me like their personal punching bag, I'd befriended Stella. Stella, who was off rubbing elbows with people who were the polar opposite of me, for the whole freaking summer.

Another one of my *moments* came on, only it didn't feel like someone had struck a tuning fork by my ear. It felt like my whole body was ringing. "Kyle, I think I'm going to throw up."

"Don't do it here," he barked. "The last thing I want to be doing before Mom and Dad get back is cleaning vomit stains out of the rug."

I pushed myself off the couch and fled to the bathroom just in time. Projectile vomit, composed mostly of half-digested booze and Indian food, spewed from my mouth into the toilet bowl. After a few painful retches, I lay down on the cool tile floor with my eyes closed and my hands clutching my dizzy head.

"Guess you overdid it," Kyle slurred from the doorway.

"I feel like death," I moaned. "I'm going to bed."

"Drink water before you sleep or you'll feel even worse in the morning."

I shuddered at the thought of ingesting anything and climbed up the stairs to my bedroom. I felt exhausted, but couldn't get the muscles in my limbs to relax. I lay down on my quilt and the room began to spin.

"Make it stop," I moaned.

The walls of my bedroom pressed themselves against me. I stared at all the antique knickknacks on my windowsill. Mr. Crankypants, a scowly ceramic gnome I'd picked up at a yard sale, stared back at me. *Oh, did you want me to do something? Like give you a hug? Because I can't. 'Cause I'm, you know, just a hunk of dried clay and glaze.*

I picked up the paperweight on my bedside table and watched the light sparkle in the bits of sea glass buried inside it. Usually, just the weight of it in my hand would soothe my nerves, and I could distract myself by making up romantic stories about the previous owner. This time, I felt nothing and let the paperweight drop from my hand onto the oriental rug.

The stuffy air threatened to shrivel my lungs, and I pushed my window open to let the cool night in. I lingered by the windowsill for a moment and then slid out onto the roof, dragging my ass along the shingles because I didn't trust myself to stand. The street below was deserted, but I could see TVs flickering in my neighbors' houses. I pulled my knees up to my chest as I heard an epic battle between two screeching cats break out in the distance.

In that moment, something inside me shifted. The pit that had been hollowed out by a bunch of tiny, icky things caved in on itself, flooding me with fear and something else I couldn't quite put my finger on. I'd spent years convincing myself that my life under the radar was enough. That it was for the best because it would keep me from turning into someone like my brother. Or Connor. Or Meadow or Will. But Stella was the thing that made it tolerable. Without her, I was just a drunk girl on a roof, teetering on the edge of the same kind of spiral she'd watched her brother slide down.

I wish I could say that in that beautiful little moment I'd decided to make the conscious leap from consumption to creation. But the reality was considerably less romantic. Perhaps some small part of me was clutching those big ideas in the back of my mind, but the actual epiphany went more like the pathetic prayer of an intoxicated seventeen-year-old girl.

Dear God. I'm so freaking bored, and it's making me think about things that are making me really sad. I really, really need something that will make me not think about these things so that I can survive this summer without using alcohol to turn my brain to mush. Thanks.

The very next day, I found myself outside Akiko Miyake's crumbling house, trying to convince her daughter to help me save my own life.

The humid Southern California air hit me like a wall the moment I stepped out of LAX. I eyed a poster for Disneyland as I stood in line for a cab. When I reached the front, a gray-haired man tipped his cap to me as he pulled up in a yellow taxi.

"Where ya headed, miss?"

I gave him the address of my hotel in North Hollywood and took a seat in the back.

"First time in California?" he asked.

"Yes." I slipped on my black-as-night sunglasses and hoped they made me look like a savvy world traveler instead of a scared-shitless co-ed who'd left the country of her birth for the first time in her life.

The cab smelled like stale body odor and my stomach had tied itself in knots. But I didn't care. That smell and those knots and that humid SoCal air were about to deliver me to the future.

— Akiko Miyake, Los Angeles, July 3, 1976

Will With Two Ls Takes the Trolley

The night of Mattie's first performance at Salone Postale, I was riding the crosstown trolley, half-hoping to see the lady with the empty cat carrier. Instead, I found myself amidst a bunch of drunk college kids who turned out to be just as obnoxious as drunk high school kids. One of them broke into a saucy rendition of "You're a Grand Old Flag," except he changed "flag" to "fag" in all the verses.

He wasn't using the word the way the guys on the basketball team did. They tossed it out as a thought-less insult, like a sharp cousin to the oft repeated and equally reprehensible "that's so retarded." But as an easily identifiable member of team-QUILTBAG, this college kid was reclaiming that three-letter word and brandishing it like a shrill fuck off. It was both a weapon and a come-on.

I should've been amused by the whole thing, and maybe if I'd been in a better mood I would've been. Instead, I dug a bottle of ibuprofen out of my messenger bag, popped three of them, and waited for my stop.

Let's back up a bit. After I swore off nights spent wallowing in my room, I came up with a plan. I'd steer Betsy away from intolerably loud parties and toward something equally fun that didn't resemble the slow, debaucherous decline of civilization. If I didn't have to spend my evenings getting sloshed with loudmouth bros, I figured I could keep up the everything-is-hunky-dory charade with Betsy for at least another six months.

"Oh my god, you're so, so right," she said when I brought it up. "Ryder and those guys are fun for, like, forty-five minutes tops. Then we always end up outside or in the kitchen, just chatting with a small group of people who are much more chill."

"Yes, exactly." I was sitting on the old sofa in her basement while she dug through a box of VHS tapes. We'd recently uncovered her dad's old VCR while sorting through stuff for a yard sale and spent hours amusing ourselves with grainy cartoons and kids' movies. "So why don't we just skip the rowdy part and go straight to chatting with cool cats who know how to keep it tidy?" I picked up one of the tapes. "This one."

"*Labyrinth*? We've watched it like twenty-thousand times already."

"We've watched it twice, and it's fantastic." Though I considered myself a Bowie fan, I'd never even heard of *Labyrinth* until I watched it for the first time on Betsy's basement sofa.

"The music is soooo cheesy." She paired her drawn

out "so" with an eye roll.

"Cheesy? Or brilliant?"

She laughed and smiled that I-ate-sunshine-for-breakfast smile. "Fine, fine. You know I can't say no to you."

She slid the tape into the VCR and curled up next to me. "Okay. So instead of hanging out with your b-ball peeps tonight, how about dinner and a movie?"

"You know me so well." I planted a smooch on her porcelain cheek.

"Apparently, Meadow is kinda-sorta seeing some guy from Newport. Should we invite them? Like a double date?"

"I guess. Are you just dying to size up Meadow's kinda-sorta new boyfriend?"

She rolled her eyes again. "He's definitely not her boyfriend. Meadow doesn't have boyfriends. She just has boys."

She certainly did, and they'd been an endless string of awful, dismissive older guys who never took her seriously and overeager younger guys who never stopped humping her shapely leg. Sometimes, I feared she'd never find a happy medium.

"If he's a creep we'll just ditch them," Betsy said.

I smiled.

She smiled back and brought her face toward mine. "You know, because I'm letting you watch *Labyrinth* for the zillionth time, you have to make out with me."

I wrapped my arms around her. "Bowie is a perfect make out soundtrack."

Labyrinth plus twenty minutes later, we took our

seats at a little hipster bistro on Wickenden Street. Meadow introduced us to her new kinda-sorta boyfriend, Owen. He looked about our age, with broad shoulders and boat shoes. The rich-kid equivalent of a basketball jock, except he probably played lacrosse.

"He goes to St. Joseph's Academy," she explained. "Not for the summer thingy. Year-round." She didn't say this to brag about her date's status, because Meadow wasn't a snob about that stuff. It came out matter-of-fact, like a piece of news no more or less interesting than the weather forecast.

It took me only ten minutes of listening to Owen prattle on about pork belly and prefects and sailing to Block Island to realize I didn't like him. I'm not a class warrior, I swear. And it wasn't even what he was saying that stuck in my craw, it was the easy-breezy way that he said it. It was the nonchalant way he brushed his hair out of his eyes. It was the casual way he rested his arms on the table and leaned back in his chair and claimed more physical space than anyone should. Aside from getting caught in a girl's dorm room after curfew, Meadow's kinda-sorta boyfriend didn't have a care in the world, and I kinda-sorta hated him for it.

"How did you two meet?" Betsy asked.

"Johnny Rockets," Meadow said.

Owen gazed at Meadow with an affectionate smirk. "She seemed like such a cool girl, I had to ask for her number. I'm always on the lookout for hot but low maintenance, amirite?"

I shit you not, he said this right in front of her. And, to top it off, he raised his hand to fist bump me.

Meadow rolled her eyes but smiled, and Betsy laughed. I honestly have no idea if comments like that pissed them off, but, as so-called cool girls, they'd learned how to tolerate that kind of bullshit without batting a perfectly-mascaraed lash.

Because I'm a chickenshit pansy, I followed bro-code protocol and fist bumped him. And I hated myself for it.

The whole point of this evening had been to avoid clueless cads like Ryder and the guys from the basketball team. And yet I found myself sitting across from one. He might've been a little more refined than the cads I'd grown so tired of, but he was a cad nonetheless.

Again, I thought of Mattie and the zero muskrats' asses that she gave. I didn't think she'd say anything to Owen the lacrosse jock, but she wouldn't have to. She'd just glare at him until he crumbled.

I coughed into my fist. "Is it hot in here? I'm just gonna step out a sec for some air."

I made my way to the sidewalk out front and massaged my throbbing temples.

"Hey." Betsy put a hand on my shoulder. "Feeling okay?"

"Honestly, no. I kinda feel like I'm gonna puke. Must've picked up a bug or something. Sorry."

"No worries. Let me go grab the car."

"No, no. You deserve a night out. I can call a cab."

"Are you sure?"

"Abso-tive-ly."

She crossed her arms and scuffed her skimmers on the pavement. "Will, are we okay?"

"What? Of course we're okay. Why would you ask?"

"I feel like you've been weird lately." She dropped her gaze. "Sorry, I'm probably just being paranoid."

I'm not gonna lie, this killed me a little. Betsy's instincts were spot on, but like many a teenage girl, she'd been taught not to trust herself. And because I was a chickenshit pansy, I was just going to let that go on happening.

"Sorry if I've been weird, Bets." I pulled her close and kissed her never-oily forehead. "It's just a bug or something. Maybe some stress about basketball next year. My coach won't shut up about college recruiters."

She nodded and gave me a peck on the lips. "'Kay. Text me later?"

"Posi-lute-ly."

I didn't call a cab. I started walking down Wickenden, past all the artsy gift shops and gourmet pizza joints and quirky breakfast nooks. And, for reasons I can't explain, I wanted to talk to my mom.

I pulled my phone out.

>Are you guys out?

>Yes. What's up?

>Nothing. Just curious.

>Are you bored with future Miss Sorority Queen? You can come join us.

>Please don't call her that. Where are you?

She texted me an address on Atwells Ave.

>You won't be disappointed.

And that's how I ended up on the crosstown trolley, listening to some college dude scream "Keep your eye on the grand old fag!" while his friends had a giggle fit.

I missed my stop and had to get off at the corner of Eagle Street and backtrack across the bridge. I don't know exactly what I'd been expecting, but it wasn't the nondescript bar that I found. It looked like any other bar, except maybe a little more rough around the edges and with shockingly poor lighting. Not the kind of place my parents hung out.

"Ugh." I pulled out my phone to tell my mom she'd texted me the wrong address. I didn't hear back.

The irony here is that I'd been fantasizing about speakeasies full of weirdos for years. And here was a real-life version of that, staring right at me, and I was too blind to see it. Instead of venturing inside, I stood on the sidewalk for an hour, annoyed about my head-ache and bro-code and my status as an insufferable chickenshit pansy. I finally called a cab and headed back to a dark house in Grayton, because my parents were still out, having a grand old time at a mysterious juice joint in Federal Hill.

The other slap-to-the-face irony—inside Salone Postale, Mattie was getting ready to take the stage for the very first time. That's how close we came to colliding, like two moons orbiting different planets that pass within light-seconds of each other.

I was more nervous for my first solo performance at a reno-
vated theater turned dive in L.A. than I'd been for any of my
performances back home. My typically iron gut revolted under
the stress, and I hugged a filthy toilet as I threw up the greasy
pepperoni pizza I'd eaten before the show. I cursed the smoggy
city and its overabundance of American junk food.

T-minus five minutes to my act, and I found myself
standing backstage, tugging on a lock of hair. All I could think of
was everything that could possibly go wrong. What if my assis-
tant tied the wrong knots? What if he didn't leave me enough
wiggle room? What if I choked?

As if all that wasn't enough, I worried my lazy boss at the
diner would fire me for ditching my apron and sneaking out
early for my performance. If I couldn't make rent, I'd find myself
sleeping in a cardboard box on skid row and performing hand-
cuff escapes on the street for pocket change.

I gasped when I felt a chunk of hair dislodge from my scalp.
My nervous system hadn't even registered the pain.

— Akiko Miyake, Los Angeles, August 7, 1978

Mattie and the Ravenous Imp

Less than a month after my first day of training, I stood backstage at Salone Postale, my palms sweating and my knees rattling. My brain kept going fuzzy on me. I couldn't believe I was about to do the very thing I'd spent at least ten years trying to avoid at all costs—putting myself on display under a massive spotlight.

It had taken Miyu almost a full week to talk me into it. "Performance is an integral part of escapology," she explained after I'd finally succeeded at picking five padlocks in under five minutes while locked in the pitch-blackness of the trunk. "It's perhaps the *most* integral part."

"I didn't start training so I could perform," I protested. "I just wanted to. For my own personal fulfillment. Or something. Besides, I'm not ready yet."

"Unless you're planning on becoming a spy, these skills you've acquired are meaningless without performance. Escapology is an art form designed to awe and inspire."

"Regardless, performance isn't for me."

She stared at me until I began to squirm. "My mother was a nervous wreck before every performance."

"You're a terrible liar," I whispered.

"But it's true. Do you know why she wore all those colorful wigs for her performances?" I pictured the unstoppable Akiko Miyake with her demure smile contradicting her bright hair—a different color of the rainbow for each performance. "She used to pull out her own hair when she was anxious," Miyu explained. "Like a nervous tic. She was practically bald by the time . . ."

I thought about all the grainy footage of Akiko I'd watched on YouTube. She always appeared so put together. Was there a rock hard kernel of fear beneath that composed surface? I tried to imagine myself in her shoes, standing on a stage in front of a crowd ready to ride an emotional rollercoaster of suspense, tension, and resolution. The very thought made my palms sweat and my mouth dry up, but something inside me—some ravenous imp who craved attention—wanted to know how it would feel.

I continued to protest even as Miyu and I practiced a stage-ready escape act, which included hours upon woozy hours of suspension training. Perhaps all that blood rushing to my head finally got to me, because my resolve crumbled and now I found myself standing next to Monty the Magician, watching a contortionist finish up her routine.

"Try to relax," he said. "They're going to love you. Most of them aren't even old enough to remember Akiko, so a live escape act will be completely new to them."

"That's reassuring," I said as my voice cracked.

He laughed. "I'll set the stage with an introduction so the crowd will be chomping at the bit by the time you get out there. What should I call you? Personally, I think Mattie the Magnificent is a little old-school, but has a nice ring to it."

Something about Monty saying my name, my actual name, flipped a switch in me. All it would take was one video posted to LifeScape, tagged with my name, and every freaking person in the 401 area-code would know what I'd been up to for the summer. In that moment, I saw me, my whole life, my name, my face, my body splayed out on the interwebs, ready for dissection.

"Oh, dear god. No no no," I begged. "You can't use my real name."

"Uhhh . . . okay. You got a nickname I can go with?"

"Miyu calls me Girl Scout . . ."

Monty shook his head as he smoothed his greasy mustache. "Too cutesy."

I wracked my brain to come up with a decent stage name. For some reason I'll never be able to explain, all I could think of was the summer I'd decided to dye my hair fire engine red. It faded into a hundred sad shades of pink after a few washes, and even Stella couldn't take me seriously.

"You look like an angry, deranged mermaid," she'd chirped as I obsessed over my reflection in a warped, antique mirror. "Like, Ariel's evil twin, bent on revenge. Oh! I've got it. Ginger the Avenger."

"That sounds like a comic book character, not a mermaid."

"Why can't she be both?"

Stella spent hours that summer concocting an elaborate back story for Ginger the Avenger. The details of the back story faded with time, but the nickname simply refused to die.

"My best friend calls me Ginger," I croaked.

Monty smiled and nodded, scratching his stubbly chin. "I like it. It's got an air of classic Hollywood glamour."

The contortionist took a deep bow and ducked off the stage as Monty closed the plum-colored curtains. I discreetly plucked at my black stretch pants, trying to unwedge my underwear from my nether region. I was far from obese, but my pants made every ounce of pudge I had stand out. I felt like I was made of curves and gobs of unruly flesh, and with my skin tight t-shirt and sneakers, I looked ready to take a yoga class, not perform for a crowd full of quirky weirdos.

Two steel cables with clips on the ends dropped from the darkened ceiling above the curtained stage. My stomach turned and I desperately wished I hadn't eaten a cheeseburger from Sid's a mere forty-five minutes before I was supposed to go onstage. Something that tasted like cheese mixed with bile bubbled up from the pit of my belly.

"Ready?" Miyu asked as she wheeled a rattling cart with the equipment for my act past me and onto the stage.

I didn't respond. My knees locked up while the rest of my legs turned to jelly. Monty gave me a gentle nudge. "Come on, kid. From what Miyu's told me, you've got this one in the bag. Go out there and make us proud." I shook my head at him, and he grabbed my wrists. "That woman is terrified of leaving her own house," he whispered. "But she has so much invested in you, she's out on that stage, ready to help you perform. And I'll be there, too. You'll be fine."

His mustachioed face looked so strangely earnest in that moment, I allowed myself to believe him. I gave him the briefest of nods and somehow willed my jellied legs to move so I could join Miyu on the curtained stage. Monty slipped between the curtains to face the hecklers at the front.

"Who wants a mustache ride?" one of them shouted.

"I want the bendy girl's number!" another one shrieked.

"I can't make any promises," Monty said breezily. "But buying me a gin and tonic couldn't possibly hurt your chances. But before we start bartering with drinks and digits, we've got an extra special tasty treat for you tonight, pleasure seekers. A delectable morsel of suspense." My stomach threatened to turn inside out, and I silently cursed Monty for referring to me and/or my act as a morsel.

"Many years ago," he continued, "a world famous escapologist graced this very stage with a few of her most stunning performances. After her tragic death, her only daughter found a young pipsqueak of an orphan digging though the dumpster in the alley behind the salon, hungry for cheeseburgers and fame. She took her home, raised her as her own, and trained her in the exquisite and death-defying art."

"What the hell?" I whisper-whined. "Why did he just invent a ridiculous back story for me?"

"His stage persona is kind of a dick," Miyu said. "The crowd knows he's all bullshit, but they love him. Just let him do his thing."

"Ladies, gentleman, non-ladies and non-gentleman," Monty bellowed, "you are about to witness that feral orphan's inaugural performance, aided by her mysterious assistant—a living shadow known only as . . . The Hummingbird."

"Oh, for fuck's sake," Miyu barked under her breath.

"Without further ado, the Salone Postale proudly presents the intrepid, the indelible, the incomparable . . . Ginger!"

A stagehand pulled open the curtain. Once my eyes adjusted to the blinding stage lights, I got my first look at the audience.

"Her hair's not red," one of the hecklers shouted. "I want my money back."

I almost passed out.

Monty winked at me. "To get your hearts racing and your palms sweating, Ginger will escape from a straitjacket . . . while suspended . . . upside down."

The crowd "oooohhhed" while Miyu slipped the straitjacket on me. I took in a deep breath, puffing up my chest as she cinched the straps around my ribcage. I knew I wasn't in immediate danger of literally dying— just dying of embarrassment—but I felt fragile, like the slightest knock might cause me to crumble into a pile of dusty bones.

She pulled the straitjacket's crotch strap tight, worsening my wedgie, then shackled my ankles with two distinct clanks. My head was swimming, but I somehow managed to register that the thick, stainless steel was cold. I took another deep breath and tried to focus on the chilly smoothness of the steel around my ankles, the scratchy canvas of the straitjacket against my arms, and the single bead of sweat dripping down the bridge of my nose.

Miyu clipped the two dangling steel cables to the imposing metal bar soldered between my shackled ankles. She tapped me gently on the shoulder, and I positioned myself on the floor, ready to be hoisted skyward and suspended from the rafters. As the steel cables cranked upward with a metallic rumble and screech, a strange sort of quiet fell over the audience. Perhaps everyone in the room, including me, was experiencing a simultaneous realization—*This is really happening. This is really happening, and we're all letting it happen.*

As their stunned eyes probed me, I realized I probably looked even more vulnerable and amateurish than I felt. I prayed there wasn't some creeper in the audience getting off on seeing a seventeen-year-old girl strung from the ceiling by her ankles. The thought made my stomach turn for the billionth time that day, and I swallowed a bitter burp.

"The intrepid orphan has a choice, sinners and saints," Monty said. "She can hang there until the blood rushing to her head causes her to pass out, or she can free herself." I looked toward him and realized he was staring at me with an uncharacteristic expression of concern.

I let out the breath I'd been half-holding and relaxed my tensed abs and shoulders. This gave me the tiniest big of wiggle room within the straitjacket, and I used it to muscle my right elbow toward the floor. The steel cables creaked and clanged as I thrashed, loosening the jacket. Aided by gravity, I forced my elbow over my head. I snagged the arm strap with my teeth and began to pull. I'd practiced this almost a hundred times, but the effort still made my jaw ache. With one final yank, I freed my arms.

It might have been my own excitement, but I thought I could feel the energy in the room shift. Someone in the back, maybe the tattooed bartender, let out a high-pitched whoop as I glanced at the hecklers up by the stage. They sat silently, staring at me with wide eyes, their drinks untouched on their table.

And out of that shifting energy, something dark and strange was born. Some very small part of me— just a smirking shadow in the cobwebs of my soul— took a breath and opened her mischievous eyes. She had gestated in a plum-colored womb, subsisting on scraps left behind by all the eccentrics who ripped their hearts right out of their chests and left them beating on a bloody stage. That ravenous orphan Monty told the crowd about spoke to me from inside. *Grow some perspective*, she said. *This, my friend, is worth all the fear in the world.*

With my newly-freed arms, I undid the crotch strap and let the jacket slip over my head and onto the stage. I felt exposed, but not in a bad way. Without all that heavy canvas, my skin could breathe and seemed to come to life, like it wanted to take on the world.

"Ladies and gents," Monty shouted. "The incomparable Ginger has freed herself from the straitjacket."

The crowd applauded and the hecklers finally snapped out of their trance. "I don't even care that her hair's not red!" one of them shouted.

"Don't stop now, Girl Scout." I wasn't sure if Miyu actually said it, or if it was just her voice in my head.

My abs protested for a moment as I hoisted my torso upward and grabbed onto the metal bar with both of my sweaty hands. I hugged the bar with my armpits and the shackles slid up my calves toward my knees, leaving me in a suspended fetal position. I pulled a bobby pin from my hair, snapped it into a pick and a torsion wrench, and got to work on the first shackle. Achy fire spread across my abs and back and through my strained thighs. When the pain became too intense to tolerate, I let go of the bar and swung back toward the floor.

"Can she do it, poets and prophets?" Monty asked. "The suspense is terrible," he said with a gleeful giggle. "I hope it'll last."

I gritted my teeth and forced myself upward again. After two excruciating minutes of sweating profusely under the stage lights, the first shackle opened with a springy, glorious pop. I dangled by one leg for a moment while the crowd cheered. I swung myself toward the ceiling again and hoisted my free leg up over the metal bar to support my weight.

I don't know how long it took me to pick the second shackle. The more deeply I focused, the more lost I got.

Time seemed to drop away. I was vaguely aware of the audience, and of Miyu and Monty, but they seemed faded, like memories confined to a photo album. The bobby pin, the shackle, my achy, sweaty fingers—these were the only things that were real. My mind felt clear, but not empty.

The second shackle gave way, and I gripped the bar with both hands and allowed my feet to dangle. The bar dropped slowly toward the stage and the moment my sneakers touched the floor, I felt like I'd just woken up from a hazy but pleasant dream. The hecklers were on their feet, and even Miyu was clapping.

"That'll do, Girl Scout," she mouthed at me.

"Ginger, the intrepid, chestnut-haired orphan," Monty said as he beckoned me toward the front of the stage. "And her mysterious assistant, The Humming-bird."

Miyu bowed and I followed suit, though my bow came out more like an awkward curtsy.

Naveen, still dressed in his marching band uniform, pulled me into an unexpected hug after I slipped between the closing curtains. "I'm so happy I gave you that flyer," he said.

"Me too."

I drove home just after midnight, my arms and legs jangly with adrenaline. I'd already used the "sleeping at Meadow's" excuse earlier that week, and knew I was going to have to sneak in and offer up some reason for breaking my eleven-thirty curfew in the morning.

My parents' room was dark when I pulled into the driveway, which I hoped would give me at least six hours to come up with a plausible explanation for my lateness. Kyle's bedroom light was still on, but I assumed he'd probably fallen asleep while playing *War is Fun* or *Super Japanese Animation Racing* or whatever brain-melting video game he was drowning his sorrows in lately.

When I shoved my key into the front door, I smiled. For the first time, I recognized the lock as an easy-to-pick, five-pin tumbler. *Keys are for suckers*, Ginger the intrepid orphan whispered in my mind. I slipped into the kitchen guided only by the light of the clock on the microwave and pulled off my sneakers. Guinan greeted me with a few sniffs before returning to her dog bed. I tiptoed toward the living room and nearly swallowed my tongue when I heard a creak on the stairs.

"Hey," Kyle whispered.

"Hey."

"Who were you out with?"

"Uhhh . . ."

He grinned at me. "Just a heads up, mom and dad were bugging me about it. They thought you might be out with some girl named Meadow. Not the one with the gazelle face from middle school, right?"

"She doesn't have a gazelle face. More like a consti-pated giraffe."

"That's more like it," he said. "Changing the subject and injecting a little humor. Now you're learning. I thought I'd never have a chance to pass down all my tricks."

With his brows raised conspiratorially over a pair of bright eyes, I saw a flash of the old Kyle. I caught a shimmer of the golden boy who could get away with murder, plotting something sneaky with Connor behind my parents' back, like claiming they're going camping with Austin and his dad for the weekend and then driving to New York City instead. Only, it wasn't Connor he was conspiring with this time. It was me.

My phone buzzed and I dug it out of my shoulder bag—a text from Miyu.

> Time to up the ante, Girl Scout. Tomorrow we cure you of your fear of drowning.

"Was that text from Meadow?" Kyle asked.

"Yeah, she can't find her wallet and thought maybe she left it in Stella's car."

He laughed. "Wow. Even I almost believed you for a second. The good thing is Dad actually seemed impressed that you have friends other than Stella. But Mom . . . Obviously she was a teenage girl once. She knows what's up."

"What does that mean?"

He squinted at me. "It's a guy, right? Connor thinks so, too."

I should've been thrilled that they'd so epically missed the mark. I should've been psyched that Connor suspected I was canoodling with someone other than him and was maybe, possibly, jealous. But really, it just pissed me off. Even my feminist mom had assumed that when a preoccupied seventeen-year-old girl periodically goes MIA, it must be because of a dude.

I glared at Kyle as I made my way up the remaining

steps. "Maybe it is and maybe it isn't," I whispered.

He snickered. "You really do have secrets." He snagged my arm just before I could slip into my room. "You don't have to listen to any of my advice, but one tip: You can squeeze an extra half-hour to forty-five minutes out of your curfew if you call home with an excuse. Watching a long movie, hit traffic, didn't realize what time is was, whatever. But don't do it every time and don't push it over an hour."

Despite his sexist twenty-one-year-old guy assumptions, my big bro really just wanted to be a big bro. "Thanks," I mumbled.

"You're welcome."

My phone buzzed a second time, right after I closed my bedroom door. I assumed it was Miyu with more ominous comments on my future training, but it was a text from a number I didn't recognize.

> Ginge! It's Stella. My roommate is a sneaky genius who gave the admins a decoy phone and kept her real one. She said I could text you. How's your summer????

In my amped up state, I wanted to give that sneaky genius a little piece of my mind. *One, that's my BFF you're rooming with. Back off, bitch. Two, thanks for letting her borrow your phone. Three, you suck for letting her borrow your phone because I have so many things tell her, but I'm not ready so just get off my freaking back, okay?*

Instead, I texted back.

> Hey. Cool. Good.
> What happened?
> What? Nothing. I said good.

>Something happened. You are being
cryptic, even for you.
>How can you tell thru a text?
>I just can.

Change the subject, you ass, Ginger whispered in my mind.

>Whatever. How's your summer?

After a long pause, she texted one word.

>Good.
>You suck.
>I'm just kidding, Ginge. :) Sorta. I
have to go but I'll tell you more later.

Maybe I was just losing my mind from a combo of adrenaline, curfew breaking, and cryptic texts, but it sounded like Stella had a secret of her own. But it was Stella, so it was probably something like radically deciding to stop using Oxford commas for the summer.

I threw my shoulder bag on my bed and started rifling through my record collection, searching for the perfect sound to both capture my night and make my heart stop going *pip-pip-pip-pip-pip*. I settled on Herb Alpert and basked in the trumpets of the Tijuana Brass but couldn't get my jangled nerves to settle. Everyone in my family, plus Connor and Stella, knew I was up to something. And I had no idea how much worse it was about to get.

My first U.S. tour brought me only to the major cities—New York, San Francisco, Boston, Chicago . . . Each day felt like a sprint. Get up, get on a plane, fly, land, perform, sleep, repeat.

My second tour gave me some breathing room. My assistant and I rented a van and I booked dates in a few smaller cities. Austin was kitschy and offbeat. Minneapolis was cold but friendly. And St. Louis had mouth-watering frozen custard.

But as we drove along endless stretches of highway, I could feel something on the East Coast tugging at me, pulling me forward like a vortex.

The night we barreled down Atwells Ave in Providence, the white lights strung over Federal Hill made my eyes widen and my grin broaden. At first, I brushed off my excitement, chalking it up to lack of sleep and too many hours of highway hypnosis. But when I took the stage at Salone Postale, I realized my instincts had been spot on. This place was different. The crowd looked like any other crowd—full of art school dropouts and irreverent beatniks—but there was something rising off of them. A hunger for something raw and real. A hunger for something they'd never seen before.

I scanned their faces. I saw them licking their chops, their pupils dilated, incisors ready to devour my act. All except one. A boy who was almost a man didn't clap or whoop or cheer. He just smirked and brushed his dark hair back. He kept his hands firmly in the pockets of his leather jacket.

I couldn't wait to meet him.

– Akiko Miyake, Providence, April 1, 1981

Mattie Has Something to Prove

My lungs were screaming at me to take a breath. My brain was knocking assertively at all my nerves and reflexes. *Hello? We're drowning here. Now might be a good time to do something.*

But I didn't give in. I knew what would happen—I'd inhale a mouthful of water that would feel like a prickly ball of fire and spend the next two hours hacking and coughing all over Miyu's bathroom floor. I could feel her hand firmly against my neck, holding my head under the lukewarm water in the bathtub. I signaled for her to let me go, but she was even more determined than me. I suffered for another ten seconds before she released me, and I yanked my head out of the bathtub and fell back onto the ceramic tile, gasping for air.

"You'll have to do better than a minute-thirty, Girl Scout."

Miyu and I had spent the better part of the last week in that bathroom, practicing deep breathing and muscle relaxation and then straining my lungs to breaking point. "I just need thirty more seconds," I said. "Two minutes and I'm good, right?"

She nodded. "Though it doesn't hurt to give yourself a little wiggle room. And during the real deal, you'll be moving around, using up more of your oxygen. Do as many deep breathing exercises as you can stand this week with this." She handed me a plastic mouthpiece with a tube on one side. "It's a lung expander. Athletes and Navy Seals use them."

"Not planning on going to the Olympics or running a black op, but okay."

"Some cardio couldn't hurt either, Girl Scout."

"Ugh. I hate running. It makes me feel clompy."

"Then do some Jazzercise or play badminton."

"You really did have a weird childhood."

She scoffed, but the slight curve of her lips told me she was giggling on the inside.

The following week, after I'd exhausted myself with an hour-long aerobic kickboxing session, we moved from the bathtub to the swimming pool in her backyard.

"It's kinda chilly," I said as I dipped my toe in.

"I don't wanna hear any whining, Girl Scout. I had this bitch cleaned just for you."

"I feel honored." My tone was sarcastic, but if Miyu had bothered to have her swampy pool cleaned, she probably had a fair amount of faith in me.

I sat on the edge by the deep end as Miyu chained weights to my ankles.

"You just want me to pick these locks underwater?" I asked.

"You say that like you think it's going to be easy."

"At this point, I could pick a lock in my sleep."

"Sleep is one thing. Completely submerged is another."

And, as usual, she was right. As soon as those weights pulled me to the bottom of the frigid pool, and I found myself staring up through the chlorinated water at the sunny sky, I forgot all of my breath training. The bobby pin slipped from my pruney fingers, and I scrambled along the bottom of the pool, searching for it as panic set in. By the time I found it, my lungs began to protest. I dropped the pin a second time and Miyu let me thrash around on the bottom for a full twenty seconds before diving down with a snorkel mask to free me.

When I surfaced, I drew in a desperate, greedy breath as I clung to the edge of the pool.

"Not so cocky now, huh, Girl Scout?"

"You bitch," I coughed.

"Just for that, next time I'll let you struggle for a few more seconds before I swim down there to rescue your ass."

That first day in the pool, Miyu had to rescue me five times. It wasn't until halfway through day two of pool training that I successfully picked one lock while submerged before panicking and throwing in the proverbial towel. But as my body grew more and more accustomed to cold water and oxygen deprivation, the more focused my mind became. My pruney fingers turned from fumbling disasters to nimble instruments of liberation.

With two weeks in the pool under my belt, I successfully picked three padlocks while submerged and increased my breath hold to a full two minutes. After doing a victory lap around the pool while Miyu did one of those obnoxious slow claps, I dried my face and damp hair with a towel.

"I'll go change and then we can head into Providence," I said.

She scowled at me.

"I conquered my fear of pool. You can deal with your aversion to leaving your house for a few hours."

It only took ten minutes of coaxing—less time than I thought—to get Miyu across the threshold and off the porch.

"Deep breaths," I said.

"You and Monty can handle cleaning the tank," she barked. "Why do I need to be there?"

"You're the one who wanted to go with an aquarium escape as my next act," I reminded her. "Plus, the tank is a prized historical artifact. Monty can't handle that kind of thing without adult supervision."

She huffed and stomped onto the stone walkway, briskly making her way to Stella's car.

"Buckle up," I sang. She glared at me and fiddled with the radio for the whole drive into Providence.

"All these stations suck," she complained as I took a right onto Atwells Ave.

"Stella's got some classical tapes in the glove box."

"Forget it. We're almost there."

I parked the Bug around the corner from the salon, and we met Monty by the back entrance. He looked like a fish out of water in the mid-summer sunshine, dressed in sweatpants and a black t-shirt that had probably fit well before he grew a paunchy beer gut. He yawned and rubbed his stubble.

"You look hungover," Miyu said.

"I may have had one too many last night," he admitted. "But I'm willing to suffer for the sake of art."

We followed Monty into the same storage room that I'd sat in for over an hour, drunk on Long Island iced teas and mythologizing a distant piece of history. As I picked up a soapy sponge and started dissolving the dust matted on the aquarium's thick glass, that history began to feel less ephemeral and more like something tangible—something I was connected to. I didn't dare hope to be as legendary as Harry or Dorothy or Akiko, but with each swipe of my sponge I could feel myself pulling their history into the present and pushing it forward. My mind slipped into that same clear, focused space I'd come to relish when picking locks or forcing my body out of a straitjacket.

"Did your mom design the aquarium herself?" I asked Miyu.

"Less talking, more scrubbing."

The three of us spent the morning and a chunk of the afternoon getting that tank to gleam like it did in Akiko's heyday. Once we got the first layer of dust off, Monty attacked the glass with a bottle of Windex while I smothered the tarnished brass with smelly industrial polish. Miyu climbed the ladder to the top of the tank and brought down the wooden lid, sticking her fists through the two handholes that had once allowed

Akiko to pick the padlock that trapped her in the tank.

"That thing probably needs to be replaced," Monty said.

I cringed. Typically, I was all for salvaging pieces of history, but the lid looked like a piece of driftwood, grayed and faded with age.

"Don't be silly," Miyu said as she knocked on the lid with her pale fist. "This is solid cherry. A few coats of varnish and it'll be good as new."

And, as usual, Miyu was right. By the time we left the storage room of Salone Postale, she'd turned the grayed lid a deep, rich brown with subtle hints of red. The glossy varnish shined so intensely I could see my reflection in it.

Miyu gazed at her handiwork with a smirk on her face. "Tomorrow, we practice with the real deal. Then, we go shopping for koi."

I thought performing would get easier, but I suppose I should have taken Akiko's habit of pulling out her own hair as a sign that it might not. The night before my first performance in the aquarium, I couldn't sleep. I stared at the ceiling, listened to a few mellow jazz records, and drank two cups of chamomile tea. Instead of sleep, I found myself getting up to pee three times and exchanging more cryptic texts with Stella.

>Is it a guy
>Et tu, Stella?
>OMG OMG who else thinks it's a guy?
>No one. Forget I said that. It's not a

>guy because it's not anything. Just me
listening to jazz records and reading a
bunch of books.
>I don't believe you, Ginge. *sigh*
>Wait – did you think my thing was a guy
because YOUR thing is a guy?

A long, suspicious pause.

>Sorry, Ginge. Gotta go.

Clearly a pattern was emerging, but I didn't have room in my pre-performance brain to worry about it. I threw my phone on the bed and stretched my shoulders. My lungs drew in a deep breath, preparing themselves for oxygen deprivation. The elements of escapology had become my new reflexes. When I didn't have anything better to think about, I found my mind inventing locks to mentally pick. As I paced around my room, each step of my routine flicked through my mind on an endless loop. Miyu and I had spent a week running through it more times than I could count. I pictured Miyu kneeling on the narrow platform at the top of the tank with big plastic bags full of koi.

"Ick," I said as she ripped open one of the bags and poured in a bug-eyed fish. The creature's orange splotches made it look like a bad piece of abstract art. "I know the koi were one of your mom's signatures, but do we have to use live fish? Isn't the escape impressive enough on its own?"

Miyu rolled her eyes. "I'm letting you add your old-ass jazz music to the routine. If you want to keep that, you need to compromise on the koi."

I thought about calling her bluff and ditching the jazz, but I'd already picked out the perfect song and spent a wad of my Café Italiano earnings on a faux-antique gramophone. Instead, I played the animal rights card.

"I feel bad for them," I whined. "Isn't it going to freak them out each time I get in there?"

"They're not like people, Girl Scout. They don't have memories. By the time you crawl out of the tank, they'll have forgotten you were ever in there to begin with."

Lucky bastards. "Ugh. Fine."

The night of my performance, I wished I'd protested harder. My nerves didn't freeze up like the first time around, but I felt queasy staring into those glassy, oblivious fish-eyes as Miyu and I rolled the tank into place, wheels grinding against the floorboards of the stage. Were they trying to tell me something?

I adjusted my robe and repositioned the bobby pins in my hair.

"Don't tug on them, Girl Scout, or they'll fall out," Miyu whispered.

Naveen sidled up behind me, and I let out a little *Eeep!* of surprise. "My band won't stop talking about you," he said. "I think they want to be part of your act."

See? People like you! Ginger called out joyously, her impish voice echoing in my mind. I tried to relax. If I didn't stop to truly enjoy these moments, they'd pass me by and I'd be left memory-less, like those fish.

Beyond the plum-colored curtains, I could hear Monty introducing me. "And now, ladies and gentlemen, to keep you on the very bleeding edge of your seats, the Salone Postale proudly presents . . . the incomparable Ginger!"

I took a ragged breath and slipped between the curtains, clutching an LP in my clammy hands. When the applause faded, I had to remind myself to swallow.

Time to move. One foot in front of the other.

I shuffled over to the gramophone at the edge of the stage and pulled the record out of the sleeve. I closed my eyes and inhaled the musty antique scent of the vinyl. Even with my nerves clanging like frigging cowbells, I took a moment to relish this little ritual. It's the little things, you know?

The hecklers up front started whistling and whooping when Fats Navarro's "Nostalgia" crackled out of the brass horn. They looked practically bloodthirsty, and I swear I could feel the energy of a mid-summer Friday night radiating off of them, vibrating all the little hairs on my forearms.

I stripped down to my bathing suit and gripped the ladder to the top of the tank with my shaky fingers. A little voice hissed through my mind. *You can't do this. You're out of your damn mind. Stop. Go back to your quiet little life.* I swallowed the voice and started the climb.

Miyu was waiting for me at the top, holding the straitjacket. She slipped the canvas over my arms, and I puffed myself up before she cinched each strap. I inhaled and exhaled, prepping my lungs as she wrapped a heavy chain around my ankles and secured it with a squat padlock. Wiggling my toes, I turned to face the crowd.

That was the moment I spotted Will Kane in the

audience, like a smirking omen of pure doom.

My heart flew into my throat, and my veins flooded with a mix of rage and nearly paralyzing terror. My knees buckled, but I managed to sit instead of falling off the platform and cracking my skull on the stage. I knew I wasn't in the right state of mind and body to perform, but backing out seemed like the worst of all options— especially with Will in the audience. Though he wasn't a guy I'd ever felt any need to impress, I was suddenly overcome with the feeling that I had something to prove.

Miyu's face blanched to an unnerving shade of pale, and she looked even more panicked than I felt. I nodded assertively at her, letting her know that I wasn't backing out. She shook her head but picked up the freshly varnished lid of the tank anyway, preparing to lock me into what had a decent chance of becoming a watery glass coffin. I shut my eyes and took a few deep, even breaths. *Now or never.*

I slid into the tank, letting the water envelop me and the weight of the chain around my ankles pull me to the bottom. A few of the koi brushed against my skin as they rushed to congregate at the top of the tank. The soaked canvas of the straitjacket stuck to my skin as I thrashed around, taking almost thirty seemingly infinite seconds to wriggle out.

Through the thick glass, I saw the audience react, but I brushed it aside. I pulled the bobby pin from my hair, pried it apart, and got to work on the padlock keeping my ankles shackled. A simple Westin four-pin. It shouldn't have given me any trouble, but it did. I couldn't get Will Kane out of my head. He was probably filming my act on his phone and already texting his friends . . . *Dudes. You know that weird quiet girl in my homeroom who's friends with that smart chick? You're not gonna believe the weirdness she's been up to.*

It was only a matter of time before I'd be plastered all over LifeScape. Then Kyle would know, and this wouldn't be like him conspiring with me to hide a boyfriend who didn't actually exist. He'd have to tell our parents.

As panic set in and my lungs whimpered in protest, the lock popped open, the sound muffled by the water. I felt relieved, but there was no joy, no serenity, no meditative moment of clarity. I just wanted this to be over as soon as possible. I kicked my way to the top of the aquarium and stuck my hands through the two holes carved in the lid. I had to pick the padlock completely blind, and it took me an excruciating full minute. My lungs were screaming at me, and I almost did the worst thing one can possibly do in a situation like this— inhale a quart of koi-contaminated water.

I shut my eyes for a moment, exhaled some of the stale air in my lungs, and commanded myself to calm down. The padlock above the tank clicked open with an almost anticlimactic *ping,* and relief washed over me as I pushed up the lid and climbed out of the tank. My angry lungs sucked in oxygen and then coughed up thin strands of mucus that I forced myself to swallow.

I climbed shakily down the ladder, back to the stage, and took a brief bow. The roar of the crowd brought no relief. All I could focus on was the pain in my chest and

Will, now on his feet, clapping along with the rest of the salon-goers and grinning at me like he was about to ruin my life.

Miyu accosted me backstage as I was drying off with a scratchy towel.

"What the hell was that?" I'd never seen her look so enraged. As refreshing as it was to see her express some genuine emotion, it scared me a little.

"I don't want to talk about it," I mumbled.

"I can't even tell you how much I want to slap you right now. But I won't."

"I don't see what the big deal is." I threw on my jeans, trying futilely to shrug off my shaky performance.

Miyu grabbed me by the shoulder. "This act involved real danger. I thought I was going to lose you."

I dropped my gaze to the floor. "I'm sorry. I know it was stupid. It's complicated. We can talk about it tomorrow, and you can scream at me some more if it will make you feel better. Right now I need to go home and . . . I don't even know yet. But something."

She narrowed her eyes at me. "Okay. Don't drive like an ass. If you get into an accident, I'll kill you.

I didn't dole out hugs on a regular basis, but I couldn't think of any other way to respond.

"Oh, jeezus," she moaned. "Don't get all mushy on me, Girl Scout."

I laughed but couldn't shake the niggling feeling that everything I'd worked for was about to fall apart.

"Later, Miyu."

I ran a comb through my wet hair, ducked out the back door of the salon into the alley, and shuffled though the dark toward Stella's Bug. Goose bumps rose on my skin in the cool, late night air and made me wish I'd put a hoodie on over my t-shirt.

"Hey."

The air in my lungs froze. I hadn't even seen him under the dim glow of the streetlight. Leaning on the hood of Stella's Bug was the unmistakable silhouette of Will Kane.

"Oh fuck," I said under my breath.

"That was a pretty impressive routine. It makes shooting free throws look like child's play. I feel like a cream puff compared to you."

His off the cuff comment boiled my panicky jitters into white-hot rage.

"You arrogant piece of shit," I muttered as I shook my head. "You have no idea what this means to me." He stood up, straight as an arrow, but I still couldn't see his face. "You have things, totally normal things, that make your life okay. Well, this is my one thing but now . . . well, it's like when they turn the lights on at the end of a middle school dance. Everyone who was slow dancing and making out stops and gets a good look at each other under the lights, and all the magic gets sucked out of the room."

He grinned at me with his perfectly-straight, pearly-white teeth.

"Don't you dare laugh at that metaphor."

"Mattie . . ."

Despite the fact that we'd been going to the same

school for three years, I was shocked he actually knew my name. I'm not sure why, but hearing him say it out loud melted all my rage away, leaving me as brittle as antique glass. I plopped down in the driver's seat of Stella's car, choking back tears. But trying to hold them back was only making it worse. So there I was, crying right in front of Will Kane as he slid into the passenger seat and shut the door.

"Tell me it's not too late," I whimpered. "Tell me you didn't already send a video or something to the whole freaking basketball team."

"It's not too late. I was actually too shocked to even think about pulling out my phone." I almost flinched when he placed his warm, slightly sweaty hand on mine. "If you don't want me to tell anyone about what I just saw, then I won't."

How can I trust you? I didn't have the wherewithal to say it out loud. The tears turned into a flood, and I felt a flush of humiliation as I sobbed into the steering wheel. Will squeezed my hand before letting go to rifle through the glove box. He pulled out a pile of napkins and handed a few to me.

"I figured Stella would have napkins," he said. "She seems like the always prepared type. Do you feel better?"

"Not really." I blew my raw nose into a napkin. "How can I? I don't even know you, and I'm counting on you to keep a secret for me."

He coughed and grabbed the door handle. I thought he was going to take off before I screamed at him again, but he sank back into the passenger's seat with a sigh. "I have secrets too, you know."

I blew my nose again as I wondered what kind of secrets a guy like Will would have. Maybe he had a geeky hobby, like stamp collecting? Maybe his parents dressed as clowns and made balloon animals in their spare time, so he never invited anyone to hang out at his house?

"I have an idea," he said. "What if I tell you something that I've never told anyone? That way, you know I won't tell anyone that you're incredibly talented and have a wicked cool hobby. It'll be like mutually assured destruction."

"Mutually assured destruction," I echoed with a nod. "I might be able to live with that. But so help me god, Will, it better not be a petty cool kid secret, like you enjoy doing calculus more than playing basketball, or you have a thing for goth chicks."

He laughed and shook his head. His hand slid over mine again as he coughed out two words—"I'm gay."

I stared at him.

A tinny chuckle escaped from his lips. "That actually wasn't as hard as I thought it would be."

I blinked at him, and, swear to god, had to bite my lip to keep from cracking up. "But . . . you and Betsy. You're like Ken and Barbie. You're like a couple out of a goddamn prom catalogue."

He flashed me a look that was almost a glare. "I prefer Bonnie and Clyde, but I guess Ken and Barbie is one way of looking at it. And she doesn't know."

"Oh my god. I mean . . . Oh my god."

"I'm a colossal asshole because she's really great." His voice cracked right in the middle of *great* and he leaned back against the seat, probably willing himself not to cry in front of me. "But you didn't know her in junior high. She was fucking insufferable."

"Betsy?"

"She always wanted to be the center of attention," he said. "She would start rumors and . . . invent . . . all this soap opera drama and thrust herself into the middle of it. She was the kind of girl who lived for crying in the bathroom at every school dance. It was pathetic. I figured we could date for a few years, so my friends would get off my back about the girlfriend thing, and then I would come out in high school and give her exactly what she wanted."

"A real reason to be a drama queen," I said as I shook my head. "Holy shit. What happened? She just randomly decided to grow up when you guys got to high school?"

"Her parents got divorced when we were freshmen. Her mom cheated on her dad and . . . at first, I thought it was just going to destroy her. But it didn't. She turned into a whole new person—an amazing person—and one of a million reasons why I still haven't come out."

"What are the other reasons? I mean, isn't it kind of cool to be gay now?"

"Maybe if you live in a TV show." He wiped a small tear away from the corner of his eye. "Anyway, my friends are the biggest reason."

I pictured Will's friends—girls like Meadow and guys from the basketball team who threw the word "faggot" around regularly, oblivious to the power it had to cut someone to his core. "Dicks," I said under my breath.

He shook his head. "They're not dicks. Actually, most of them are dicks. They don't beat up on gay kids or anything, but they have this idea in their heads of who I am. You know—that's Will, he's a cool cat who would never hit on another dude. Everything would change if I told them."

"You don't think they'd get over it? Don't you think having a gay friend might make them better people?"

"It took me years to come to terms with it, so I don't expect any of them to get over it overnight. And anyone who didn't care about the gay thing would still care about the Betsy thing. I know you probably think Meadow's just a snooty bitch, but really, she's terrifying. She'd go to the ends of the earth for Betsy."

"You know you don't have to be friends with those people. I have one friend—literally, one friend—and I've somehow managed to survive. There are other guys at our school who are out."

"I know, and I'm just as scared of them as I am of my friends. They'd see me as another jock, indistin- guishable from all the jocks who shoved them in the hall when we were in junior high and pretended it was an accident. Plus, I'm not into any of the stuff they're into. EDM at high volumes gives me a headache, and I don't have any plans to shave my body hair."

I snorted. "Stereotypes make for poor excuses."

"Believe me, I'm full of poor excuses."

"Me too," I mumbled. "Who else have you told?"

He looked me square in the face, his brown eyes wide. "No one. Literally, no one. Not even my parents. The only person on earth who knows is a guy I hooked up with at summer camp a few years ago."

"Would your parents be upset?"

He squinted at the dashboard. "That's not it. Like, they'd both probably be shocked, and my dad might be a little disappointed that this grand vision he had for his son's perfect little life wasn't going to pan out quite as he'd expected. But he'd act like everything was fine. He does the same thing when he's pissed at my mom, and it's infuriating. Though he has a huge tell. He rubs his nose like he's about to sneeze. You know, with rage."

"And your mom?"

He shook his head. "My fucking mom. She'd be thrilled, but here's the thing: She loves gay men, but they're like works of art to her. Not actual people."

Something strange hummed through my veins. Warm and icy at the same time, it took me a moment to realize it was power, but not the kind I wanted. This kind of power made me squirm and itch all over. I liked having the power to keep an audience on the edge of their seats. I didn't like having the power to destroy someone's life at the drop of a whisper.

"Who knows about your double life as an escape artist?" he asked.

"No one from school," I said. "Not even Stella."

"Your parents?"

I shook my head. "My brother doesn't know either. Just people at the salon and my mentor, Miyu." In my head, I laughed at myself for calling Miyu my mentor. The word didn't really suit her. It made her sound wise and deeply sane instead of crotchety and reclusive.

"Why haven't you told anyone?"

I tapped my fingers on the steering wheel while I tried to come up with a good answer. "First off, my parents would kill me and then have Miyu arrested for child endangerment. But that's maybe a tenth of why. The real reason is kinda like you and your guy friends. No one would ever look at me the same way again." I inhaled and exhaled a ragged breath. "And there's . . . there's something about sharing a thing you really, truly care about. I'm not talking about hearting stuff on LifeScape. When something's so important that it becomes a piece of you, sharing it exposes you."

He nodded and stared out the windshield at the darkened street. "Yeah. But you're sharing it with a room full of complete strangers."

"But that's the thing. I'm just a stage persona to them. They know Ginger, not Mattie. And, until tonight, the salon felt like another dimension—I honestly couldn't imagine anyone I knew showing up."

"Never say never, I guess." He raked his fingers through his dark hair. "Can I come see you perform, or will it still be like the end of a junior high dance?"

"Do you really want to see me perform, or do you just want to keep tabs on me now that I know your deepest, darkest secret?"

"Is 'both' an acceptable answer?"

I stepped out of the bathroom and threw the pee stick across the room. It bounced off the boy's shoulder and landed on the carpet of our living room with a little thud.

The boy smirked and brushed his dark hair back. "Ew."

"Ew? Look at it. There's a plus sign. Do you know what that means, asshole?"

"Why are you freaking out?" A strand of his dark hair came loose and swung down over his eye. "This is the United States, not medieval Japan. We have ways of taking care of it."

I had, of course, considered this as an option and was still considering it. But his nonchalance brought out something dark in me. I wanted to pick up the ashtray on the coffee table and smash it against his face, break his nose. All of his mysterious charms—his black leather jacket, his trademark smirk, the casual way he held his chopsticks—now seemed like a cruel joke.

"Get out of my apartment. And don't ever come back."

– Akiko Miyake, Providence, February 14, 1982

Will With Two Ls Answers the Question of the Day

Why?

I know. I didn't have to tell her. I easily could've said *nighty-night, have a nice life!* and hightailed it out of there, leaving Mattie to cry her little heart out into the steering wheel of Stella's car. And I almost did. I had my hand on the door, and I was ready to run into the night and pretend I'd never been to Salone Postale or seen one of my classmates risk her own life for some seriously breathtaking art.

Yes, I said it. *Art.* The Houdini-knockoffs I'd seen on TV were cheesy as all get out. Laughable. Literally unbelievable, as in I didn't believe the performers had pulled off their feats without crutches and camera tricks. But what Mattie had done rattled me to my very core. It pulled at heartstrings I didn't even know I had. Because unlike the TV-Houdinis with their showboating and their '80s leotards and their flashy misdirection, Mattie's act was more raw than the bruised ego and flayed knee of a kid who trips on the stairs in front of everyone on the first day of junior high.

In those last few seconds before she burst out of the aquarium, when an expression of complete and total terror crossed her face, I stopped breathing. And not because I thought she might actually drown in front of a crowd of Providence hipsters and weirdos, but because it was obvious that fear had its sticky paws around her throat and she didn't let it stop her. She pushed through the terror like a survivor clawing her way out of a hideous, burning car wreck.

When Mattie took her bow that night, my mom elbowed me, almost knocking the seltzer and lime I'd been ignoring out of my hand. "Wasn't that outstanding, Willem? And she looks so young. Like a fresh-faced Marina Abramović, don't you think?"

I blinked a few times before responding. "I know her."

My mom's face lit up so bright it practically caught fire. "You do? How?"

"From school."

She cackled. "Well, my faith in the public school system has officially been renewed. You have to go congratulate her."

I shook my head. "I know her, but I don't really *know* her, you know?"

"Ah, the tedious intricacies of teenhood. Get over yourself and go talk to her. Monty will let you back-stage."

For the record, arguing with my mother—not just

about this but about anything—is pointless. So I stalked off, slipping through the crowd as they applauded for the gal who gave zero muskrats' asses. But I didn't go backstage. I needed fresh air to reset my lungs, which were still recovering from the seconds I spent too dumbfounded to breathe. I found a fire exit and headed into the night.

Stella's unmistakable Volkswagen greeted me in the alley behind Salone Postale.

"Oh, hey, little jalopy," I actually said out loud.

Then, of course, I laughed at the fact that I was too chickenshit to go say two words—*hi* and *congrats*—to a girl I sat only two feet away from almost every day in home room. *What was the big deal?* She had no idea I occasionally indulged in detailed daydreams frequented by a cast of offbeat characters that included her. With her, I could still be Cool Will. Cool Will who played basketball and had a hot girlfriend and didn't mind going to parties where everyone got splifficated and engaged in mindless, meaningless conversation at nearly intolerable volumes.

So Cool Will leaned on the hood of that car and waited for the escapologist to emerge. And when she did, wet and shivering and as frizzy as ever, it became abundantly clear she didn't cotton to Cool Will. In fact, Cool Will seemed to really piss her off. When she called him an arrogant piece of shit, he shrank like the pansy he truly was into the most dimly lit corner of my soul. He left me hanging out to dry on the asphalt with a gal who'd once been unreadable and now seemed to be posi-lute-ly spilling over with feels.

"Mattie." I said her name because I couldn't think of anything better to say. Though I didn't know quite why, it snapped her out of her righteous hissy fit.

I knew she was going to cry, and I almost couldn't take the juxtaposition between the intrepid orphan who'd flipped death the bird and this tearful mess whimpering in the driver's seat of her best friend's shitty car. I would've done almost anything to make it stop. So I got in the car and reached for her hand. She flinched a little, like she wanted to yank it away but didn't want to be rude. I told her I wasn't going to tell anyone about what I'd seen on that stage.

To my horror, my words brought on a rather hideous crying jag. Mattie, god bless her, is by no means a pretty crier. Her puffy face flushed a splotchy red, and snot oozed out of her crusty nose.

Eager to do anything I could to clean up the mess, I fished through the glove box and pulled out of wad of napkins.

She laughed the saddest little laugh as she wiped her face. It sounded so hollow, so unfunny, it broke the shit out of my already broken heart.

"I don't even know you, and I'm counting on you to keep a secret for me," she said.

When she said this, I almost took off. My sweaty fingers were poised on the door handle when an odd little itch, like a tickle deep in my chest, pulled me back. I wish I could say it was my altruistic need to soothe Mattie's hysterics. I wish I could say I told her because I saw a bit of myself in her maudlin meltdown. I'd even settle for being able to say I saw our little conundrum as a prime opportunity to turn her from a fantasy friend into a real life pal.

Sadly, the itch was none of those romantic things. It was, in fact, my own selfish need to push past the fear and let someone know who I really was. A real life someone, not some single-serving acquaintance I had a roll in the hay with at b-ball camp when I was fourteen. Someone who wouldn't care because she had nothing whatsoever invested in me. And Mattie—all weepy and snotty and frizzy and apparently leading a double life— seemed like a safe bet.

So I scraped together my meager scraps of courage, took a shaky breath, and coughed it out.

I didn't regret it right away. Maybe I was just hyper-ventilating, but I felt like I'd run a marathon and was ready to dust off my sneaks and run another. If Stella's Volkswagen had a sunroof, I might have floated right up into the dark Rhode Island sky.

The lighter-than-air high didn't last, of course. As soon as Stella's jalopy was out of sight and I was left to my lonesome on a deserted stretch of cracked pavement, a text from Betsy knocked me right back down to the earth.

> Enjoying quality time with your fam? Miss you oodles, mostest adorbs boyfriend. XOXO.

I texted back:

> I'd be having more fun with you, I'm sure. Don't get into too much trouble without me.

What I really wanted to say was, *I'm not adorbs, I'm*

a two-faced asshole. Please, please get blotto and cheat on me so I don't feel like such a dick.

"Well . . . I've got good news and bad," the doctor said as he removed his slime-coated gloves. "The bad news is she's comin' out backwards."

His efforts to turn her around had obviously failed. "Fucking hell," I moaned. "I can't have a C-section. I have a performance booked six weeks from now."

"Don't panic yet." He scratched his salt and pepper beard. "The good news is I feel confident I can deliver this baby vaginally if you're on board."

"Is that safe?"

"It carries risks. But I consider myself a farmer first and a doctor second. I've delivered literally thousands of calves and piglets. A good third of those were breech."

My first instinct was to tell this backwoods hick that my baby was not a farm animal, thank you very much. But something about his even tone and the scuffs on his work boots set me at ease. I'd expected a very no-nonsense doc with a stick up his ass when I arrived at the hospital. A doc with a sensible haircut who would go home afterward to a trophy wife and a few trophy kids and a golden retriever. This man with a flannel shirt on under his white coat was an entirely different shade of medical professional.

"Okay. I trust you."

The Hummingbird emerged ass-first at 7:34 p.m., a screaming, fluttering red bundle of life.

— Akiko Miyake, Providence, November 15, 1982

Mattie and the Myth of the Blank Slate

I found myself floating in an endless aquarium. A school of koi swam by, tickling my arms and legs with their slippery fins. I dove deeper and breast-stroked into a cozy sea cave. Waiting for me, I found a table set for a tea party. The octopus with the top hat—the one from the Mollusk Brigade poster—waved two of his eight arms toward an empty chair.

"Tea?" he asked when I took a seat.

"Why not? Thank you."

He wrapped one of his arms around the teapot and poured. "Tell me your troubles, child."

"Ugh. Where do I start?"

The cave shook and the sea floor rattled beneath our feet. Or arms, in the case of the octopus.

"What's happening?" I asked.

He adjusted his monocle and opened his mouth to speak. Instead of words, he bleated an old-fashioned telephone ring.

I woke up to the sound of my phone ringing as it did the twist on my dresser.

I crawled out of bed. "Um, hello?"

"Ginger!" the person on the other end of the line shrieked with joy.

"Hey, Stella."

"Oh, Ginge—I mean Mattie. Are you in one of your moods?"

I yawned. "No. Sorry. I was just out late."

"Oh," I could practically hear the smirk in her voice. "Doing what? Something with your mystery man?"

Oh fuck. "Uhhh . . ."

"Oh my god! Were you really out with a guy?"

"No! I mean, why does everyone think that? But, sort of?"

"Mmmmmkay."

Keeping everything from Stella would be like trying to hold back a flood with a single grain of sand. It was too big. Better to lock myself into an inevitable reveal than wait for a worst-case scenario to happen. "Yeah, I'm sorry. I have some stuff to tell you, but not over the phone."

"But I won't see you for two more weeks," she protested. "I won't be able to stand it."

"You're one of the most patient people I know, Stell. You'll live. How's St. Joe's?"

"Do you actually care, or are you just trying to change the subject?"

I stole a line from Will Kane. "Is 'both' an acceptable answer?"

Stella laughed. "I can never stay mad at you. You're

too funny. It's been super fun so far. The teachers are amazing."

"Has Marlon Blando been bugging you nonstop?"

"Who?"

"That guy from your Honors English class."

Stella paused and then exploded with laughter. "Holy crap, is that what you call him?"

"In my mind," I admitted. "I guess I never said it out loud before."

"Wow." Another long, suspicious pause. "You know who's actually really cool?"

Yes, I'm just dying to know what fascinating, Ivy-League-bound go-getter will be replacing me.

"Hrmph. Who?"

"Frankie Campos."

"Hm."

"You know who I'm talking about, right? He goes to our school. He's that fourteen-year-old prodigy who skipped two grades."

For college app resume: Excels at being ditched by best friend for nerdy pubescent boys.

"I think you need to work on your definition of cool, Stell. I had an art class with that kid, and he spent most of it sitting in the corner like a creeper, reading H. P. Lovecraft and making sculptures that looked like swords and guns."

"Ugh, don't be so judgy, Ginger. Someone can be into antique weapons and still be cool."

"I do like antiques," I admitted.

"Awesome. Once summer session is done, we're going to hang out with him."

"Whoa. My love of antiques will only get you so far. You mean, like, *hang out* hang out with him? Like, outside of school?"

"Yes, outside of school. We get out of St. Joe's the Friday after next. Plan something fun for us! Seriously, I expect the Friday night to end all Friday nights."

If Stella was dying for a debaucherous night out, I shuddered to think of the fun-void she'd been stuck in. "You *and* Frankie?" I asked.

"Yes, me *and* Frankie. Keep an open mind for once, Ginge. Please?"

"Okay, okay. I just don't want his parents to send the cops after us if we're ten minutes late bringing him home."

"Won't happen. Okay, I gotta go prepare for a presentation on David Foster Wallace. I'll call you two Fridays from now."

At least with Stella back I could stop using Meadow Winters as my go-to excuse. "'Kay. Bye."

I hung up and realized I had two unread text messages. The first was from Miyu.

> The salon wants you back on the 13th, Girl Scout. I want to see you redeem yourself in the tank. This time, you choose the restraints.

It took me a moment to realize the thirteenth of August was the Friday after next. *Shit.* How was I going to juggle Stella, her new buddy Frankie, and an escape act in the same night?

The second text was from a number I didn't recognize.

>What up, Mattie-O? It's Will. Want to
hang out today?

Against my better judgment, I made plans to meet up with Will. I took a quick shower, threw on jeans and a t-shirt, and headed downstairs.

"Pssst. Mattie," a voice called from the living room.

I trotted in to find Connor and Austin curled up on the couches, still reeking of booze. Austin was dead to the world, and Connor was staring at me with bleary, red-rimmed eyes.

"Too drunk to drive your asses home last night?" I asked.

"I blame Austin," he said with a yawn. "He's the one with the car."

"Right. Did you need something? I kinda have somewhere to be."

"Off to see your Secret Agent Lover Man? Austin, wake up. Mattie's about to tell us about her summer fling."

Austin grunted and rolled over. Two months ago, this surely would've ended with some serious Bear Poking and Connor tossing out the c-word or the b-word or telling me to fuck off. And I was tempted. Connor had already done half the work for me. How easy would it have been to play coy, drop a hint or two, let him follow a trail of breadcrumbs into a hedge maze grown from lies?

Instead, I walked away without saying another word.

"Seriously?" The last thing I expected him to do

was crawl out of his sarcophagus of blankets and come after me. "Fuck, Mattie, I was just kidding," he said as he grabbed my shoulder. "Really, I'm just curious. If you found someone you really like, then I'm happy for you. I mean that."

"Great. Later."

"Whoa, really?"

"Connor, I'll be honest. I'm not exactly sure where this conversation is going, but I have zero interest in it."

Silence.

"Can you please let go of my shoulder?"

Without another word, he stalked back to the couch, rubbing his sleepy eyes with the tips of his fingers. I shook my head and continued down the hall.

"Mattie, come in here for a sec," my mom shouted from her mom-cave. *Uh-oh.*

"Are the wonder twins up yet?" she asked as I entered her den. Guinan yawned and sniffed at me, and I gave her a quick pat on the head. The earthy scents of old vinyl and yellowing newsprint filled my nose, and the stacks of records lining the walls comforted me, even though my mom and I didn't exactly see eye-to-eye when it came to music.

"One of them was stirring," I said without elaborating.

"I'm just glad they didn't drive home drunk," she admitted. She took a long sip of coffee and looked up at me, over the tops of her glasses. "We need to chat about colleges."

Ugh. "Like, this second? I kind of made plans with someone."

She laughed. "If you'd like to do this later, you can *kind of* pencil me into your busy schedule."

"Now's fine."

"Perfect. I believe I asked you almost two months ago to line up some tours. Why has that not happened?"

A little gurgle of dread wound its way through my guts. "Can't this wait until school starts? I have, like, stuff going on right now." *Shut up, Mattie.*

"There's no better time to look at colleges than right now, when you're not busy with school."

I almost said *But right now I'm busy with stuff I actually care about.* Instead, I coughed out a squeaky "'Kay."

"Not so fast," she said when I turned to leave.

Oh fuck.

She slid her glasses down the bridge of her nose. "Are you planning on properly introducing us to Mr. Stuff Going On Right Now?"

Double fuck. "Uhhhh . . ."

"Mattie, you're a smart girl. We give you the same kind of freedom we gave Kyle because we trust you. But I want to know you're being careful. Safe. You know what I'm saying, right?"

"God, Mom. Eww."

She cocked one eyebrow at me. "That's not an answer to my question."

"Okay, jeezus. Yes, I know what you're saying. And if at some point this summer I find myself within arm's length of some guy's thing, I'll be sure it has a condom on it."

She just blinked at me. And though I'm pretty sure I maintained my Impenetrable Look of Teenage

Disgust, my insides were screaming *holy shit holy shit holy shit*.

She pushed her glasses back up and returned to her zine. "Well, then. You're free to go now."

"Thanks," I mumbled as I zipped out of the mom-cave, eager to get as far from that awkward mom-convo as humanly possible.

<hr/>

By the time I found a parking space and stumbled into Três Amigos, I found Will already sitting at a booth for two, clenching his jaw and tapping his fingers on the tiled table top. I slid into the seat across from him.

"Hey." I meant for it to sound breezy and carefree, but it came off as aloof.

"Hey," he mumbled back. "I hope you didn't feel obligated to have lunch with me."

"Um, no." *Smile and say something nice, goddammit. Your secret life depends on this guy.* "I like Mexican food." *Ugh.*

"Oh," he said as he picked up a menu. "Good."

I could practically hear crickets chirping as I sat there, pretending to look over my menu while I obsessed over the fact that I couldn't come up with some innocuous topic of conversation that would keep us occupied for another forty-five minutes to an hour. The sound of my own swallowing rang in my ears. Will wiped a sheen of sweat off his forehead and thanked the waitress when she brought us glasses of ice water. I ordered the first entree on the menu because I had been too busy being neurotic to pick a meal I actually wanted to eat.

"So . . ." Will said once the waitress had taken our order. He tapped the tabletop a few more times and then folded and unfolded his hands while he shifted in his seat.

"For fuck's sake, Will With Two Ls," I spat out. "I don't even know what I just ordered. Your anxiety is making me anxious. There's no reason for the two of us to be nervous. That's what the mutually assured destruction is for. It negates the need for nerves." I took a breath. "Yes, too much alliteration. Sorry."

Will blinked at me for a few seconds and then cracked up. "Did you just call me Will With Two Ls? Is there a Will With One L I should know about?"

Son of a bitch. "Wil Wheaton," I said out of the corner of my mouth.

"Like, from *Star Trek*?"

"Yes, from *Star Trek*, but you completely missed the point of my rant."

He leaned back against the booth, studying me for a moment. "I'm not nervous you're going to expose my . . . you know. *You* make me nervous."

I rolled my eyes. "Yeah, I know I can be a little awkward and weird. Thanks for pointing it out."

"No, no. That's not at all what I mean. You're like . . . the opposite of those things. You're one of those people who has everything together. You don't let hang ups get in your way. I'm not quite there yet."

My eyes widened. "You couldn't possibly be more wrong about me. My entire life is one giant hang up.

That's the reason I got into escapology in the first place."

"Go on," he prodded me after a brief span of silence.

"You know how people are always like, 'what doesn't kill you makes you stronger'? They think all experiences are good experiences as long as you learn from them. Like, if you hate high school it's fine because it'll make you a better person."

"It's such bullshit," he said with a disarming amount of seriousness.

Something warm and spiky pulsed through my veins, like hot oil popping in a wok. It made my heart beat faster and my tensed shoulders turn to jelly. "Yes. Oh my god, I can't believe you feel the same way."

"It's like the myth of the blank slate."

"The what?"

He coughed to clear his throat. "People say high school doesn't matter because you can just go college and reinvent yourself. I used to believe that, but my cousin was a loner in high school, and now he's constantly trying to make up for it. When I see him overcompensating like that . . ." He shook his head. "Fuck, it's exhausting. You can't just wake up and decide to be a different person because you've moved into a dorm room. All that damage done in high school is going to follow you, like a sad little ghost you can't shake."

My mouth went dry as I stared at him. I took a sip of water to regain my bearings.

"Are you okay?" he asked.

I nodded. "I've just never heard someone put it so

perfectly." I smiled at the waitress as she set a plate of enchiladas in front of me.

"But what does this have to do with your escape act? Did you finally say 'screw it'?"

I shook my head. "No, but . . . I don't know. Skating by didn't seem like enough anymore. I needed a good distraction."

Will raised his eyebrows. "Some distraction."

"You're right. It's more than escapism. Watching escape acts on YouTube wasn't cutting it anymore. I felt like I needed to put myself out there." I shoved a bite of chicken enchilada into my mouth. Maybe I was just high on the rush that comes with a good old-fashioned honest conversation, but the spicy flavors exploded in my mouth. It was the best enchilada I'd ever tasted.

"How did you end up at Salone Postale last night?" I asked.

"I went with my parents," he admitted. "They're regulars. And they think I need to be exposed more frequently to 'transgressive culture,' as my mom puts it."

"Transgressive culture, huh? That sounds like something my mom would say."

Will polished off a taco in three massive bites and flagged our waitress down for another glass of water. "What's Mattie short for?" he asked once he returned his attention to me. "Madeline?"

"It's not short for anything."

"You have a nickname for a name. Groovy."

I shrugged. "I'm named after Mattie Ross from *True Grit*. It's my dad's favorite movie. My parents are weird."

"If naming your kid after a character from a movie

makes you weird, my parents are abso-tive-ly just as weird."

"You're named after a character from a movie?"

"Sort of," he admitted with a grin. "My mom's favorite movie is *The Last Temptation of Christ*. She named me after Willem Dafoe."

"The actor? Does that mean your first name is really Willem?"

He nodded. "Not many people know that. Now you have two secrets on me, Mattie-O. I'm going to need some more juicy tidbits from your dark and mysterious life."

"I hate to disappoint you, but you already know everything that's worth knowing."

"Oh, come on. There must be something. Do you have a super-secret significant other who causes super-secret drama?"

I rolled my eyes. "No. But . . . I do have a best friend who's about to give me a major headache."

"Stella?"

"Yeah. She's been at St. Joe's all summer, and apparently Frankie Campos is her new best bud."

"That kid who skipped five grades?"

"Yes, though I'm pretty sure he skipped only two. The two of them get out the Friday after next, and she wants to hang out."

"And?"

"And I have a performance that night."

"Oh." He grinned at me as he mixed his rice and beans together. "So what's your plan?"

"No freaking idea."

Will scanned me with his brown eyes. "You kinda want to tell her, don't you?" he whispered.

That warm, spiky feeling pulsed through my veins again, like jump-out-of-your-skin joy cut with fear. That same feeling you get on a rollercoaster, right at the top of the lift hill. "It's not that I want to tell her. I just . . . she's my best friend. I can't keep this from her."

"You should invite her to the salon. We could have a little coming out party for you."

I forced a laugh and put my fork down. My hands were shaking.

"Are you okay?" he asked again.

I let out a deep sigh and buried my face in my hands. "Yeah," I mumbled. "This is hard for me. Just thinking about Stella in the audience makes me feel like I'm about to throw up."

"But you'll get through it," he said. "Then it'll get easier. At least, that's what I always tell myself when I think about coming out."

I nodded. "But what about Frankie?"

Will steepled his fingers under his chin. "Can he be trusted?"

"How should I know? I've never even had a conversation with him."

"Has *anyone* from school had a conversation with him?"

"Good point."

"What are you going to do for your act?"

"Since I almost drowned last night, Miyu wants me to redeem myself with another aquarium escape. But I get to pick the restraints. And the music."

"Cool," he whispered with wide, glistening eyes. "Can I help?"

Eighty-seven days. That's how long it's been since I slept for more than three straight hours. The day nanny is the only thing standing between me and a nervous breakdown.

During the three a.m. feedings, I have to will myself not to be resentful. Some nights, I don't go back to sleep. I just sit in a rocking chair by her bassinet and cry.

But can I blame her, even when she's squawking and fluttering and producing more shit than any tiny human should ever be able to? She had no choice in this.

And really, I should be thanking her. The sleep deprivation. The sore nipples. Her little squishy, needy face. All of it's transforming me into something stronger. Something forged by fire.

When I get back to the stage, the world won't know what hit it.

— Akiko Miyake, Grayton, February 10, 1983

Will With Two Ls Puts Cool Will in his Back Pocket

After I disclosed my deepest, darkest secret to Mattie and watched her drive off in Stella's jalopy, I rode home in the back of my parents' Lincoln, feeling rawer than Mattie's escape act. A shiny little trinket I had guarded fiercely since fifth grade had just slipped from my hands into the murky depths of a bottomless well. I was never going to get it back.

"Are you okay, sweetie?" my mom asked as she glanced at me in the rearview.

I nodded because I was afraid to open my mouth. I thought if I started saying actual words, I wouldn't be able to keep the rising tide at bay. A storm surge of tears and fear and self-loathing would spew forth and scare the ever-living shit out of my parents, who were under the impression that I'd grown into a well-adjusted, albeit disappointingly pedestrian, red-blooded American boy.

151

She pursed her lips at the mirror. "Did you get a chance to talk to your friend from school?"

Really, Mommy Dearest? She clearly needed a refresher course in leaving well enough alone.

I took a deep breath to keep myself from puking weepy, desperate word-vomit all over my dad's pristine leather seats. "Yeah. Though she's not really my friend."

My dad laughed. "Smart. You don't want to get stuck in the friend zone."

"What? No! I have a *girl*friend, remember?"

"Never hurts to keep your options open," my mom grumbled. "What did the two of you chat about?"

I clenched and unclenched my fists and cracked my knotty knuckles. "I don't know. Nothing. I said, 'Hi' and 'Congrats,' and she said, 'Thanks' and 'Aren't you psyched to be a senior?'"

My mom whipped her head toward me, the streetlights glinting in her sharp, narrowed eyes. "What? 'Aren't you psyched to be a senior?' There's no possible way those words came out of that girl's mouth. Young artistes of that caliber don't care about high school."

For fuck's sake. I cursed my mother for being maddeningly perceptive and for allowing the least Mattie-esque sentence ever uttered to pop out of my mouth.

Of course, she couldn't let it go. "You didn't go talk to her, did you?"

"No," I lied.

"Please tell me you weren't on the phone with the Stepford Wife."

"Marjorie," my dad chimed in.

"Okay, okay," she said, finally throwing in the towel. "I'll try to be a little more laissez-faire."

Thank fucking god.

The twenty-minute drive home seemed to last for a tense century, with my mom huffing in the passenger seat and me still trying to hold back the storm surge. When we drove past Grayton Elementary, I choked on a pathetic little sob and covered it with a cough. I thought it would all come pouring out of me once I crawled into bed, but I was too exhausted to cry and too tired to sleep. I lay there for hours, squirming under my covers and wishing I could take back the whole day.

I didn't think Mattie would tell anyone, but in the dead of that long night, I couldn't stand for anyone to know. Not even her. Especially her. Mattie ate her own fear for breakfast, and I let mine drag me around on a leash. I couldn't be that secretless guy. Not yet.

As the sleepless hours ticked by, my common sense and typically even keel deteriorated. I bordered on delusional, grasping at straws, determined to fix the unfixable. *I'll call her tomorrow and tell her I was just kidding. I'll tell her I lied because I felt sorry for her.* And while I waited for her at Très Amigos the next day, I had every intention of doing so.

But I didn't have to, because Mattie made it okay. More than okay, because that's the magic of Mattie. She resides at that strange little way station between stark reality and larger than life fantasy. She wants so much more than just-the-facts-ma'am. She lives for those miraculous moments when you stumble upon something that's somehow truer than the truth.

With four little words, and without even realizing what she was doing, she carved out a safe place for me to be someone other than Cool Will. She called me Will With Two Ls.

He was just a joke at first. A goofy nickname for a Will who's buddies with a Wheaton fangirl. By the afternoon, he became the charming stage assistant to Ginger the intrepid orphan and budding escapologist.

On the way to Miyu's house, Mattie popped an old-fashioned cassette tape into Stella's ancient Volkswagen stereo. I almost had a conniption when the familiar crackles of "My Blackbirds Are Bluebirds Now" came on.

"Oh my god . . . is this Annette Hanshaw? You listen to jazz?"

Mattie's eyes bugged out of her face. "Yeah. I can't believe you know Annette Hanshaw."

"Have you not noticed how much Jazz Age slang I throw around? The '20s are probably my favorite decade. I mean . . . good god . . . the art, the fashion, the music. Maybe the 2020s will be cool."

"We can only hope. I've always felt like I got screwed by the time lottery. Are you ready to meet Miyu?"

"Is she expecting me?"

"Hell no. If I'd given her a heads up, she would have barricaded the door."

"Oh. When you put it like that, she sounds like a real peach."

"It'll be fine," she said, though she sounded far from one hundred percent sure.

We pulled up to one of those old Grayton villas. I realized I'd driven past it at least half a dozen times and probably raised my eyebrows over the knee-high lawn. It never occurred to me to wonder who lived there. I followed Mattie up a stone footpath and watched her ring the bell by the ornate front door. A few beats later, a little panel with a hummingbird carving flipped open.

"Who's the Jehovah's Witness?" the woman behind the door asked. Based on Mattie's description of her mentor as a sharp-tongued recluse, I could only assume it was Miyu. And, for the record, she'd already won me with that line.

"This is Will."

"Hey," I chirped.

"It's okay. He's cool. I almost drowned because of him, but we worked it out."

"I'm so happy for you," Miyu deadpanned.

"No you're not. But you're going to let him in. He's going to help me raid your attic so I can plan my next act."

Miyu slammed the hummingbird panel shut.

"So," I said. "Does that mean I don't get to give her a free copy of *The Watchtower*?"

"It means she's either loading her shotgun or checking herself out in the mirror before she opens the door."

The door flew open and Miyu stood over the threshold, her dark hair freshly finger-fluffed.

"So predictably vain," Mattie mumbled.

"I will let the Jehovah's Witness in on one condition," Miyu said without even a hint of a smile. "He takes over as your stage assistant so I can stay backstage where I belong."

"Miyu, Will doesn't—"

"Yes," I squeaked over Mattie's protest. "Oh my god, a thousand times, yes. Miyu, you're the cat's meow."

Miyu gave me a cool once over with her steely eyes. "If you say so, Jehovah."

"Thanks for consulting with me first," Mattie whined.

"I thought you didn't have any friends," Miyu said. "I'm jumping on the first opportunity that presented itself."

I turned to Mattie with my best puppy-dog eyes. "I won't do it if you don't want me to."

Miyu cackled from the doorway. "If you can resist that dimpled pout, you're a stronger woman than I, Girl Scout." *Yessss.*

"Goddammit," Mattie huffed. "Will, you're officially my new stage assistant."

I couldn't think of anything to say, but I'm certain I had one of the goofiest grins of all time plastered on my face.

Mattie shoved her way inside, scowling at Miyu. "We're off to the attic."

We climbed three flights of stairs wrapped in threadbare oriental runners and scaled a ladder I had to pull down from the ceiling in the third floor hallway.

"Holy cannoli," I whispered. "It's like the Xanadu of antiques."

I'd been in my fair share of grandmas' attics, but I'd never seen anything like this. Dusty credenzas carved out of solid cherry. Wrought-iron coat trees with glass birds perched on the hooks. Boxes spilling over with Christmas ornaments and stained glass lamps. A menagerie of abstract lawn sculptures.

Mattie pointed at the sculptures. "Totally late-80s art deco, don't you think?"

I barely heard her because something hanging on a dress from across the attic had drawn me in. I had to climb over an old Schwinn and a collapsed tent to get to it. The crust of black sequins sparkled even in the dim light.

"Whose was this?"

Mattie glanced over. "Ah. One of Akiko's costumes. She had quite the career."

"She was an escape artist? Is that how Miyu learned all this stuff?"

"Yep."

"Who designed her costumes?"

"No idea." She popped open a black trunk lined with red velvet.

I massaged the hemline between my fingers. The stitching was so precise, so perfect. "It's really excellent work. And it looks formal, but it's designed for movement. Genius."

Mattie squinted at me. "Genius? Seriously? I thought you had an aversion to stereotyped interests."

"That's not what I said. And it's not like I give a shit about fashion trends or runway models. I just like the idea of handcrafted art you can wear. I probably get it from my mom. The woman has more hand-stitched jackets than a boutique in SoHo."

I might have a contentious relationship with my mother, but if nothing else, she'd instilled in me a deep appreciation for beautiful things made with passion. I'm not talking about the kind of high-priced bullshit you find on Fifth Avenue. I'm talking about one-of-a-kind artifacts that change the way you feel when you put them on. Art that transforms.

"I guess I'll buy that," Mattie said. "I do have kind of a thing for vintage clothing. You know, stuff from back in the day when everything wasn't made in a sweatshop and falling apart after the first wash." She grinned at me. "So, do you and the guys from the basketball team talk about wearable art?"

I have to admit, I loved that Mattie and I had bulldozed through the walking-on-eggshells phase of friendship and gone straight for asking each other pointed questions. "What do *you* think?" I coughed.

"I think you should come help me dig through this stuff."

I knelt beside the trunk. "What are we looking for?"

"Something the salon-goers will dig."

We dug through piles of straitjackets, nets of chains, enough shackles to lock down a small army, and a slew of antique locks, all polished more lovingly than most prized pieces of jewelry. I pulled out a pair of rusty antique handcuffs that had probably been used to transport prisoners in the late 1800s or keep drunken sailors from rattling around in the brig.

Mattie shivered as she stared at them. "Those are super creepy. All that rusty iron . . ."

That's how I knew we'd found the right restraints.

There's nothing I wanted more in that moment than to watch Mattie take on something that scared her enough to give her a case of the shakes with just a glance. Cool Will couldn't handle that kind of audacity, but Will With Two Ls was more than ready to live vicariously through his new partner in mutually assured destruction.

Will With Two Ls didn't daydream about sipping bootleg cocktails at speakeasies with imaginary friends. He didn't have to because he and Ginger the intrepid orphan frequented Salone Postale on the regular. He didn't mope around in his room listening to show tunes and old jazz records. Instead, he and Ginger drove down back roads on hot summer nights listening to them together.

I didn't have to be Will With Two Ls all the time because, lord knows, I wasn't quite there yet. I got all fluster-cated anytime I even thought about showing up at one of those intolerably-loud-vomit-parties as Will With Two Ls. Ryder, inevitably drunk on vodka, would predictably lose his shit over the thousand-and-one times he'd changed in front of me in the locker room. His zozzled ass wouldn't even hear my adamant claims that overbearing close-talkers did zilch for me. And in a tragic turn of events, Betsy would drop all of her quiet sophistication, regress into junior-high-drama-rama, lock herself in a bathroom and sob over a vanilla-scented candle for hours. Meadow would glare at me from a dark corner, plotting dastardly ways to avenge her BFF.

I could still pull Cool Will out of my back pocket

when I needed to and tote him around like a shield. But by dubbing me Will With Two Ls, Mattie had thrown open a dusty trapdoor and shown me an escape route. I was ready to take only the smallest of baby steps. Though, that day in Miyu's attic, I saw the light at the end of the tunnel winking at me, coaxing me forward with the spark of better days to come.

The woman from TV tapped her pen against her lips. "Do you ever get scared?"

I curled a strand of my bright pink wig around my index finger. The Hummingbird was flitting around behind my chair. I'd bought her a foam samurai sword to keep her entertained during the interview. She sliced through the air with grand swishes, vanquishing imaginary foes. Swish!

"Mom-mom-mom-mom," she babbled. "Look, look!"

"Hush," I said. "In a minute, Hachidori." I turned back to the TV woman. "What was the question?"

"Do you ever get scared?"

"Of course," I replied with a smile. "What I do is very risky. It can be a matter of life and death. But there's also a deep sense of serenity. There's a moment, just before I free myself, that feels so small and yet so big at the same time. It lasts for just a second, sometimes less, but it encompasses everything."

"Does your life flash before your eyes?" the TV woman asked.

I laughed. "Maybe something like that. But I don't see it. I feel it, like a thick mist condensing deep in my chest."

– Akiko Miyake, New York, November 19, 1985

Mattie, You're Giving me that Look

"Deep breaths," Will said as I parked Stella's Volkswagen in her driveway.

My sweaty palms kept slipping on the steering wheel. I wiped them on my jeans before pulling the keys out of the ignition. I followed Will's advice and sucked in a lungful of oxygen before opening the driver's side door.

"Okay, wish me luck."

"You don't wish performers good luck, Mattie-O. You say 'break a leg.'"

Frankly, I didn't need luck or a broken leg to pull off my plan without a single hitch. I needed a freaking miracle.

I stalked up to Stella's front door and rang the bell. The door flew open less than a second later and Stella's spidery limbs trapped me in one of her classic hugs.

"I missed you, Ginger."

"I missed you, too," I admitted with a sigh. "Like, a

lot. Is Frankie here yet?"

"Yeah, he's in the kitchen. Did you take good care of my baby?" She glanced toward the Bug, her brows knitting. "Is your brother in the car?"

Will waved from the passenger seat and I shoved Stella into the foyer and shut the door.

"Look. I can promise you a fun night, but you and Frankie are going to have to abide by a few rules."

An olive-skinned early adolescent emerged from the kitchen, gangly limbs dangling from his torso. "Salutations," he mumbled.

I grabbed him by the shoulders and shuffled him next to Stella. His stiff arms and the look of mild shock on his face told me he wasn't used to being touched, especially by insistent teenage girls. "Please listen carefully. Rule number one—under even the most extreme of circumstances, you will never, ever speak of the things you see tonight, no matter how thrilling or surprising or ridiculous you may find them. Sub-rule one-dash-a— no photos or video evidence allowed. If I see either one of you pull out a phone, I will run that phone over with the Bug."

"Ginge, you're scaring me."

"Rule number two," I continued. "One of our fellow students is waiting in the car. You will treat him like a normal human being, and you will not, for any reason, ask him why he is hanging out with me."

Stella glanced at Frankie and he nodded.

"Rule number three—you will not over-consume alcohol, no matter how many free drinks people hand you. I will not have time this evening to be a drunk person's babysitter."

Stella scrunched up her face. "Mattie, Frankie's totally cool, but I don't think bringing him to a house party is a good idea."

"Good lord, Stella. Do you think when you're away I turn into a teenage cliché? We're not going to a house party. Though there will be drunk people. And loud music. And possibly some debauchery."

"I'm so confused," Stella whined.

"Confusion aside, can I count on you to abide by these three rules? Don't talk about what you see, don't be a twerp to my new friend, and don't go on a bender."

She threw her hands up. "Yeah. Sure. I guess."

I grabbed Frankie's shoulders again. "What about you?"

His dark eyes blinked at me. "I've always fantasized about being drafted into a shady, international spy organization with no formal ties to the government. This is almost as good."

"Fantastic. Let's roll."

Twenty minutes and one awkward drive full of silent pauses later, the four of us piled into a corner booth at Pink Ginger. Sugar-coated Japanese pop music blared from a speaker behind the sushi bar and the scents of soy and raw fish assaulted my nostrils.

"I'll have the Sushi Regular," Stella told the waiter.

Will ordered the same, I ordered two Philly rolls and a seaweed salad, and Frankie ordered chicken teriyaki.

"Not a fan of raw fish?" I asked.

"I don't eat anything with a face," he replied.

Will busted a gut.

"You do realize chickens have faces, right?" I asked.

"Oh, birds don't count," Frankie explained with a shake of his head. "They're, like, tiny, soulless dinosaurs. I have no moral qualms about eating them." He glanced from me to Will, then cracked a huge grin.

"You're screwing with us," I said.

"Maybe a little," he said with a shrug.

Will cracked up again, and Stella raised her eyebrows at me. I wasn't sold on Frankie the Wannabe BFF Thief yet, but he was growing on me. I studied his face, trying to decide whether he was the type who would blackmail an older woman once he found out about her double life.

"You're giving me that look," he said.

"What look?" I asked.

"That look that white people give me when they're trying to figure out whether I'm white."

Will and Stella both exploded with laughter. "So busted," Will sang.

I shot Frankie a scowl. "For your information, that's not what I was thinking about. But I will admit I wondered on the car ride over here."

"I'm Azorean," he explained.

Will squinted at him. "Is Azorea a fictional land in one of those online RPGs?"

Frankie blinked and pursed his lips. "I have no idea. But I'm not from Azorea. My family hails from the Azores."

"Islands off the coast of Portugal," Stella said, saving us from making more awkward guesses about what and where the Azores were.

"Groovy," Will said. "I gotta iron my shoelaces."

Stella's face got all serious as soon as he left the table and headed toward the restroom. "Will Kane? How did this happen?"

I grinned when I realized Stella was just as weirdly suspicious-slash-jealous of Will as I was of Frankie. "Rule number two," I reminded her with a smirk.

"Oh, I'm well aware of rule number two, Ginge. You said we couldn't be twerpy to your new friend. You didn't say I couldn't bug *you* about how it came to be that he's hanging out with the three of us."

"Touché," I grumbled.

"I don't see what the big deal is," Frankie said. "He seems like a nice guy."

"Turns out he *is* a nice guy," I said.

"Don't change the subject just because Frankie doesn't understand the Cianci Regional social fabric."

"Holy super-snob, Batman, you're doing it again. We don't live in a poorly-written, low-budget drama, Stell. This is real life. Sometimes, in real life, interesting people find other interesting people and decide they want to hang out with them."

"That seems reasonable," Frankie chimed in.

Stella raised one eyebrow, flashing me a look of incredulousness I could never pull off, even if my life depended on it. "What, exactly, does he find so interesting about you?"

"I don't know what you're implying, but our friendship is completely non-sexual."

Stella and I fell silent as Will returned from the

bathroom and slid into the seat next to me. "Were you guys gabbing about me?" he asked.

Stella took a sip of her water to avoid answering, and Frankie's olive skin flushed beet red.

Will fixed his eyes on Frankie. "Out with it, kid. Were they talking about me?"

Frankie's lips quivered for just a moment. "Do I have to answer? This just got really awkward. Even more awkward than the car ride over here."

Stella snorted and buried her face in her napkin. Will chuckled, and I tried to hold it together but couldn't.

Frankie crossed his arms. "I know awkward comedy is popular these days, but personally, I don't find it all that funny."

We couldn't contain ourselves as the waiter set our plates in front of us. The poor guy just shook his head as he walked away.

Will turned to Stella as he unwrapped his chopsticks. "In all seriousness, I hope you don't think I'm trying to replace you or encroach on your territory or anything like that. Mattie's the bee's knees, but you guys have history I can't possibly compete with."

Stella nodded. "Noted. Thank you, Will."

Frankie shot me a knowing glance. "It's like when a new *Star Trek* series starts. Just because the new captain has a mind-blowingly awesome back story doesn't mean he or she tops Kirk or Picard."

"I told you," Stella said.

"Goddammit," I said as I shook my head.

That increasingly familiar feeling, like distilled lightning, pulsed through my limbs. For a fleeting moment, I had hope that my night might actually work out as planned.

I pulled Stella through a crowd of smokers standing on the sidewalk outside the bar above Salone Postale. Frankie and Will followed us through the bar and down the staircase to the cough-syrup-colored door.

"Rule number one," I reminded Stella and Frankie before I opened the door.

"How did you find this place?" Stella whispered over the clink-and-chatter of bar noise.

"Naveen from Bollywood Palace told me about it."

She smirked. "I'm impressed, Ginge. You've definitely branched out over the summer. Though I don't know why you'd need to keep this place a secret."

It's not too late to back out. I swallowed a lump in my throat and pulled a chair out for Stella at a reserved table by the stage.

"Reserved seats," Stella squealed when she picked up her place card. "This is so cool."

"I feel so privileged," Frankie said. I couldn't tell if he was serious or not.

The hecklers greeted me with a cheery chorus of heys. One of them winked toward Stella. "Who's your friend?"

"She's underage, you creep."

"Don't worry, we'll take good care of her," he shot back.

The fiery-haired, tattooed bartender popped over to

our table with two glasses on a tray. "Midori Sours, on the house," she said as the placed them in front of Stella and Frankie.

"Oh, we don't really drink." Stella waved the glass away.

"It tastes like candy. You'll like it," the bartender said before trotting back to the bar.

"Um . . . okay." Stella pouted as she gingerly picked up her drink like it might explode in her face.

Frankie immediately began sucking down his Midori Sour. "Mmm. Melon-y."

I pointed at him. "Rule number three."

"You guys aren't sitting with us?" Stella asked.

"Will and I are needed backstage. I promise that will make more sense soon."

She pulled her lips into the corner of her mouth. "I haven't seen you in two months. I thought we were going to actually hang out tonight."

"We will, we will. I promise. Will and I have to go take care of something first, then we're all yours for the rest of the night. Okay?"

"I guess," she sighed.

"Frankie, keep her entertained while we're gone."

He nodded as he slurped down the last of his drink.

Will and I ducked backstage and found Miyu and Monty waiting for us.

"Finally," Miyu barked. "I thought Monty was going to have to tell the crowd you choked to death on a cheeseburger."

"It's the only way I could ensure they didn't riot in the event you were a no-show," he explained. "Pleasure to see you again, Will."

"You too, Monty. What's the skinny, Miyu?"

"I had to prepare the tank by myself. And I'm constipated. Thanks for asking, Jehovah."

"Are you ready to go?" Monty asked.

I was already stripping down to my swimsuit and slipping into my robe. "Yes," I said with a nod. *Deep breaths.*

Miyu and Will rolled the koi-stocked aquarium onto the stage. I could hear the wheels clacking against the floorboards as I swept my hair into a low pony-tail and shoved a few bobby pins into place. The crowd hushed as the stage lights came up and Monty emerged from behind the closed curtain.

"Good evening, ladies, gents, denizens of the night."

"Tell the barmaid to get these kids some more booze," one of the hecklers shouted. I could only assume he was talking about Stella and Frankie.

"You're not going to win any points by referring to her as a barmaid, darling," Monty cooed. "We have a splendiferous, phantasmic, far-out evening planned for you, sinners and saints. Guaranteed to amaze. And we're going to start things off right."

"With plate-spinning!" one of the hecklers shouted.

"We can do better than that," Monty replied. "First up, we have the young orphan you've all come to know and love."

The crowd whooped, sending a surge of confidence through my guts and bringing a smile to my face.

"The girl who forces you to stare into the face of death and love it," Monty bellowed. "Salone Postale's poster girl for the ages . . . the incomparable Ginger!"

Will linked arms with me as the curtain opened. "Go get 'em, doll," he whispered.

Monty handed me the mic. I gazed out into the crowd for a moment before saying, "Hello." The timbre of my own voice echoed in my ears. It sounded almost disembodied, like my mind couldn't believe that word, spoken to a room filled mostly with strangers, had come from me.

"She speaks!" one of the hecklers shouted.

"It's shocking, I know," I said with a grin. "I wanted to take a moment to let you all know that The Hummingbird has retired. This tall drink of water, known as Will With Two Ls, will be my assistant for the evening."

Will waved to the crowd, and one of the hecklers screamed, "L is my favorite letter!"

He picked up the rusty antique handcuffs and showed them off to the crowd. "Tonight, I'm going to escape from these," I said. "But first, I need a volunteer."

The hecklers chanted a chorus of, "Pick me! Pick me!"

I pointed to one of them, a thirty-something wearing skinny jeans and glasses, and he hopped onto the stage.

"Not that I think anyone in the crowd would dare question my legitimacy, but I want you all to know I'm the real deal. Will With Two Ls, if you would be so kind as to cuff our volunteer." The crowd cackled, whooped and whistled as Will clamped the hand-cuffs on the heckler, swaddling his pale wrists in rusty iron. "Now, sir, give us your honest impression of this evening's restraints."

The bespeckled heckler made a show of struggling, but it didn't take long until he was sweating with genuine anxiety under the stage lights. I held the mic to his lips. "Yeah, these cuffs are serious business."

The crowd cheered. "There you have it, ladies and gents," I said. "Serious business."

Once Will had freed the heckler with an antique skeleton key, I returned the mic to Monty. "You'd make a decent MC," he whispered. "Should I be worried?"

I shook my head. "You've got your gig, I've got mine." While Will climbed the ladder to the platform at the top of the aquarium, I pulled an Annette Hanshaw record from its sleeve and placed it lovingly on the gramophone. The audience clapped in a rare expression of reverence when "My Inspiration Is You" came crackling out of the brass horn.

I joined Will on the platform, where he placed the handcuffs on my wrists. I'd been avoiding direct eye contact with Stella, but I glanced over just before Will blindfolded me with a swatch of black silk. Her eyes blinked at me, and her jaw hung open. Frankie looked no worse for the wear as he downed his second Midori Sour.

Will tapped me on the shoulder, giving me the a-okay to drop into the tank. The cool water shocked my skin, sending my heartbeat into overdrive. I'd run through this routine so many times, I was counting on my muscle memory to take charge without a second's hesitation. But it didn't happen. The water pulled the loosely tied blindfold off my face, leaving me with a perfect view of the crowd and turning my fingers into trembling amnesiacs.

Stella and I stared at each other. She'd covered her gaping mouth with her pale hands and the sight of her shocked eyes filled me with dread. My heart pounded in my chest, and I almost inhaled a mouthful of koi-flavored water. With the seconds ticking away, I hardly had time for a moment of clarity, but it became abundantly apparent that practice and performance were entirely different beasts, especially with my best friend in the crowd. In my panicked mind, I heard that kernel of paralyzing fear chime in. *What if they let your secret slip? How can you trust Frankie with this? You don't even know him!*

I shut my eyes to block out the crowd and pictured Ginger the intrepid orphan, manacled with the antique handcuffs and chained to the floor in the cabin of a rapidly sinking ship. Seawater filled with happily flapping koi poured in through the portholes, soaking her tattered Victorian clothing and splashing against her face.

The octopus in the top hat floated by, his monocle glinting in the cabin's dim lantern light. *Do you plan to die today, child?*

Fuck no.

I clawed my way through the paralysis and yanked a bobby pin from my hair.

As my burning lungs screamed for air, my oxygen-starved brain realized my fear had never truly been rooted in the possibility that Stella and Frankie would spill my secret. I mean, Frankie didn't even have any friends. Who would he tell? The truth was I didn't know if I could stomach my best friend seeing me at that tricky point where all my strengths and vulnerabilities converged like the contents of a potent emotional reactor. For those two minutes under water, I condensed every fiber of my being, exposing the strangeness at my core. What if the person who was supposed to know me better than anyone didn't like what she saw? I wondered if my partner in mutually assured destruction felt the same kind of icy-hot panic course through his veins when he thought about telling Betsy Appleton the truth.

My pruned fingers shook as I picked at lock number one. In practice, I'd adjusted to picking locks while restricted by the handcuffs. But even in the near-weightlessness of the water, the cuffs seemed so heavy. The iron wrapped around my wrists felt like it was squeezing the life out of my whole body. My heart rate picked up, threatening to fly off the rails.

A brief jolt of relief shot through me when the first handcuff sprang open. Only one handcuff to go and then the padlock on the lid.

By all means, take your time, the octopus deadpanned in my mind. *It's not as if your very life is on the line.*

Once the second handcuff sprang open, I thrashed my way to the top of the aquarium. I was so dizzy from oxygen deprivation I could barely see, but I caught flashes of white and orange fins flicking through my peripheral vision. I thrust my fists through the holes in the lid and commanded my shaky, shriveled fingers to focus. I pictured Ginger kicking her way through the seawater, beating down the locked door of the sinking ship's cabin and scrambling to a lifeboat. Through the water, I heard the padlock pop open with a muffled *ping!*

The second I surfaced and pushed myself out of the tank, the roar of the crowd filled my ears. "My Inspiration Is You" came to a perfect denouement and crackled to a close. Will grasped my arm and dragged me onto the platform as I gasped for air. He looked like a ghost ready to toss his cookies.

"Jeezus, Mattie-O. No wonder Miyu didn't want this job. I thought I was going to have a heart attack and then have to dive in there mid-v-fib and fish out your drowned corpse."

"Not today, Will With Two Ls," I sputtered before launching into a coughing fit.

"Let's hear it, ladies and gentlemen," Monty said into the mic, "for the incomparable Ginger and her new assistant, Will With Two Ls!"

Will helped me down the ladder, and we took brief bows and waved to our audience of mostly-strangers before slipping backstage. Before I had a chance to dry off, Stella's spidery arms were trapping me in another hug.

"Ginge, I don't even know what to say," she said. "I don't think I've ever been so scared."

I didn't have a response so I just whimpered and hugged her back.

"That was hard for you, wasn't it?" she whispered. "To share that with me?"

"If you're totally freaked out, or mad I didn't tell you right away, I get it. But we're still friends, right?"

"Oh, Ginge. Of course we're still friends. There's nothing you could do to make me not want to be friends with you, except maybe kill someone or, you know, kick a puppy really hard."

That warm, spiky feeling flooded through me again, like tiny tendrils from the core of my being pushing their way to the surface of my skin, reaching out into the void for someone else's tendrils. But this time that joy and fear was mixed with relief. I felt weightless, like all the bricks of dread I'd been collecting had imploded in a single, dusty burst.

I nodded, and Stella wrapped me in a towel.

It's probably fitting that after I disclosed my secret to Stella in the most dramatic way possible, I found myself alone with her in a sort of confessional booth—the downstairs bathroom at Will's house—pulling her hair back into a sloppy ponytail right before she retched and puked.

"No more tequila," she moaned with her head clutched in her hands. "Ever."

The two Midori sours she'd sipped before I went on must've loosened her up because the hecklers somehow talked her into doing shots with them. She downed a shot of mid-shelf Kentucky bourbon with a squinty pout. Then she slurped up a shot of Jäger. Then, like she'd been doing it for years, she topped that off with a shot of cheap tequila and a grin.

To my horror, she got up to dance with the hecklers when Mollusk Brigade went on and planted a fat, wet kiss square on Naveen's lips.

"She broke rule number three," Frankie said.

"Yep. She totally did."

And now she was curled up in front of the toilet, pulling off her cardigan and wrapping it around herself like a sad little blanket. She squinted up at me, her typically-sunny face now a bleary-eyed mask of drunken misery.

"Ginge, I have something to confess. I wasn't going to tell you about my summer fling because it didn't exactly end on a high note. But I want every last detail on how you turned yourself into badass with Will Kane as your Vanna White, and I'm almost certain that telling you this next thing is the only way I'm going to get it out of you."

"Um . . . okay."

"So here goes. I hooked up with a guy at St. Joe's. More than once. And . . ." She retched again but didn't puke. "You know him."

I blinked at her a few times. "It's not Frankie, is it?"

"Oh my god, Ginge, no. No! He's adorable and funny, but he's much too young for me. And for you. I hope you're not thinking about corrupting such an . . ."

"No. Got enough on my plate, thanks. So if it's not Frankie . . ."

"Marlon Blando," she whimpered. "I still can't believe you call him that."

"Oh," I said.

"Go ahead. Judge me. Get it over with."

"Stell, I'm not going to judge you. I'm not like that. Am I?"

She just laughed. "Maybe all that oxygen deprivation's changed you."

"So how was it?"

She gave me a shrug. "Okay? Certainly nothing like some of the horror stories I've overheard in the bathrooms at school. But Marlon . . . ahem . . . Evan and I are not meant to be."

"What went wrong?"

She shook her head and moaned into the floor. "Nothing! Well, we did actually get into a fight over *Alice's Adventures in Wonderland* because he refuses to acknowledge its literary significance. But that fight was sort of fun. Most of the time he would just talk and talk and talk and, oh my god, Ginge. I was so bored."

"Imagine that," I said with a snicker.

Her nostrils flared. "See? There it is."

"What?"

"You're getting judgy."

"Oh. Sorry."

She sat up and sighed. "It's fine. Anyway, I couldn't stop thinking about how he would go on and on and not really say anything and I thought, 'Do I sound like that? Am I just as boring and too caught up in good grades and college apps to even realize it?'"

I laughed as I leaned back against the sink. "Is that why you went overboard tonight?"

"Maybe."

"Stella, can you just take stock of where you are for a sec?"

"Will Kane's bathroom?"

"No. Well, kinda. Think about the night we just had. If you were boring, would you have had that kind of night? If you were so consumed with grades and college to the point where you talked about nothing, would you even be friends with a kid who quotes *Star Trek* and a girl who escapes from a fish tank in front of strangers?"

"No?"

"No. So there you go."

She giggled and kicked her flip-flops off while she gave me this weird, knowing look.

"What?" I asked.

"You. You sound . . ." She waved her hands like she was trying to snatch the right word out of the air. "Confident. Yes, that's it. It's cracking me up."

"Thanks? Hey, so I promise I'll tell you all about my wild summer. But right now I'm going to tell you about something else. Remember when my brother threw that huge party like a year ago?"

"Yeah?"

"I slept with Connor that night."

She stared at me for a second and then laughed into the floor, her hair spilling across the tile like a mop. When she looked up and opened her mouth, I thought she was going to tell me how silly I'd been. Instead, she retched again and spewed into the john.

"Unacceptable," I shrieked as I scooped The Hummingbird out of a pile of padlocks and handcuffs. "Are you high? These are not toys." The Hummingbird let out an ear-piercing wail, as if I'd just snatched a fresh cone of fudge-ripple ice cream—her favorite—out of her hot little hand.

"I'm so sorry, Ms. Miyake," au pair number seven groveled. "She begged me all morning. I thought a few minutes would be okay. I was watching her carefully."

"No excuses," I squawked. "You're fired."

"Please don't do this, Ms. Miyake. I love little Miyu."

"Oh, shut it, Esther. You love your work visa, not my kid."

My brutal honesty must've been the final straw for the moon-faced girl. She pursed her thin lips and glared at me from behind a monstrous pair of glasses that made her look like a pale frog. "Before I go, I just want to say you're not at all how I thought you'd be."

"Blah, blah, blah," I shot back. I'd become impervious to the ineffectual whining of these naïve, European post-adolescents. "Did you think I'd be all smiles as we jet-setted around the country? Did you think you'd be rubbing elbows with stars and sipping champagne?"

The Hummingbird howled and beat her little fists against my chest. I pretended she was mad at Esther instead of at me.

– Akiko Miyake, Orlando, July 4, 1987

Will With Two Ls Meets
Francisco of the Sacred Sword

If there's anything to be gained from frequenting intolerably-loud-vomit-parties, it's the ability to wrangle a drunk person.

Once it became abundantly clear that Stella was three sheets to the wind and then some while we were at Salone Postale, I pulled her into a hug. "Hey, buddy."

"Will! Will, you're the best. Isn't this place the best? I'm having the *best* time."

"I can see that, Stell. You know what? The fun doesn't have to end. We're going to have a slumber party at my house."

"A slumber party," she slurred. "Heck yeah! I haven't had one-a those in . . . Your parents won't mind?"

"They're away for the weekend. Thank god."

"Yay! Your parents are the *best*."

I guided Stella into the backseat of her little jalopy and tried to keep a lid on her while Mattie drove to my house. Frankie called his mom from Mattie's cell and rattled off something in Portuguese.

"Isn't Frankie the best, Will?" Stella asked. "He's bilingual!"

And now she was lying on the tile floor, trying to get Mattie's attention.

"Ginge, I have something to confess."

I snagged Frankie's arm and pulled him into the hall. "I think that's our cue, kid."

Unfortunately, the two of us didn't move fast enough to avoid overhearing Stella tell Mattie that she'd fooled around with some guy at St. Joe's.

"Don't ever repeat what you just heard," I told Frankie.

He yawned and shook his head. "Stella's personal life is old news. Currently, all I care about is finding a semi-comfortable place to collapse."

Frankie followed me up the stairs, and I dug out a t-shirt and a pair of sweat pants for him. He changed in the master bathroom and came out looking like a little squirt who'd raided his dad's closet. I saw him eyeing my parents' king-sized bed.

"Have at it. I'll wash the sheets tomorrow. They'll never even know you were in there."

He flung himself onto the down comforter and flailed his skinny arms and legs. "Are your parents obscenely rich? Because this bed is huge."

I laughed through a yawn. "We had a pretty good night. It's been a while since I've had that much fun."

Frankie sighed one of those melodramatic sighs that early-adolescents pull off so well. I'd like to think I'd grown out of that, but my parents would probably say otherwise.

"What's up, kid?"

"Nothing. It *was* a fun night. I had a really fun summer, actually. But all that just reminds me I have one more year of high school looming ahead, like a giant cloud of suck."

I should've laughed, because almost everything that popped out of that kid's mouth was a hoot and a half. Instead, I recognized him for the first time as a fellow in-betweener. A guy who belonged neither here nor there. A wanderer without a tribe. Frankie was too smart and too wonderfully weird to appeal to any of the freshman pipsqueaks his own age, but it's not like any of the seniors wanted to hang out with him. Well, except Stella. And me. And Mattie, who'd done her best to resist a new pal and been won over anyway by clever *Star Trek* references.

I nodded, and he must've taken it as a sign to keep talking, which I guess it was. He told me about how anxious he sometimes got in his own neighborhood—a neighborhood that I'd occasionally ventured into to track down a taco truck that Betsy loved, knowing that she and I could leave anytime we wanted and go home to our safe little suburban capes in Grayton.

"It's home, but smart and scrawny doesn't get you very far there, you know? Sometimes the guys in my building look at me like I'm from another planet."

He told me about how his dad was still back in the Azores, and he hadn't seen him in almost a year. He told me about how he missed him but worried that he didn't miss him enough, and it made me think about how often I took my own parents for granted.

And he told me how excited he wants to be for college but how he can't quite get there and how scared he is of living on his own at fifteen.

I was standing at the edge of eighteen and terrified of the same thing.

At some point, he turned to me and said, "Sorry. I ramble when I get tired, and I'm probably raining on your parade. You're one of those people who likes high school, right?"

This time, I did laugh. Hard. I felt that little tickle in my chest again, even more insistent than when I'd come out to Mattie. Maybe telling her had torn off some kind of floodgate. It'd certainly felt that way as I tossed and turned in my bed the night before we met up at Très Amigos and she dubbed me Will With Two Ls. And this might've been the gin and tonic still buzzing in my head, but I wondered if colliding with Mattie, in Salone Postale of all places, had sent up some kind of magical, invisible beacon, drawing fellow in-betweeners and strange cats toward us the way speakeasies used to.

"It probably looks like I'm one of those people, right?" I said to Frankie as I plopped down on the bed. "Because I play basketball and have a cool girlfriend and go to parties and yadda-yadda-yadda. But here's the thing—my cool girlfriend and all those supposedly cool people at those parties? None of them know I'm gay."

For a second, I couldn't believe I'd said it. But there it was, hanging in the air between me and a sleepy, brilliant kid who didn't fit in anywhere and whose dad was literally an ocean away.

He blinked at me. "Wow. I guess that kinda makes things more complicated for you then."

"You could say that."

"Wait, am I the first person you told?"

"No, the second. I told Mattie first."

He nodded. "Good, good. I don't think I could handle that kind of pressure. Mattie's really neat. Do you think she'd hang out with me again?"

"Abso-tive-ly."

"Great. Hey, Will?"

"Yeah?"

"This was a really good talk. But my brain registered what you just said as some bastardized combo of absolutely and positively. I think that means I'm going to start hallucinating pretty soon if I don't get some sleep."

"Goodnight, Frankie."

"Goodnight."

I padded down the stairs and opened the fridge. Mattie wandered in as I was unwrapping a cheese stick.

"String cheese?" I asked.

"I just watched Stella toss her cookies. I don't think I can handle food."

"She's pretty zozzled, eh?"

"Two months at a prep school can do strange things to a person. Where's Frankie?"

"Asleep on my parents' bed."

"Aww. Did you read him a bedtime story and tuck him in?"

I laughed. "We kind of bonded, actually."

"Yeah?"

"I just came out to him."

Her eyes bugged out. "Really?"

I relayed my heart-to-heart with Frankie while Mattie stared at my string cheese.

"Admit that you're hungry even though you just watched Stella spew."

"Fine." She stole a piece of my cheese, and we chewed in silence for a few beats. "Can I ask you a really personal question?"

"Shoot."

"Do you and Betsy have sex?"

I can only imagine the look that crossed my face. "Uh . . ."

"You don't have to answer."

"No, it's a fair question." Betsy and I had had the sex conversation at least a dozen times over the course of our relationship. In junior high, we were still too young and she was too Catholic. Like, confirmation-in-a-white-dress kind of Catholic. She told me she was saving herself for marriage, which sounded pretty damn fantastic to me, assuming I grew the cojones to come out before the two of us ended up walking down the aisle.

The day her mom moved out, she declared herself officially non-Catholic. But when you grow up with something like that, you don't just throw it off in one fell swoop. Over the years, we'd added more and more to our repertoire, and I knew it was only a matter of time before she'd want to start shopping for condoms and take the plunge.

"What does she think you're doing tonight?" Mattie asked.

"I told her I was going with my parents to Martha's Vineyard. She texted me a few times to check in, but she won't call me until Monday because she doesn't want to interrupt the family time I'm not actually having. It kills me that she's such a perfect girlfriend. Like, she's dedicated but never clingy. What about you? Do you have a secret guy I don't know about?"

She chuckled. "No, but my whole family thinks so because I've hardly been home all summer. Wait, how do you know I'm not gay? Is gay-dar a real thing?"

I laughed. "You could be attracted to all sorts of people for all I know. But I've seen you stare at Naveen on occasion."

"Ugh. Great." She stole another piece of my string cheese.

"Have you ever been with a guy?"

She stopped chewing and stared across the kitchen, like she couldn't decide how much she wanted to tell me. "Yeah. One of my brother's friends. It wasn't serious, though."

"Oh. Sorry."

"Why?"

I shrugged. "Not-serious sounds good in theory but is kinda messy in real life."

"Like you and the guy at basketball camp?"

I nodded and swallowed a little lump in my throat and tried to push him out of my noggin.

"Yeah," Mattie sighed. "I don't even know how to feel about it." She laughed. "I was just about to ask you not to say anything to Stella, but I realized I just told her. You think she's so drunk she won't remember?"

"Either way, you know your secret's safe with me, Mattie-O."

I put my arm around her and handed over the last of my cheese stick.

Stella woke up the next morning with her first hangover, and if the perma-grimace on her face was any indication, it was a doozy. But I could treat a hangover almost as well as I could wrangle a drunk person, so I took her to breakfast at the greasiest spoon I knew—a little railcar diner in Warwick.

Mattie and Frankie came with us, of course, but the of two of them got sidetracked by an antique store on the way there.

"Oh my god, is that Bill Shatner's first spoken word album on vinyl?" Mattie squealed as she pressed her hands to the glass of the front window.

"Where?" Frankie asked.

"Over there, by that kitschy nightstand with the nobs that look like dice."

Frankie crossed his arms. "It's probably a reissue."

"It looks vintage from here," Mattie said. "Should we bet on it? Loser buys breakfast?"

"We'll meet you guys there," Frankie said.

Stella grimaced at me. "Why is the sun so bright?"

I pulled her toward the diner and the two of us slid into a booth near the back, in the dimmest spot I could find.

She scanned the menu for a bit and then dropped her head down to the table. "Everything sounds disgusting."

The waitress cocked an eyebrow at the two of us when she came over. "Rough night?"

I smiled and ordered two coffees, two large orange juices, and breakfast sandwiches with double bacon.

"Yep. Sounds about right," she said before she ducked back into the kitchen.

"Ever been as zozzled as you were last night?" I asked Stella.

She lifted her head up off the table and shot me a look that was almost-but-not-quite a glare.

"What?" I asked.

"I appreciate you taking care of me last night and making sure I didn't drunkenly stumble home to my own house. But I still don't trust you, and I have no idea what your intentions with my best friend are, but they can't possibly be good."

"Stella, I swear I—"

"Will, cut the crap. My head feels like it's being continually run over by a truck, and I simply do not have the patience to deal with you acting like you're all innocent." She huffed and started shredding a sugar packet. "I know I smile and nod like I don't care that you and your friends either ignore me or make snide comments behind my back. But sometimes, like right now, I really do mind."

And there it was again. That tickle crept into my chest as I stared at a stripped-down no-bullshit version of a girl I'd been in honors classes with for three years and, obviously, hardly knew.

"Stella, I promise I'm not trying to get in Mattie's pants."

She rolled her eyes.

"No really. Because . . ."

She glared at me again. "You think she's not good enough for you?"

"No!" I shut my eyes and clenched my fists under the table. "Look, I'm sorry my friends are assholes. Will you just listen for a sec?"

"I'm listening," she said icily.

"Stella, I'm gay."

I'd expected her to react like Mattie did, except maybe with repressed giggles instead of hysterical laughter. But she just stared at me, and then shifted her gaze to the window. I could've been wrong, but I thought her eyes got a little misty.

"Oh."

"Say something other than 'oh,'" I begged.

"How many people know?"

"Three. Including you."

She nodded and we were both quiet for a bit before she spoke again. "It's funny how sometimes everything starts to change all at once. First Mattie. Now you've just torn my stereotypical basketball-guy schema for you to pieces. And this time next year we'll all be at college orientations."

"Yeah," I said.

"And I always thought I'd be ready for it. More than ready—excited even, after three years at a school where I'm just 'that brainy girl who drives a Bug.' And it's amazing. Beautiful, really. But it's also . . . a lot."

I grinned at her. It's true that Stella and I had never exchanged more than a few pleasantries in any of our classes together, but I wasn't at a total loss. "It's no use going back to yesterday, because I was a different person then."

She smiled back. "Lewis Carroll. Well played, Will Kane. I guess you've been paying more attention than I thought."

When the waitress brought our food, Stella scowled down at her double-bacon sandwich oozing with processed cheese.

"Can you trust me on this one?"

"I suppose," she sighed. "But just this once, and only because you quoted my favorite author." She took a hesitant little bird bite. "Oh my. Why is this disgusting grease-fest so scrumptious?"

A poem:

"Hachidori, you need to finish your math homework."
"Hachidori, please make your bed."
"Hachidori, turn that music down so I can get some sleep."
"Not until you start training me" is always the response.
God help me, I've created a monster in my own image.

— Akiko Miyake, Grayton, March 4, 1991

Mattie as Moral Support

The night before the first day of our senior year at Cianci Regional, Will picked me up at my last gelato-scooping shift at Café Italiano.

"Are you ready for this?" I asked as I slid into the passenger seat.

He rubbed his palms against his jeans. "I guess so. You know my mom."

"Not really. But you told me once that gay men are like pets to her or something. And your dad has a tell when seething on the inside, right?"

"Yeah. Rubs his nose like he's about to sneeze."

"I'll keep an eye out for that," I promised.

On the way to Will's house in Grayton, we listened to some of my favorite Ella Fitzgerald tunes with the windows down, dousing ourselves in the humid late-August air. As much as I loved the fashion, the over-the-top slang, and the social turbulence of the 1920s, I'd been trying to convince Will that jazz continued to get better after his favorite decade.

"This is actually really good," he admitted. "But it makes me think of my grandma's record collection."

"Then your grandma is wicked cool," I argued. "You have to remember that all old people were young once. Try to imagine your grandmother when she was our age, sneaking out of her house to go to a jazz club so she could have a few sips of booze and slow dance with sailors."

"I doubt any of that happened," he said with a laugh.

"Then pretend it did. It'll be like a tiny bit of radical nostalgia."

"What?"

"You know, like how Frankie writes Lovecraft fanfic full of people of color even though Lovecraft himself was undeniably racist. Or like how you fantasize about the best parts of the '20s, but you don't actually want to live in the '20s."

"It sounds fucked up when you put it that way. It's cherry picking."

"It's cherry picking, but it's not fucked up. All the things you love from back then were actually part of a huge cultural shift. They were signs of rebellion. Isn't that why you like them?"

As Ella's caramel voice warmed my ears, my mind sifted through the last week of our summer. Will, Stella, Frankie and I had spent almost every waking moment together. Even when I had a shift at the café, the three of them would hang out there for hours, downing lattes and filling out college applications on their laptops. After work, we'd drive over the border into Massachusetts and comb through dusty antique stores, me hunting for old LPs and knickknacks, and Frankie hunting for pocketknives with decorative handles. Frankie even came with me to Miyu's a few times. The two of them would sip bitter tea at the dining room table and chat about Lovecraft while I picked and polished locks.

"Have you seen Betsy at all this week?" I asked when we pulled into Will's driveway.

"We went out to breakfast on Wednesday."

"That's it? She's supposed to be your girlfriend and you saw her once this week?"

"I'm trying to distance myself from her. I'm hoping that will make it easier when I finally . . . you know."

"Wow. Do you think she's suspicious or anything?"

He shrugged. "She's still trying to be that supportive girlfriend. She's like, 'If you need space for a little while, take it.'"

"Jeezus," I said as I unbuckled my seatbelt. "You must really hate yourself."

Will glared at me, his brown eyes like sharp slivers, and I felt like such an ass. "Sorry. Not at all what you need to hear right now. Let's shift our focus to the task at hand—your parents."

We found Will's dad in the kitchen, sipping a glass of red wine and slicing up a block of cheese that had undoubtedly been purchased from the "fancy cheese" section of the grocery store. He looked a lot like Will, but paunchier and with a receding hairline.

"So nice to meet you, Mattie." He smiled and extended his hand for me. "We've heard so much about you. Can I get you a lime rickey?"

"Yes. That sounds fantastic."

"Will used to love lime rickeys as a kid." His dad explained. "But his basketball coach has a pretty strict no-sugary-drinks rule."

"Dad," Will whined.

"I don't play basketball," I said. "Bring on the sugar."

"Your mentor doesn't enforce a strict diet?" he asked.

My throat shriveled up, and I realized I'd forgotten that Will's parents were regulars at Salone Postale.

Will jumped in to save me. "Miyu works Mattie to the bone, but she doesn't really care what she does on her own time."

A slim woman, swimming in a cloud of jasmine perfume and decked out in skinny jeans and tall black boots, waltzed into the kitchen. Her eyes, the same brown as Will's, lit up when she saw me. "My god, she's even more darling off-stage."

She hugged me, enveloping me in her jasmine perfume, and my face flushed. "You must be famished," she said. "Do they feed you at the gelato factory?" she asked with a raised eyebrow.

I laughed. "I get one bowl of gruel a day."

"And she's funny!" Mrs. Kane declared. "See, Will? The good ones have a sharp sense of humor."

Will grumbled something I couldn't make out, and I wondered if his mom had just compared me to Betsy.

"Help yourself to some artisan cheddar," Mr. Kane said as he handed me a sparkling lime rickey in a highball glass. "Dinner will be ready in about twenty minutes."

We chatted while we munched on cheddar so sharp it could cut diamonds, and Will's parents grilled me on my burgeoning career as an escapologist.

"We never got to see Akiko perform," Will's mom explained. "I never truly understood why people were so in awe of her until I saw you perform. It's so much more than a death-defying stunt. You raise it to the level of performance art."

"You really think so?"

"Of course," she said between sips of wine. "What you do is literal and figurative at the same time. That's an incredibly powerful thing."

"And I love all the little touches you add, Mattie," Mr. Kane said. "Especially the jazz records and the old gramophone. Your personality really shines through during your performances. How did you become interested in escapology?"

"I think it was the stories, mostly," I replied. "All the major players have such great stories. And there's something inspiring about the act itself."

"Most definitely," Mrs. Kane agreed. "The struggle is compelling."

We sat down to a spread of braised short ribs, grilled asparagus, and roasted red potatoes. I dug into my short ribs, shoving delectable chunks of grass-fed beef into my face. Will stared at his mom, his plate untouched.

"Are you all right, sweetie?" she asked.

He cleared his throat and wiped a thin sheen of sweat from his brow. "Yeah. I, uh, need to tell you guys something. I invited Mattie for moral support."

Mr. and Mrs. Kane exchanged a quick glance while I swallowed a huge bite of short rib and put my fork down.

Will exhaled a deep breath that rattled in his chest. "I'm gay."

I looked from Mr. to Mrs. Kane and back again. They both gawked silently at Will. I found myself staring at Mr. Kane, waiting for him to rub his nose, but his hands stayed in his lap.

Mrs. Kane spoke first, her eyes glistening with tears. "Oh my god, sweetie, I'm so glad you told us. Honestly," she added as the clutched the collar of her sweater, "I'm so relieved. We were so worried you were going to be terribly uninteresting."

Will rolled his eyes and a brief snort escaped from my lips.

"Marjorie," Mr. Kane protested. "I'm not sure 'uninteresting' is the right word for it."

Mrs. Kane ignored him. "Does this mean you've broken things off with that awful girl?"

"Mom," Will moaned. "I don't know how many times I have to tell you, she's not at all like she was in junior high."

"Oh, I know, Will," she sighed before taking a small sip of wine. "She traded all of her wilted-flower theatrics for vacant optimism and soft-focus dreams of sorority pins and white-picket fences."

On a scale of one to walking in on your parents having sex, this dinner party had officially reached watching your art teacher split her pants while bending over to pick up a paintbrush. Hard as I tried, I couldn't wipe the grin off my face. Mrs. Kane represented the worst of the over-privileged and over-educated salon-goers, wearing her counter-culture banner like a cleric's robe. She looked down her nose at people like Betsy, no matter how kind and well-adjusted they were. But she did it so well, it was awe-inspiring.

"Why don't we get back to what really matters," Mr. Kane suggested. "Our son was brave enough to tell us something very personal about himself. And his friend was here to support him." He'd obviously become skilled at defusing tension between his wife and son.

"You're absolutely right," Mrs. Kane admitted with a nod. "In this heteronormative world, coming out is never easy, even to your family. Especially when you're still a teenager. I'm very proud of you, sweetie. You know that we love and accept you, no matter what. And as an added bonus, gay men are almost never bored or boring."

I shot Will my best It Could've Been Worse look. He rolled his eyes again and grinned at me as his mom proposed a toast.

"I'm sorry," Will mumbled later that night as we drove to my house along back roads that stretched out like dark ribbons from the interstate.

"For what?"

"My mom is . . . I don't even know."

"I see what you mean, but I think she's hilarious. And it's always nice to know there are people out there who are even more judgmental than me."

I expected him to laugh, but he didn't. "Promise me you're not going to be like her."

"What?"

"Like, when we're real adults . . . in our thirties or whatever . . . promise me you won't get like that. You won't look down on people because they shop at J. Crew and don't know who Cindy Sherman is."

I should have been offended that he assumed I could ever be like his mother, but all I could feel was that warmth flooding through me again and collecting around my heart.

"You just said, 'when we're real adults,' like we'll still be hanging out when we're thirty."

"Won't we?" he asked.

"I hope so," I said with a nod. "I usually don't let myself think that far ahead. But I hope so."

We sped through the night in comfortable silence until Will pulled into my driveway. "See you at the sausage-grinder, Mattie-O."

"We have homeroom together, don't we?"

He laughed. "Yeah. I forgot about that."

I tapped on the hood of his car and waved before heading into my house, hoping to get a good night's sleep before I had to face my last year at Cianci Regional. Guinan met me at the door with her paws clacking against the kitchen floor and her wet nose sniffing my hands.

I dug my phone out of my bag and realized I'd missed a text from Miyu.

> I gave you the week off but now it's time to get yr head back in the game. Yr

next act is all you, Girl Scout. Sink or
swim.

Guinan whined for attention. "Hey, girl," I whispered as I ruffled the fur on her pointy ears. "Tomorrow's gonna be a long, weird day."

I woke up after a night of sipping martinis in front of the TV with a dull ache radiating through my skull. "Hachidori," I moaned, "can you mix me a bloody mary? And don't forget the celery."

I gasped and bolted out of bed the second I realized I'd left her locked up in one of my trunks. I could hear her muffled whimpers as I fumbled with the key, and she exploded as soon I lifted the lid.

"You forgot me!" she screamed, tears streaking down her red, quivering face. "How could you forget me?"

My head throbbed. "Don't yell. I'm sorry. You're the one who wanted me to train you. How many times have I said you'd be better off at a summer camp, running around with other kids?"

"I could've died in there!"

"There are holes in the lid. You couldn't have died. I wouldn't let that happen."

"You're missing the point."

I took a deep breath and exhaled through my nose. "I'm sorry, Hachidori. What's the point?"

"The point is you're the worst mom ever."

— Akiko Miyake, Grayton, March 15, 1993

Mattie vs. the Sausage Grinder

Stella and I arrived in homeroom a solid fifteen minutes early. Despite our punctuality, she was still percolating with anxiety and kept sighing and humming to herself while we drove to school in her Volkswagen. Her nerves must've been telepathically signaling my nerves, because my palms wouldn't stop sweating, but I swallowed my complaints. The first day of school was always a big deal for her, like an overachiever's holy day. I figured she'd settle down by lunch.

"Hey, Mattie," Meadow said as I took my seat behind her.

"Hey, Meadow." I smiled to myself as I thought about how many times over the summer I'd used her as an excuse for staying out until the early hours of the morning.

"How was your summer?"

I had no idea how to answer that. "Um . . . you know . . . fine. Stella had fun at St. Joe's."

"Oh, that's right," she said as she examined her cuticles. "That'll probably be a big booster for your college apps."

Will breezed into the room and set his messenger bag on his desk. Maybe the tension was all in my head, but I felt like I could cut it with a knife. I stopped breathing as I wondered whether he'd acknowledge me and Stella—and risk exposing himself in the process— or pretend this was just another day at Cianci Regional.

He surprised me by not just exchanging *Hi!*s with us, but by launching into a convo with Stella about the first book on the Honors English syllabus.

"I'm surprised it's a modern selection," he said. "I thought we were going to be relegated to Victorian-era classics forever."

A chat about non-historical fiction wouldn't hold my attention on a good day, but I was so fascinated by Meadow's reaction to this sudden sea change, Will and Stella could have started conversing in Pig Latin, and I wouldn't have known it. Meadow and I weren't exactly friends, though I'd known her long enough I could recognize when something was bothering her. As she stared at Stella and Will, her hazel eyes narrowed and her brows knitted ever so slightly. Her lips, undoubtedly glossed with all-natural chapstick, puckered into a perfect O. She clearly didn't understand why Will was investing so much of his conversational time in Stella and, therefore, didn't like it.

Will and Stella chuckled with each other, though I had no idea how Honors English could possibly be funny. I watched as Meadow's expression softened into cool, collected acceptance. Then she laughed when Stella asked, "How many structuralists does it take to change a light bulb?"

As we got up to leave for our first classes of the day, Meadow pulled Stella aside. "I'd love to do a quarter-page in the yearbook about your experience at St. Joe's. Do you think you'd have time to meet with me later this week?"

For more than a brief moment, I wanted to swing my book-laden backpack right into her dewy-fresh face. In less time than it would take for me to beat the yearbook staff to a bloody pulp, Stella had gone from someone Meadow didn't deem worthy of direct eye contact to someone she could use like a piece of social currency. For a moment, I saw the world the way Will's mom must see it—a place full of shallow automatons who place all their chips on empty status symbols instead of . . . I didn't even know. There had to be more important stuff than whatever Meadow had on her mind.

But I wasn't Will's mom, and that rage quickly faded to pity. Meadow was so caught up in Meadow-land, she'd never stumble upon the hidden jewels of the world, like Salone Postale. She'd miss out on getting to know people like Frankie because they didn't serve any obvious purpose for her. And she'd never really connect with people like Will, because they'd be too afraid to confide in her.

"You okay?" Stella asked as I shuffled out of homeroom and into the hallway.

I nodded. "I didn't know quite what was going to happen."

"Me either. Did you see Meadow's face?"

"She looked like she'd just sucked on an exceptionally sour lemon."

"I guarantee she'll forget all about that yearbook thing by third period. Au revoir, mademoiselle." She smiled and waved before heading off to Honors English.

Though I'd been dreading my first day back at school, it helped that my first class of the day was an elective with Liam titled *How to Read and Write Like an Historian*. He'd confided in me before summer break that, behind the principal's back, he referred to it as *How to Tell When Your Biased Textbook is Lying to You*.

"Mattie McKenna!" he shouted from his desk when I walked in.

"Yup, it's me." A few fellow students had already taken their seats, thus I felt obligated to refer to him by his last name. "Hey, Mr. Prentice."

"And how was your summer?"

"Pretty fantastic, actually." I paused for a moment to consider how much I wanted to reveal. "I think I've found a creative hobby I can stick with."

He took his sneakered feet off his desk and adjusted his tie. "That *is* fantastic."

I took a seat near the front, between a junior with earbuds jammed in her ears and a fellow senior who smelled like he'd forgotten to take a shower that morning. Liam passed out our textbooks—fat, aged tomes titled *Manifest Destiny: America Moves West*.

The junior next to me ripped out her earbuds. "Isn't that, like, kind of racist? There were people here before all the whities moved west."

"Precisely," Liam proclaimed with a smile. "But this textbook was used at this very school until as late as 1992. We aren't going to use this textbook as a bible. We're going to dissect it. We're going to learn that history can't always be separated from mythology and mythologies aren't set in stone. They serve the purpose of those telling the story. Before the end of the semester, you'll complete an independent project in which you dissect a text of your own choosing."

The smelly senior raised his hand, sending a cloud of body odor wafting in my direction. "Does that mean once we're done reading this huge, boring textbook we have to read another huge, boring textbook?"

Liam stared at the smelly kid for a beat, and, though I have no idea how, managed to not roll his eyes. "No. I'm using the term 'text' loosely here. You can choose anything you want as long as it purportedly documents an historical event. And it doesn't have to be a book. It can be a song, a film, a poem scrawled on a cocktail napkin for all I care."

As Liam continued his lecture, I couldn't help pondering the awesomely endless possibilities for my independent project. Should I dissect one of my dad's favorite Westerns? Or was I finally ready to share a bit of my own obsession with the world? Houdini and H. P. Lovecraft, Frankie and Miyu's fave horror legend, had collaborated on a supposedly true story that might be ripe for historical analysis.

Bzzzzz. The vibration of my phone in my back pocket pulled me out of my nerdy daydream. I knew it couldn't be Stella. She'd never text in class. I willed myself to ignore it and focus on class. When it buzzed a second time, my fingers began to tingle. After the third buzz, I couldn't take it. I pulled it out of my pocket and tossed it in my lap. Will had sent a text to me, Stella, and Frankie.

> ›Betsy just posted this photo of the two of us on her LifeScape page with the caption "my most fave person ever." Kill me now.

Will gazed out from the photo with the best smile he could muster as Betsy, all porcelain skin and wispy blonde curls, planted a massive kiss on his cheek.

Frankie had replied to Will's text.

> ›She looks like she's going to suck all the skin off your face.

Stella had broken her self-imposed rule of never texting in class and chimed in.

> ›I hate to say this, but maybe it's time to rip the Band-Aid off?

I picked my phone up out of my lap and followed Stella's text up with:

> ›The longer you wait, the more she'll hate you. Also, your face would look gross with no skin.

When I looked up, I realized Liam was staring at me. I shoved my phone back into my pocket and apologized. The girl with the ear buds snickered.

"Did your new hobby lead to a few new friends this

summer?" he asked.

"Something like that."

"Great. Just try to keep your phone out of sight so I don't have to take it away."

By lunchtime, Stella's nerves had given way to caffeine-fueled excitement.

"The new AP Chemistry teacher is brilliant, Mattie. We're so lucky to have her."

I nodded, though even the smartest woman on earth couldn't teach me how to comprehend chemistry. Fortunately, I had no plans for a career in the hard sciences.

As we headed toward the cafeteria, a redheaded woman bounded toward us through a throng of students.

"Is that Ms. Simmons?" Stella asked.

Oh fuck.

Our effervescent and always dedicated guidance counselor sidled up to me with her big, bright blue eyes. "Mattie, can I borrow you for a minute? If you want, you can bring your lunch to my office."

I took a deep breath and followed Ms. Simmons down the hall, carrying my PB&J in a paper bag.

"Am I really worthy of first day treatment?" I asked as I took a seat in her office. My face twitched as soon as I got a look at those god awful Successories posters behind her desk.

"Mattie, most of my students fall solidly into two camps. Those I'm not worried about, and those I have no hope for. You don't fall into either camp."

My throat went dry and I crumpled the edges of the paper bag with my sweaty fingers.

"You had almost three months to think about our last conversation. Any thoughts? Do you think you can pick a few extra-curriculars you can live with?"

"Definitely not. But I have a plan. Kind of."

"Okay," she chirped. "What, exactly?"

"Um . . . I can't tell you."

She stared at me for half a minute before picking up a pencil and snapping it in half between her clenched fists. "Sorry," she said with an almost frightening degree of composure. "Sometimes I need to do that to keep myself sane."

"I would have gone for one of those posters behind you," I quipped.

"Let's change the subject. Do you know what schools you want to apply to?"

"Not yet. I'm going to look at a few in September."

"Excellent. I would suggest applying to at least three. And you'll need one hell of an essay and a fantastic letter of recommendation from a teacher. I'm sure Mr. Prentice will be happy to help you out."

"I think I can handle that."

"Do you have any ideas for your essay?"

"Yes. But I can't tell you what they are. They have to do with . . . you know . . . that other thing I can't tell you about."

Ms. Simmons's narrowed eyes and flared nostrils conveyed her disgust loud and clear.

"You'll just have to trust me," I said.

"Mattie, I've been doing this for eight years. I trust

high school students about as much as I trust people who email me claiming to be Nigerian royalty."

I couldn't help but snicker at that. "You know, you should really drop the peppy act. I think this snarky-scary version of you would be much more effective with people my age."

Her lips curled into something almost resembling a grin. "I'll keep that in mind. Am I going to get anything else out of you today?"

"Probably not."

"Then go eat your lunch and hit the books. You promised me you'd up your GPA this quarter."

As I left her office, my phone buzzed in my back pocket. I pulled it out to find a text from Miyu.

> I booked you for Oct 31st, Girl Scout. Salone Postale takes All Hallows' Eve seriously. You better deliver.

Stella and Frankie stayed after school to go over an AP Chemistry assignment, and Will offered to give me a ride so I wouldn't have to take the bus.

"I haven't taken the bus since Stella got her license," I said as I buckled my seatbelt.

"I took it once last year when my car was in the shop. It was pretty demoralizing. And louder than a bag full of feral cats."

I invited Will in for an afternoon snack and a brainstorming session for my next escape act.

"Miyu booked me for Halloween night," I mumbled as Guinan greeted us at the door. "I might as well be performing in front of the doors of Macy's on Thanksgiving Day. I don't know if I can take the pressure."

Kyle stumbled into the kitchen with Connor and Austin in tow. The three of them looked like they'd just woken up and were still recovering from yet another night of drinking.

"'Sup," Kyle said as he nodded toward Will.

"Um, hey," Will replied.

Kyle and Austin continued on to the fridge, but Connor lingered by the doorway, smirking at me. "You're not going to introduce us to your friend?" he asked.

"Nope." I took two apples from the fruit bowl and headed upstairs with Will.

"That's him, right? The guy she's boning?" Connor asked Kyle, loud enough for me to hear. "God, I thought she'd be less of a bitch once she started gettin' some on the regular."

Will stopped dead in his tracks on the stairs, and I knew exactly what he was thinking.

I sighed and nodded.

"Oh my god, Mattie. Colossal asshole might have been an understatement."

"I know." I pulled him the rest of the way up the stairs.

"The blond guy's kinda cute," Will said once we were safely in my room.

"His name's Austin."

"Cool name," he said with a grin. "Sounds like he should be the rough and tumble hero of a romance novel or a character on an old-school soap opera. Seems a little mopey, though."

"They weren't always like that. Even Connor. When we were kids he . . . he was always a jerk, but he wasn't so mean about it. They used to be fun."

"What happened?"

I spilled the story of my brother and his two supposed best friends to Will, starting with Austin moving into town and ending with my brother's college fail and subsequent inability to get his life back in gear.

"I hate to say it, because they've been friends for so long, but the three of them are toxic to each other."

Will nodded as a grin crept over his face. "Oh. Oh, man. I have an idea."

"What?"

"It's obvious, right? You should invite them to see your next act."

I blinked at him. "Are you high? They are the last people on earth I'd want to share this with. Especially Connor."

His eyes got all wide. If he were a cartoon, I would've been able to see a thought-bubble above his head, bursting at the freaking seams. "Just hear me out. It kills so many birds with one stone. One, you get to show them that your summer hasn't been all about some hotsy-totsy guy. Two, you might actually inspire them to . . . I don't know . . . get off their drunken asses and do something with their lives. Three, and I know this is selfish, I might get to hang out with Austin for a night.

"No. No way, Will. They'll think I've lost my damn mind. Even worse, they might tell my parents."

He squinted at me. "Stella was cool with it."

"Stella's my best friend. Of course she was cool with it."

"And yet, just talking about sharing it with her got you all in a tizzy." He tapped his forehead. "I remember these things."

I planted my feet on the Oriental rug. "That's not going to work on me. This is completely different and you know it."

He watched me pace the edge of the rug. If I forced myself to be brutally realistic, I knew Austin probably wouldn't care one way or the other. And my brother? Well, he'd either be so horrified he'd tell Mom and Dad, or he'd be psyched out of his mind that I'd pulled him into my grand conspiracy. Truly, it was the mischievous conspiracy to end all mischievous conspiracies. If just slipping me a bit of parent-management advice had brought out a flash of the old Kyle, maybe Will was right. Maybe, with this, he'd find a way to climb out of his gloom spiral. But it was a big maybe and carried the even bigger risk that he'd rat me out for my own good.

And Connor. *Ugh.* Just picturing the smirk on his face made me want to scream into a pillow. He would either pick and pick and pick at me until I'd revealed every last freaking detail of my double life or, worse, he'd do that aloof, cool-guy thing he does and say nothing at all. I'd be left with my neurotic imagination running wild over what might be going through his head behind that punch-worthy smirk.

"Can you at least think about it?" Will said.

I walked the length of the terminal, trying to find a signal for the blasted contraption I'd bought on a whim. It seemed anytime I actually wanted to place a call on my new phone, there was no tower to be found.

I climbed over a railing and inched toward a window. One little bar appeared, and then another. Success!

The Hummingbird didn't pick up. The sound of my own voice on the answering machine grated against my ears. "You can't even bother to pick up the phone, Hachidori?" I said after the beep. "Ugh. I'll be boarding in a few minutes. I'll call you when I land in L.A. Try to drag yourself off the couch and pick up the damn phone, all right?"

Ten minutes later, I shuffled down the jet bridge with the other first class passengers and collapsed into my seat. I took a deep breath and felt my lungs shrivel up. My palms had already slicked over with sweat. I could free myself from chains and cages, but flying always made me feel trapped.

"Can I get you a drink, Ms. Miyake?" a stewardess asked, her lips shellacked in pink.

"Scotch. Neat. Please."

I swallowed half a Valium dry and put on my eye mask. Before my scotch arrived, I slipped into a deep, drug-induced sleep.

I didn't wake up until an oxygen mask fell from the overhead compartment and smacked me in the face.

— Akiko Miyake, Houston, December 3, 1999

Mattie Knows It'll Never be a Cakewalk

On the first Saturday in September, I turned eighteen the same weekend Frankie turned fifteen. To appease my mom, and because Stella declared it "mandatory," we spent the morning touring colleges. Stella and Frankie were both smitten with Watson University, an intimidating institution on the coast of Massachusetts.

"Oh my god, they have such an amazing neuroscience program," Stella gushed as we strolled across the quad, buffeted by a mid-autumn sea breeze. "I think I'd give my left arm to get in."

Will and I exchanged resigned glances. Watson's campus boasted a number of architectural wonders, and a progressive history program, but Will and I didn't have a snowball's chance in hell of getting in. Even with three years of varsity basketball under his belt, Will would need to up his GPA a full point before the Watson board would give his application a serious look.

And if I applied, my resume would surely end up on a cork board in the employee break room, so the admissions staffers could have a good laugh while they sipped their morning coffee.

Will stood a much better chance of getting into Bristol College, a little liberal arts haven forty minutes from Tivergreene that I was fully prepared to hate. My disdain lasted all of ten minutes because of my insta-crush on our tour guide, a chubby-cute sophomore with a Charles Mingus t-shirt. *Charles Mingus* for frig's sake! I could practically feel my mom giving me a self-satisfied See I Knew You'd Like College look from thirty miles away.

As an added bonus (like my mom rubbing it in from afar), he recognized Will and me from the salon.

"Hey-o," he said as he pulled us aside. "Always nice to have a few local celebrities on the tour. When's your next act?"

"Halloween night," I replied. "Be there or be square." *Or please just be there because you are adorable.*

But don't think for even one second that I was all *Rah! Rah! Bristol!* just because of some cute Mingus fan (I can be a silly girl, but not that silly). Their history department was so legit I'd actually already read books by some of the visiting professors.

"What do you know about the fine arts department?" Will asked. "Do they look down on fashion design?"

"Not at all," our tour guide said. "My roommate is an FA major with a concentration in fashion. They take it seriously here."

With his grades, extracurriculars, and overall winning personality, the admissions board at Bristol would eat up Will's application with a spoon. But my grades fell below the median for Bristol and my mediocre SAT scores weren't doing me any favors. I'd have to play up my new hobby on my app, or languish for four years at some party school where, inevitably, my party-girl roommate would sexile me on a nightly basis.

After a long day of trekking through student centers and flipping through course catalogs, the four of us headed to the edge of East Providence for a birthday dinner at Frankie's. I wore my blue and white party dress from the '50s with the Peter Pan collar and cap sleeves.

"Oh meu deus!" Frankie's mom proclaimed when I walked into the kitchen of their second floor apartment. "You look like Donna Reed!"

"Like Donna Reed after a stint in prison," Will whispered in my ear. "The don't-fuck-with-me version of Donna Reed."

I stifled a giggle and inhaled the rich, buttery scent of something that had been cooking low-and-slow all day. Frankie introduced us to his two older sisters, twins who had graduated from Cianci Regional the same year as my brother.

"How is he?" one of them asked as she set the table.

"Fine," I said without going into any details about my brother's current state of affairs.

The other twin glanced at me as she emerged from the balcony with two folding chairs. "I heard he dropped out."

Her sister snapped at her in Portuguese before I even had a chance to reply. "It's not easy for people our age," she said. "Even with a college degree, good jobs are hard to come by."

"Even bad jobs are hard to come by," the other twin mumbled.

Frankie's mom had made him his favorite meal for his fifteenth birthday—traditional Azorean pot-roast with a side of Portuguese sweet bread.

"We can make hot dogs if you don't like Alcatra," she assured us.

But no hot dogs were harmed in the making of this birthday party, just a hunk of beef Mrs. Campos had simmered and roasted to juicy, tender perfection. Even after I'd stuffed myself, Frankie's mom tried to heap another ladleful on my plate.

"I can't," I protested as I dropped my napkin like a white flag of surrender. "I'll explode."

Frankie's twin sisters conspired in Portuguese, then slipped out of the kitchen and returned with a chocolate cake topped with enough candles to burn down a city block. Frankie and I blew out the candles on the count of three and dished out thick slices of cake and scoops of coffee ice cream. The cake melted in my mouth, and I downed every last bite, despite my stomach's gurgling protests.

After dinner, Will and Stella washed the dishes, standing hip to hip at the kitchen sink. I volunteered to help but Mrs. Campos wouldn't have it.

"Birthday girls don't wash dishes," she said.

Instead of watching Stella and Will scrub glassware,

Frankie and I headed to his storage locker in the basement so I could check out his collection.

"You're lucky the police don't know about this cache," I said as I surveyed the hodgepodge of carefully organized knives, swords, and other miscellaneous instruments of death. "They'd send a SWAT team in here."

Frankie laughed and took a seat at a small desk where he probably spent hours ensuring his collection remained shiny and sharp. "I think the police have bigger fish to fry. There was a drug bust a few blocks down about a month ago."

"That's kinda scary."

He shrugged his bony shoulders. "I am lucky the school doesn't know about it. They'd probably have me committed."

"Good point. You'd be guilty of being weird." I shuddered to think of the amount of time Frankie would have to spend with Ms. Simmons if she found out about his antique weapon collection.

He snorted. "Already guilty of that, I'm afraid. Which reminds me, I keep meaning to ask if you've read *Under the Pyramids*."

"That's the story Houdini wrote with H. P. Lovecraft, right? About vacationing in Egypt. I was actually considering analyzing it for my history class."

Frankie laughed. "I'm not sure how historical it is considering Lovecraft added an army of half-animal mummies to the tale."

"Nothing wrong with a few embellishments here and there. Some stories deserve to be larger than life.

That's how mythologies are born."

I pointed to a crossbow with a skeleton of iron and wood. "Wow. Where did you get this?" A few specks of rust had crept onto the mounts, but the polished wood looked like it had been painstakingly cared for. "Early twentieth century?" I guessed.

He nodded. "Handmade in 1908 by a Portuguese craftsman. You can take it down, if you want. It's not loaded."

I slid the crossbow off the pegboard and ran my fingertips along the taut string.

"My uncle was a collector, too," Frankie said. "He bought that in the Azores. That's where a lot of these pieces came from. I inherited them."

"Does a lot of your family still live there?"

He nodded. "My mom came here by herself when she was pregnant with my sisters. She lived with a friend of hers for a while before she got a job and could afford a place of her own."

"Where's your dad?"

"Still in the Azores. He stayed because my uncle was sick. He comes to visit once or twice a year. They're still married, but sometimes I think they're happier living apart."

"Stella's parents are like that. They separated when we were in middle school. It was hard for her at first, but I think she's glad they got it over with and met other people they don't fight with all the time."

Frankie nodded again and gazed at his feet. A new topic seemed to be in order.

"So, do you think you'll apply to Watson U?"

"Yeah, I guess. It's a really good school."

"You sound like you're bursting at the seams with excitement."

That coaxed a brief smile out of him but it didn't last. "I know I should be excited about college. They say everyone who hates high school likes college. But I doubt it'll be like that for me. I'll still be younger than everyone else. And I'll still be me."

I leaned against the squat little desk, still holding the crossbow. "If it makes you feel any better, I don't think college is all it's cracked up to be, even if you've made it all the way through puberty by the time you get there. For most people, it's probably a slightly less sucky version of high school. I'm actually beginning to wonder if life, in general, is a progressively less sucky version of high school."

"I don't know whether to be comforted or horrified by that," he said.

"Sorry," I laughed. "I'm trying to make you feel better, I'm just not doing a good job. I guess . . . It'll never be a cakewalk for weirdos like us, you know? But that doesn't mean we're not allowed to be happy." In my mind, the monocled octopus and Ginger the intrepid orphan gave me a round of applause. *That'll do,* the octopus said with a wise nod.

Frankie's eyes dropped to one of the desk drawers. He opened it and pulled out a slim little book with a gold cover. "So, I have something for you."

"You didn't get me a present, did you?"

He laughed. "No. At least not one I paid for. And I'm not actually giving this to you. I'm just letting you borrow it. And it comes with conditions."

When he handed it to me, I realized it wasn't a novel, but something handwritten, like a journal. I flipped through the first few pages and skimmed a passage about a Japanese schoolgirl trying to score a gig as a magician's assistant.

Those handwritten words made me choke on my own breath. My mouth went dry and I almost dropped the crossbow I'd tucked under my arm. "Oh my god, Frankie. Akiko's diary? Where did you get this? Has this just been lying around Miyu's house since her mom died?"

He shook his head. "Akiko didn't write it, Miyu did. So, it's not really a diary. It's a mock diary. A miary? A mock-oir?"

The ridiculousness of the word "miary" didn't even register. "Miyu wrote it? But . . . why . . . I mean . . . she kinda hates her mom, right?"

Frankie squirmed and scrunched up his button nose. "Miyu and I converse about Lovecraft. Psychoanalyzing her mommy-issues is way, *way* out of my wheelhouse."

"Frankie, help me out here. I have to know why, and if I ask her she'll never give me a straight answer." A wave of adrenaline coursed through me, almost as sharp as the rush I got from performing. "Holy frig. I just realized this is the perfect text for my history project."

"What about Lovecraft?"

"Screw Lovecraft."

Frankie's mouth puckered like he'd just smelled a rotten egg, and he slipped the journal out of my trembling hands. "I'm going to chalk that last statement up to excitement and forgive you. But you may want to reconsider Lovecraft. Like I said, the miary comes with conditions."

"Like what?"

"Miyu said I could let you borrow it only if you promise not to ask her about what you read. Technically, you're not allowed to quote-unquote 'bug her with questions about her mom again.' Ever."

I took a deep breath to keep myself from having a knock-down, drag-out tantrum. I felt like a kid being tempted with a silky smooth premium chocolate bar— the kind sprinkled with delicately toasted almonds and oozing with caramel filling—only to be told that if she eats it she can never have another piece of candy again.

"Frankie, that is bananas."

He laughed. "Of course it is. We're talking about Miyu here. Have you made a decision?"

"Ugh." Unable to resist the mouth-watering deliciousness of the historical morsels potentially hidden inside, I took the journal.

"You're welcome," Frankie said with a grin.

I gave him a friendly punch in the arm before shuffling back to the pegboard to hang the crossbow in its place. "You know, a few escapologists have used crossbows in their routines. They chain themselves to targets and escape before being impaled with arrows."

Frankie's dark eyebrows flicked upward. "You think you're ready for that?"

I imagined arrows piercing my skin, gliding between my ribs, making mincemeat out of my internal organs. Drowning was certainly preferable to death by impalement, but maybe it was time to put up or shut up. I had, after all, just crossed that arbitrary line between kid-dom and adulthood. And the salon-goers would go nuts over the genuine possibility of blood-drenched gore, especially on Halloween night.

I whipped out my phone and texted Miyu to let her know I had an idea for my next act.

For the rest of the month, I pulled triple duty as a young escapologist practicing for her next performance, a (mostly) diligent student, and an eager college applicant. Will and I submitted our applications to Bristol College on the same day. Ms. Simmons encouraged me to apply to a safety school, so I said I would, then procrastinated until the early acceptance deadline passed.

At least I had a good excuse. The "miary," as Frankie had dubbed it, called to me on a nightly basis. I'd tuck myself in bed, crack open that gold cover, and get lost in those handwritten pages. I didn't know why Miyu had written it or how much of it was true, but that didn't make it any less engaging. I'd seen a few interviews with Akiko, though they never probed this deeply. This was the unabridged version of her story, told in her own voice.

Except it wasn't really her voice. It was her voice filtered through Miyu, which only made it more fascinating.

Two weeks after submitting my application to Bristol, I sat in Liam's class, trying to come up with some sort of unifying theme for my history project. *Prickly young woman struggles to come to terms with her mother's death? Recluse hides in her crumbling villa and relives her mother's life on paper?* I knew those obvious clichés would never fly with Liam.

My phone danced in my back pocket—a text from Will.

>Did you get an interview?

Before I had chance to text back, Ms. Simmons popped her rosy-cheeked face into the doorway.

"Can I borrow Mattie for a minute?" she chirped. Her blue eyes glistened in my direction.

Liam happened to be in the middle of an intense lecture on cultural bias and waved me toward the door without giving Ms. Simmons a second glance.

As soon as we were safely in the hall, she dropped the act, her typically cheery guidance-counselor expression melting into a grimace. "I don't know what you put on your application, but Bristol wants to set up an interview with an alum."

My insides shriveled into a tight little knot, and I was vaguely aware that I couldn't feel my hands. "That's . . . um . . ."

"It's excellent, assuming you don't blow the interview."

"Yeah. Okay, great. When?"

"This Friday."

But it's already Wednesday! "Does it have to be so soon?" I asked.

"Believe me, you don't want to keep them waiting."

"Fine. Friday works. What about Will?"

"I'm not permitted to disclose any information regarding his application to you." She bit her lip and squinted at me. "I will say that when it comes to Will, I'm not worried. You, my dear, are another story."

To keep my mind off my pre-interview jitters, I spent the afternoon at Miyu's training for my next act. Miyu and Frankie sat by the pool, soaking in some mid-autumn sunshine and taking turns reading passages from *The Shadow over Innsmouth* to each other as I practiced picking locks while chained to a dining room chair Miyu had dragged out onto the patio.

As I stabbed at a weighty padlock resting on my hip, I boldly ignored the conditions of the miary. "Did she really pull out her own hair when she was nervous?" I asked. "Even when she was a kid? I thought you just told me that to make me feel better. And I always heard that she went into that magic shop in Shinjuku and wouldn't take no for an answer. In your version, she seems so timid. Is that how she told the story or did you write it that way because you . . . you know . . . still have beef with her?"

Miyu ignored me but Frankie stopped reading and shook his head. "You're making me look bad."

"Don't be silly," I argued. "She knew I'd never follow the rules."

Miyu grunted and told Frankie to continue *The Shadow over Innsmouth*.

"Fine, fine, fine," I said. "Can't you at least tell me the magician's name? I want to see if I can track him down. You know, for my project. Technically, that question doesn't break the rules. I'm not asking you *about* the journal or your mom, I'm just asking for a small piece of info that's missing."

"Don't split hairs," she barked, arms crossed against her chest. "Cub Scout, shut her up."

Frankie got up from his lawn chaise and grabbed the back of the chair I was chained to. "Please don't be mad at me. You did this to yourself."

With a single push, he knocked me and the chair into the frigid pool. The chains pulled me right to the concrete bottom. Despite the shock, I had the where-withal to keep my grip on the bobby pin. I picked the remaining lock, fought my way through the chains, and kicked my way to the surface.

"You bitch."

Miyu laughed. "She wasn't infallible, you know. At the end of the day, she was still just a person."

"Wait, what?" I coughed as Frankie ran out of the house with a towel. "Of course she was a person. That's why I want to know more about her. Was your dad really a deadbeat? How could she fall for such an obvious asshole?"

"Oh, for fuck's sake. No more questions or I'll make Cub Scout withhold that towel. You'll have to climb out and air dry your ass."

A brisk fall breeze coated my arms with goose bumps as I beached myself like a fully-dressed whale on the poolside patio.

"Whatever," I said as I took the towel from Frankie. And then I had an idea.

"Hey, Miyu. Do you have a favorite memory from when you were a kid?"

Her eyes flashed with rage. "Do I need to have Cub Scout push you back in the pool?"

"But I'm not breaking the rules. I promised not to ask any questions about your mom, and I didn't. That question was about you."

One of her eyes twitched as she stared at me.

Frankie took the towel from my hands. "Uhm. I'm just gonna go toss this down the laundry chute."

"Follow me," Miyu said as he scampered off.

Still shivering, I trailed after her, inside the house and up the stairs to the second floor. I'd been up to the attic a few times, but the bedrooms on the second floor had been off-limits to me, their doors always shut. When we passed the bathroom where I'd practiced breath training, I knew where we were headed.

I suppose I expected Miyu's bedroom to look like the rest of the house—a dusty shrine. What I found was something that looked more like my brother's bedroom. Messy. Colorful. Lived-in.

Miyu pointed at something in the corner, by the closet. My breath caught for a sec when I saw it. A Houdini-themed vintage pinball machine.

"Wow," I whispered.

"Every time my mom performed at the Black Cat Cabaret in Chicago," Miyu said, "I would sneak off to a little pizza place a few blocks away to play this. I figured she had no idea what I was up to. Then, when I turned ten, she surprised me with this. And it's not just a replica. She literally went into that pizza place and bought the machine from them."

Miyu and I played a few rounds, which didn't take

long because I couldn't hang onto a ball for more than a minute or two. I thought I might like pinball more than all the flashy games my brother played, but the clanging and banging rattled my nerves. Frankie eventually made his way upstairs, freaked out over the pinball machine, and threatened to beat Miyu's high score. I hung back and then took the chance to look around Miyu's private sanctuary, figuring I'd probably never be allowed in again.

She hadn't made her bed and random piles of clothing—some folded, some not—dotted the hard-wood floor. Three of the four walls were lined with ceiling-high bookshelves. The woman owned enough trade paperbacks to open a small library. Next to her dresser was a small oak desk, clearly meant for a school kid, but it was obvious she still used it. The typewriter sitting on top had a fresh piece of paper already dialed in and behind it sat a veritable wall of typed and hand-written pages, all stacked on top of each other with a few random journals thrown in here and there.

"Did you write all this?" I asked. "Have you written things besides the miary?"

She looked up from the pinball machine. "Did you think that I just sat around all day, waiting for you to show up?"

"Honestly? Kind of."

On Friday morning, as I waited for the Bristol alum in the conference room by Ms. Simmons's office, I couldn't keep my palms from sweating. No matter how many times I wiped them on my skirt, a salty flood would rise up out of my skin.

I jumped when the door sprang open.

"You must be Mattie. I'm Katrina." Katrina looked only a few years older than me, with jet-black hair, Betty Paige bangs, and deep red lipstick. The left leg hem of her dark gray pantsuit had frayed, and her scuffed heels had seen better days.

She flung her jacket over her chair and collapsed into her seat. "Promise me, whatever you do, you won't let anyone talk you into going to law school."

"Okay. I don't really have any interest in being a lawyer."

"Fantastic. Then you've already got that going for you." She reached into her shoulder bag and pulled out a messy stack of papers. "So, your essay was quite entertaining," she said with a grin. "You're either bound for the creative writing program, or you're an exceptionally talented young lady."

"Does that mean you thought it was BS?"

She shook her head and fished a pen out of her bag. "It doesn't really matter. Applicants say all sorts of outlandish things in their essays, believe me. The point is that it was well-written. And creative."

I leaned back in my chair. "It matters to me. I've worked pretty hard. Would you like to see me pick a lock?"

She laughed. "That's a joke, right? That's good. A sense of humor is always a point in your favor."

I put on the most serious face I could muster. "It's not a joke." I leaned down and dug through my backpack for a Westin four-pin. Katrina let out a tiny whimper when I dropped it on the table with a metallic *clank!* I pulled a bobby pin from my pocket, snapped it in half without batting an eye, and tackled the padlock. She let out another barely audible whimper when it popped open.

"I would have brought a straitjacket," I said, "but I thought that might be a little melodramatic for an interview."

Katrina peered at me, her deep red lips curling into a smile. "It's really true?" she whispered. "You're, like, a teenage Houdini or something?"

"Or something. Houdini performed most of his escapes hidden behind curtains or facades. I don't hide. All of my escapes are in full view."

She clicked her pen as she squinted at me, then scribbled a few notes on the messy stack of paper. "Let's presume you're telling the truth. You don't need a college degree to pursue . . . uh . . ."

"Escapology."

"Right. You don't need a degree to pursue escapology as a career."

"I love escapology. And I love performing. But I still want to be a historian."

She steepled her fingers on the table. "What do you like about history?"

"The stories, mostly. Most people my age see history as a dry, crumbly thing. You know, words on paper about dead people. But those people were young once. They were like us, up against the world, ready to make it their own. The past grounds us, places us on a timeline, but it's always open to interpretation."

"Is there a particular historical period you're interested in?"

"I've loved the Jazz Age for as long as I can remember. But I can find something worthwhile in almost any historical period. Even in the face of tragedy, there's always something to connect with, some forward momentum to cling to."

"Hm, that's an interesting answer." She cleared her throat. "Your grades and your test scores fall a little bit below average for Bristol."

"I'm aware."

"Can you reassure me that you're academically prepared for a school like Bristol?"

"I've always done well in subjects that interest me. As long as I'm engaged, I think I can handle it."

She clicked her pen one last time, scribbling a final note. "Mattie, I can't make any promises during this interview. But I can say I think you'll fit in nicely at Bristol."

The octopus gave me another round of applause while Ginger did a few cartwheels through my mind. I wouldn't have been able to wipe the grin off my face if my life depended on it.

I'd been dead for only three weeks when the social workers showed up on the snow-dusted porch of my villa in Grayton. They hadn't been able to find The Hummingbird's father or get in touch with my family in Japan. No matter—her father was a deadbeat, and her grandparents didn't even know she existed.

But a lack of relatives willing to open their homes meant The Hummingbird would be swallowed by a nebulous entity known as "the system."

"Did you pack some clothes?" a thirty-something in business casual asked. She sounded like she was trying to affect an air of compassion, but she'd done this too many times. She wanted to care, but no longer had the energy.

The Hummingbird slumped her shoulders and shook her head, a curtain of dark hair guarding her tear-streaked face.

The thirty-something sighed. "I know you don't want to leave. And I know packing will make it real. But you'll want your own stuff when you get to the group home."

"Fine," The Hummingbird huffed. "But I'll pack what I want to pack, and you'll shut up about it."

She took her time stomping up to the attic and filled a suitcase with locks and chains.

— Akiko Miyake, Grayton, December 24, 1999

Will With Two Ls Gets Crafty

Two weeks before Mattie's All Hallows Eve performance, I drove to Miyu's to help Frankie with construction. I might not strike most people as a handy guy, but my mom had sent me to more than enough art classes as a kid to prepare me for a papier mâché apocalypse. No matter the medium, I can squeak by in a pinch.

Miyu greeted me at her front door without a hint of a smile. "Jehovah."

"What's the word, Hummingbird?" I waggled my eyebrows for emphasis.

Her non-smile dropped to a sneer. "Yes, you think you're cute. You've made that quite clear. Cub Scout's in the garage."

"Groovy. Where's Mattie?"

"Training in the living room. She needs concentration so please keep your dimples outside."

"Understood. Hey, Miyu, is there a sewing machine up in that attic?"

She blinked her dark eyes at me. "Probably yes. Why?"

"Um, I need one for a thing."

Her nostrils flared. "I don't know why teenagers feel the need to be so vague when they want to withhold information. If you don't want to tell me what you need the sewing machine for, then just tell me it's none of my damn business."

"It's none of your damn business."

"Very good, Jehovah. I'll have Mattie dig it out for you."

"No! I mean, the thing is kind of a surprise. For Mattie."

"Ugh. Fine, I'll drag my ass up there and dig it out myself. You owe me, Jehovah."

She shut the door and I moseyed off the porch and into the garage. The squeal-and-buckle of a drill filled my ears as I gave Frankie's makeshift workshop a once over.

"Sandpaper, stat." He didn't even look up at me.

"You got it, kid. Four-hundred grit?"

"That should be sufficient."

We sanded and sanded and then sanded some more until I feared we might sand away the whole project. *The Karate Kid* had been among Betsy's dad's old VHS tapes, and I kept hearing Mr. Miyagi's instructional mantra in my head. *Sand the floor, sand the floor.*

"We're gonna be able to kick some serious ass when we're done with this," I said.

Frankie glanced over at me. "Huh?"

"*Karate Kid*? No?"

"Huh?"

"Never mind."

Once all that sanded wood reached a state of sheer splinterlessness, Frankie opened a few windows and busted out a can of varnish. Maybe it was all the fumes going to my head, but an hour into varnishing, all I could think about was wood grain and even coats and polish-polish-polish. It reminded me of coloring as a kid. It didn't even feel like a chore after a while. It just felt like everything.

The clack of boots on concrete pulled me out of my varnish-trance. Miyu and Mattie stood in the doorway, eyeing our progress.

"Wow," Mattie breathed.

Miyu just scowled.

"What?" Frankie asked.

"Yeah, what?" Mattie said. "I think it looks great."

"The craftsmanship isn't the problem. You did a lovely job, Cub Scout. I'm just not sure your muse understands the gravity of this."

Mattie huffed. "First, please don't ever refer to me as a muse. Second, it's not like this is my first rodeo."

That line made me picture Ginger the intrepid orphan as a rodeo clown, complete with blood-red overalls, but that's beside the point.

"This is fundamentally different from everything you've done before," Miyu explained. "You under-stand that, don't you?" A little edge had crept into her voice. With most people, it would've made me squirm, and maybe pretend to take a call on my cell so I'd have an out. But getting her knickers in a knot was Miyu's way of showing Mattie she cared. I'm not ashamed to admit it warmed my heart as much as the possibility of Mattie's demise scared the ever-living shit out of me.

"I understand that I could die, if that's what you're trying to say. But my last two acts also involved real danger. You said so yourself."

"Not like this. If you'd really gotten into trouble in the aquarium, you know Monty or I would've fished your ass out and pumped the water out of your lungs. I can't help you with this one. If you fuck it up, it's irreversible."

That word hung in the air like an ice-cold mist.

"Technically, I'm an adult," Mattie argued. "So if I fuck up, it's on me and no one else."

Miyu squinted at Mattie. "You still haven't told your parents, have you?"

Mattie buried her face in her hands. "Ugh. Miyu, if even ten percent of that diary is true, then your mom, who built her whole life around escapology, had second and even third thoughts about training you and putting her own kid in harm's way. And my parents aren't world-renowned escape artists. They're Mr. and Mrs. Suburban Rhode Island."

I expected Miyu to throw up her hands or bark at Mattie—*You know nothing, Girl Scout!* Instead, she crossed her arms and tapped one of her knee-high boots on the concrete floor. "I'll just say this. If my mom were alive when I was your age, there's nothing I'd have hidden from her. You never know how long you have."

Instead of responding, Mattie glanced over at me—*Please help.*

I replied with a shrug. If I had any sage-isms or

words of wisdom rattling around in my noggin, my mouth couldn't find them. I was still too shocked by Miyu's rare display of genuine feels.

A deep sigh escaped Miyu's permanent non-smile. "Cub Scout, I need your help with something."

She clacked out of the garage with Frankie trailing after her.

Mattie sank down onto a reclining beach chair, shut her eyes, and rested her clasped hands in her lap.

"Tell me about your mother," I quipped in a terrible Austrian accent.

"Oh, Will." She didn't laugh but I got a smile out of her.

"If you do decide to tell your parents and they disown you, you could always move in with me."

That made her laugh. "Marjorie would love that."

"She's your biggest fan."

Before I left that night, Frankie snuck a portable sewing machine he dug out of Miyu's attic into my parents' Lincoln. When I got home, I flipped through the sketches I'd done the night before, tracing the lines with my finger. Then I did a few test projects with the sewing machine. A quilt square I'd probably never turn into a quilt. A little felt messenger bag for Mr. Crankypants, Mattie's ceramic gnome. I just wanted to get a feel for it. My stitching on the quilt square came out all helter-skelter, but I'd settled down by the time I got to the strap on the mini-messenger bag. All that stuff from Home Ec 101 and the zillion arts and crafts workshops my mom sent me to started coming back, like the instinctual dynamics of riding a bike.

My phone buzzed as I was slicing through fabric with a pair of shears. I should've ignored it.

>Hey. Did you want to see me at all this week?

It was from the Bonnie to my Clyde, of course. Only there was no *dearest adorbs boyfriend* or *love you oodles* or *XOXO*. She knew something was up.

>Of course. Brunch on Sunday morning?

>Fine. Pick you up at 10:00.

I thought about texting back an *I love you* or posting a cute photo of the two us on LifeScape. But the end was coming, I could feel it. Adding more lies to the giant pile of lies wasn't going to accomplish anything at this point other than making me more of a liar.

So instead of trying to placate my main squeeze, I took a deep breath and picked up the shears. I fell into that same all-consuming space I had in the garage while varnishing Frankie's construction project. Only this time, it was even better. Because this was my project.

In her childhood on the road, The Hummingbird had learned to tune out the noise of highways and city streets and cabarets and amphitheaters. But the dingy group home the thirty-something brought her to was host to a chaotic chorus that set her teeth on edge. I could see it in her face, in the way she set her jaw as she sat on her bed with its little pancake mattress. There was the chitter-chatter chitter-chatter of all those white girls, punctured by the occasional shout or curse word. The incessant squeak of sneakers on lineoleum. And, underneath it all, the rattle and hum of the air circulator.

When it got unbearable, she'd pull out a padlock and pick it with a bobby pin.

– *Akiko Miyake, Providence, January 12, 2000*

Mattie vs. That Old Kernel of Fear

On the night before Halloween, known to most New Englanders as Cabbage Night, I slipped the following hand-written note under my brother's bedroom door.

Dear Mr. McKenna,

You are cordially invited to an evening of Halloween merriment. Please bring yourself and your two dearest friends (you know who they are) to 555 Atwells Avenue in the sparkling city of Providence in the great, sea-kissed state of Rhode Island on October thirty-first. Arrive no later than eleven o'clock, post-meridian, and do not speak of any spectacles you witness. If you can keep a secret and an open mind, you and your cohorts will, in all likelihood, thoroughly enjoy yourselves.

Sincerely,

Your sister, Mattie Ross McKenna

The second my fingertips pushed the note out of reach, I wanted to snatch it back. I jiggled the door-knob. *Locked.* I considered picking it but that kind of invasion of my brother's lair made my stomach turn.

I paced around my room for a few minutes, then pulled out my phone to text Stella, Will, and Frankie.

›I just did it. God help me.

Stella replied:

›Don't second-guess yourself, Ginge. After it's all over, you'll be happy you did it.

Will texted:

›You are going to blow their minds

Frankie chimed in:

›Now I'm even more nervous. Do I have to be onstage?

I set my phone on my antique nightstand, put on a Hank Mobley record, and crawled into bed. I must have lay there for a full hour, letting that kernel of fear deep in the pit of my stomach squeak and scream and huff.

When I'd had enough of my insomnia, I got up and flicked on the stained-glass lamp on my desk. Like a beacon of hope promising glorious distraction, the gold cover of Akiko's diary glowed under the yellow light.

I picked it up, slipped back under my quilt, and let those precious snippets of Akiko's life wash over me.

"It's going to be fine, Mattie-O," Will said as we drove to my house after school on Friday, also known as D-Day.

My pre-interview jitters last week paled in comparison to these jitters. My hands weren't just sweating, they were shaking. Everything was set—Miyu and I had checked and rechecked all the equipment for my act, the dress rehearsal at the salon had gone off without a hitch, and Will, Stella, Frankie, and I had all told our respective parents we'd be sleeping elsewhere for the night. But my meticulous pre-Halloween arrangements offered no comfort. I folded myself into my lap and buried my head in my arms.

Will parked the car and untangled me. "Deep breaths."

My dry throat pinched my airway. "I can't do this."

"Yes, you can. You can and you will." He got out of the car, and I heard the trunk pop open. "I have a gift for you," he said through the driver's side window. "Let's go upstairs so you can try it on." He had a cardboard box tucked under his arm and a garment bag slung over his shoulder.

I let out a sigh of relief once we made it up to my room without running into Kyle. Will put the box on the bed, hung the garment bag on the back of my bedroom door, and placed his warm hands on my shoulders.

"I didn't do measurements because I wanted to surprise you. So I had to guess, but it's totally alterable. We still have almost eight hours until show time."

"You have something for me to wear *tonight*? But I've been training in sweats and a t-shirt, this could—"

He fixed his brown eyes on me. "Relax. I've already cleared this with Miyu. She says you'll be fine."

He unzipped the garment bag and pulled out a *dress*. "Dress" wasn't even the right word for it. Like a tangible fragment ripped right out of a gauzy, jazz-soaked dream, this was the most Mattie-esque garment I'd ever laid eyes on. I couldn't get my mouth to form actual words. The best I could muster was a quiet "Oh . . ."

"Do you like it? I know you have an aversion to contemporary knockoffs, but I was hoping you could make an exception."

"Will . . . it's . . . I don't even . . . where did you get it?"

He stared at me like the answer was obvious. "I made it. Will you please try it on? I'm dying here."

I took the dress off its padded hanger and whipped off my shirt.

"Really?" he protested. "Right here?"

"What do you care? Just turn around."

"You can't change in the bathroom?"

"I don't want to risk running into Kyle."

Will walked himself into a corner and covered his face with his hands.

I slipped the dress over my head and let the seafoam green satin and black beading fall just below my knees. The dress's straight lines hugged my hips and the square neckline made up nicely for my lack of eye-popping boobage.

"Can I look yet?"

"Yes."

Will uncovered his eyes and gave me a onceover. "I should probably take the bust in like a quarter-inch, but I have to say . . . I'm kind of impressed with myself.

And I took a cue from Akiko's old costumes. It looks fancy, but it's chock full of elastic. You should be able to move any way you need to."

"What's in the box?"

"Remember when we were antique-ing in Fall River before school started and Frankie made you go with him into that back room to look at some knives or something but then didn't buy anything? I asked him to distract you so I could buy this."

He dipped his hands into the box and pulled out a hat. Not just any hat—a seafoam green cloche hat with a black band and little upturned brim. I imagined the hat's previous owner as a young girl spending her first year in the big city, working as a typist by day and frequenting galleries and jazz clubs by night. She wasn't a knockout gal guys would notice right away, but those she ensnared in a cozy, bar-side chat couldn't get enough of her sharp wit and her sly smile as she batted her lashes beneath the brim of that hat.

"Oh my god, Will. You really shouldn't have."

He laughed and gently placed the hat on my head. My dark hair poked out beneath the brim, glistening in the mirror.

"Look at that," Will said. "You really do have a little bit of red in your hair. The green brings it out."

I wanted to hug him, but it didn't seem like enough. Instead, we sat at the end of my bed, my toes skimming the Oriental rug and his hand clasped in mine. My mind fumbled for the right words, but they just wouldn't come. Instead of solidifying that moment with the perfect words, I mumbled, "You're like my fairy godmother," and then immediately wanted to slap myself.

Will laughed again. "Lord knows I'm nobody's fairy godmother. And you know it's not like that. We've helped each other." He squeezed my hand. "These past few months . . . I honestly can't remember ever feeling so . . . I don't know. Happy's not quite the right word. Maybe . . . so on the verge of feeling like a real person."

"You've always been a real person. People are still real, even when they hide things. And I know it sounds cheesy, but I'm proud of you for coming out to your parents."

His smile began to droop, though I wasn't sure why. "Thanks, Mattie-O. But we both have to admit I got lucky in that department. Not everyone has parents like mine. Some people get it from all sides, you know? Not just their friends, but their family, too. And their neighbors, their churches. I can't even imagine."

"It's still a start."

He shook his head. "It's a start, but I'm beginning to wonder if it ever really ends."

"What do you mean?"

"If I come out in high school, I still have to come out in college, and then at work. It's like I'm facing an endless line of people assuming I'm something I'm not. And it's great that more and more people are cool with it in this day and age, but I'll always have to deal with the possibility that someone won't be. And what if that uncool person ends up being my college roommate, or my boss, or my father-in-law?"

Will's words struck a nerve, knocking something

loose in my brain that I'd managed to bury until that moment. That first night, right before Will and I became partners in mutually assured destruction, he'd told me my escape act made him feel like a cream puff. But now I felt like the cream puff. I finally saw the fundamental difference between our secrets—no matter how strange people thought my hobby was, it would never threaten to knock me down the ladder of privilege.

My excuses for living a double life appeared to be dwindling by the minute.

I still couldn't think of anything meaningful to say, so I just leaned my head on his shoulder. We sat like that for a long time.

Seven jittery hours later, I stood behind the bar at Salone Postale wearing the seafoam green dress and matching cloche hat. I ducked into the shadows when Stella came through the cough-syrup-colored door. Kyle, Connor, and Austin trailed behind her. I shuddered as they stepped over the threshold. The boundary I'd spent the summer building now officially had a gaping hole. My brother and his two best friends didn't know it yet, but they'd just crossed over from their world into mine.

I watched from behind the bar as Stella showed them to their reserved table. Connor already had that *look* on his face. That look that made me want to punch him because he seemed poised to scoff at anything and everything. I thought he might actually laugh out loud while the performer onstage finished up his lengthy monologue about the rules of interdimensional time travel.

Naveen tapped me on the shoulder, dressed in his Mollusk Brigade uniform. "Ready?" he mouthed.

I nodded and waved at the rest of the Mollusk Brigade members standing behind him. They smiled at me, their instruments in hand. The monologist finished up his sci-fi warbling and the plum-colored curtains closed as he exited stage left. My stomach did a backflip as soon as Monty took the stage.

"The witching hour is nearly upon us, gremlins and ghouls. In less than an hour, All Hallows' Eve will come to a close. But before we send you all into the night, we have one more act—a capstone to our evening of macabre revelry."

"Bring on the Houdini chick!" one of the hecklers bellowed.

"In due time, my good fellow," Monty said with a wink. "Tonight, sinners and saints, she's got something the likes of which this hallowed stage has never seen. She's got special guests. And it might get messy."

The hecklers whooped, whipping an already amped-up crowd into a frenzy.

"Without further ado, the death-defying orphan you all know and love. The indelible . . . the incredible . . . the incomparable Ginger!"

Monty ducked offstage as the lights dimmed and Mollusk Brigade launched into a funeral dirge. They marched in an ominous line toward the stage, their horns droning and drums pounding. I followed behind them, head bowed. I spotted Will's mom at a nearby table. She waved and I gave her a brief smile.

As we passed the table I'd reserved for my brother, I could hear Connor over the din of the funeral dirge. "Holy fuck, Kyle. That's your sister. Jesus Christ. She's finally going to kill herself, and she's going to do it in front of us."

Connor's comment should have pissed me off, but all I could do was laugh. Kyle and I made eye contact, and I flashed him the most confident smile I could muster. He didn't look reassured.

I climbed the stairs onto the stage where Will, wearing an old-fashioned straw boater hat and a seafoam green vest and bowtie, handed me a mic. Frankie stood next to him, dressed the same and shaking like a leaf.

"It'll be fine, kid," I whispered before putting the mic to my lips. "Hello," I said to the crowd.

The hecklers whooped again. "Who's the noob?" one of them shouted.

"I know most of you are familiar with my assistant, Will With Two Ls. The young man standing next to him shall be known as Francisco of the Sacred Sword. He, ladies and gentlemen, is my weapons expert."

"Fran-cis-co!" The hecklers chanted. Frankie smirked at me, and I could almost see his rattled nerves starting to settle.

"Simmer down, groundlings. It's story time," I said. "In the year nineteen hundred and twenty-six, when this establishment was still a post office, my great-great-grandmother frequented many of the bars in this neck of Providence. But on October thirty-first of that year—the very same day that Harry Houdini met his maker—my great-great-grandmother's jazz-soaked life was almost snuffed out when she came face to face with a vicious serial killer known as . . ." One of the girls from Mollusk Brigade filled the silence with a drum roll. " . . . Olneyville Ollie."

A few salon-goers gasped and one of the hecklers bellowed, "Ollie, ollie, oxen-free!"

"As a stevedore down at the docks, Ollie had seen his fair share of shady importing and exporting. But property crime wasn't enough for Ollie. He had a thirst for blood, and a soft spot for brunettes. And Ollie didn't shoot his victims or carve them up with a knife. He hunted them like game through the urban jungle . . . with a crossbow."

The hecklers whooped and the fiery-haired bartender whistled from her post at the back of the room.

"When Ollie spotted my great-great-grandmother," I continued, "flicking her cigarette outside a speakeasy just a few blocks from here, he loaded his bow and gave chase. My great-great-grandmother saw his shadowy figure barreling toward her and took off, weaving through darkened streets and courtyards."

I glanced over at my brother's table. Kyle and Austin blinked up at me. The *look* had been completely erased from Connor's not-so-smug face. I could tell he had no idea what to make of Ginger the intrepid orphan or this zany story about her great-great-grandmother. But if Will could come out to his parents, surely I could handle revealing my alter-ego to my brother and two twenty-somethings I wasn't even related to.

"When Ollie began gaining on her, his mouth watering and bearded face sweating, she thought she'd breathed her last breath. Even from ten smoots away, she could smell the stench of the docks on him, and it sent a shiver down her spine. Ollie licked his chops as he loaded his bow and let an arrow fly. My great-great-grandmother ducked into an alley just in time to hear it whiz by her left ear. She was certain his next arrow would find its way straight through her skull, but in the corner of her eye, she saw a glimmer of hope—a jack-o-lantern left out on a back stoop. She snatched it up off the stoop and flattened herself against the side of a brick tenement.

"Ollie, of course, thought he'd backed her into a corner. He loaded another arrow into his bow and lurched toward the alley, whistling a haunting sea shanty. My great-great-grandmother's heart hiccupped each time one of his big, black boots hit the concrete. Just as Ollie reached the alley and his sea shanty filled her ears with dread, she darted out and smashed that jack-o-lantern right into his hairy face. He reeled back, covered in pumpkin, and she ran. Her heels pounded the sidewalk until she finally caught a cab at the corner of Atwells and Knight.

"Tonight, in honor of my great-great-grandmother, I will escape from a net of chains, or meet a gruesome death by the point of an arrow."

The hecklers practically lost their drunken minds as the curtain opened to reveal a tableau of jack-o-lanterns and an apparatus that Frankie had spent a week helping Miyu and me build. One of them knocked over a full beer, soaking their table, though none of them seemed to notice.

I gestured to a taut, loaded crossbow poised to rocket an arrow straight at the heart of a Mattie-sized slab of pine. The arrow's steely point practically glowed under the stage lights.

"Francisco of the Sacred Sword, will you please tell the crowd what we have here."

I handed the mic to Frankie, and he cleared his throat. "Um . . . yes . . . this is an antique recurve, pull-lever crossbow handmade in Portugal in the early twentieth century. I've loaded it with a modern 400-grain bolt—that's a fancy term for, um, a big deer-hunting arrow. The trigger has been rigged with a thick twine brushed with a small amount of liquid butane. You know, lighter fluid. Once your restraints have been secured, I'll release the safety and ignite the twine. You'll have roughly two to two and a half minutes to free yourself or . . ."

I stole the mic back. "Be honest with me, Francisco. If I don't manage to escape, will this crossbow kill me?"

"The bow will launch the bolt at approximately three-hundred-fifty feet per second. At this distance, it would go straight through your chest, likely piercing your heart. Death, at that point, would be inevitable."

"There you have it, ladies and gents. I know you're chomping at the bit, so I won't waste any more of your time with chit chat. Will With Two Ls, if you would be so kind."

Will took the mic from my hand and Mollusk Brigade resumed their funeral dirge as he began chaining me to the slab, which Miyu had sardonically dubbed "the torture board." Through the sheer fabric of the dress, I could feel the iciness of the steel criss-crossing my torso. When Will clicked the last of the four padlocks into place, I swallowed a lump in my throat and watched Connor cover his eyes with his hands.

"So help me, Mattie-O," Will whispered. "You are not allowed to die on me tonight."

The arrow's pencil-sharp point stared me down. "Not planning on it," I mumbled. My breath had gone ragged. Had I lost my mind? Is this really what it took to pull my brother out of the doldrums? Maybe I should've just bought him a few cheesy posters like the ones in Ms. Simmons's office.

Too late, Ginger giggled in my mind. Will nodded and Frankie pulled out a Zippo. His fingers shook as he set the twine ablaze. The hecklers looked possessed, the fire glinting in their wide eyes. Frankie gave me and the band a thumbs up, and Mollusk Brigade abruptly ceased their funeral dirge and launched into a skronky rendition of "Muskrat Ramble."

I snaked my arm upward, far enough to pluck a bobby pin from beneath my hat, and went after the first padlock. My vision swam and, for a moment, I thought I might pass out. I'd expected my performance nerves to give me a hard time but hadn't prepared for the mind-numbing terror that flooded through me as I stared at the antique crossbow, illuminated in horrific detail by the stage lights, in front of an audience that included my brother and his friends.

Think of all the blood, Ginger whispered.

Like an idiot, I let my gaze fall on Connor. The story of my double-great-grandmother had wiped the smug grin off his face, but seeing me tied up onstage had apparently replaced that look with a pale, wide-eyed expression of horror. For a split second, that old kernel of fear squawked in the back of my mind. *If you wanted him to take you seriously, maybe you should have picked something less extreme.*

I closed my eyes, drew a deep breath and commanded my brain to stop dredging up images of gaping chest wounds, splintered ribs, and jaded paramedics shaking their heads. *Damn kids think they're invincible,* they'd say. I pictured my ghost screaming at them. *Don't you get it? I know I'm not invincible. I've built my whole life around my keen awareness that I'm the polar opposite of invincible in every possible way. That's the whole freaking point of these onstage antics.*

As I continued to hack away at the padlock, I unwittingly made eye contact with Kyle. If watching his kid sister flirt with the very real possibility of death didn't make him realize life was worth living, I didn't know what would.

My muscle memory finally woke up from its terror-induced stupor and an almost undetectable grin crossed my face when I felt the first lock pop open, loosening the chain binding my calves to the slab. I had to stretch sideways to pick the second lock. My obliques whimpered under the strain and the lock became a stubborn hunk of metal. I forced myself to focus, allowing the world to drop away. All I could hear was the sound of my own breath and my blood beating in my ears. The second lock sprang open, but I didn't give myself even a nanosecond to celebrate. Two locks still stood between me and my life.

Lock number three took me less than ten seconds to take down, giving my hips a much needed quarter-inch of freedom. But my fingers had a sheen of sweat by the time I tackled lock number four. The bobby pin nearly slipped from my hand, and my heart almost stopped when I pictured it clattering to the floor. Olneyville Ollie's sea shanty filled my mind's ear, a reminder that death itself was gaining on me. As I stabbed desperately at lock number four, I tried not to think about how few seconds stood between me and an arrow through the heart.

When the lock finally clicked open, the chains slid downward, clanging on the floor. The sound made me painfully aware that "Muskrat Ramble" had screeched to a halt and the crowd had gone completely silent. Fearing I might be too late, I shimmed to the left just in time to hear the crossbow click into action.

The crowd let out a collective gasp of horror when the arrow slammed into the slab of pine. The sheer force of it knocked the wind right out of my lungs. With my feet still tangled in the pile of chains on the floor, I realized I couldn't move. I looked down, praying that I wouldn't see a mass of red blossoming against the seafoam green of my dress. The arrow had pinned the fabric hugging my torso to the so-called torture board, but missed my skin by a fraction of an inch.

I yanked the arrow from the wood and thrust it into the air, a tacit sign of victory.

After a few seconds of stunned silence, the crowd erupted and the band resumed their rendition of "Muskrat Ramble" at a volume that somehow seemed louder than their usual deafening cacophony.

I tried to take a bow, but the hecklers stormed the stage. The one with the glasses attacked me with a bear hug while the others whooped and started smashing the jack-o-lanterns. Pumpkin shards rained down all over Mollusk Brigade, but they played on, filling the room with brassy, victorious noise.

Monty bounded onto the stage with a mic in his hand. "Happy Halloween, poets and profits. And good-night!"

With the blood drained from his face, Will took my hand. "It's going to be like that every time, isn't it? I'm going to have white hair by the time I'm twenty."

"You'll look very distinguished with white hair," I replied.

Will, Frankie, and I waved to the crowd. I shot a quick glance toward my brother before we scurried offstage. He had his hands over his mouth and looked like he'd sweated enough saline to fill a kiddie pool. Connor looked like he'd seen a ghost, or like he was about to spew all over their reserved table. Of the three, only Austin looked jazzed. He whistled and shouted, "I know her!" with his fists in the air.

Miyu met us backstage, hands shoved in the pockets of her hooded sweatshirt. "That'll do, Girl Scout. That'll do."

I laughed and threw my arms around her. "I can't remember if I ever said thank you. In case I didn't, thank you."

"In case I forgot to tell you you're a sap, you're a sap. That said, I don't wholeheartedly regret inviting you to tea."

Monty and Miyu surprised me with a backstage after-party, complete with a jazz trio and copious amounts of cheap champagne in plastic stemware.

"I promise I'll pay for your dry cleaning," I told Naveen between sips of bubbly.

"It's not your fault those loonies at the front table lost their minds over your act," he said. "Who can blame them? Besides, we're just psyched we got to be part of the highlight of the evening."

Miyu sidled up to me with a glass of champagne. "I'm just going to say one thing, Girl Scout. She would've been impressed."

"You really think so?"

"Yes."

"I think she'd be impressed with both of us. Look at you, out at a party."

"Why do you have to turn into an after-school special every time I say something nice to you?"

I just smiled.

Stella made her way toward me and blushed when she spotted Naveen.

"Do you think she remembers trying to make out with me?" Naveen asked.

"Obviously," I said.

"Right. I'm gonna go . . . uh . . . not be here." He took off before Stella's arrival would make things awkward for the both of them.

"He hasn't forgotten I tried to make out with him, has he?" Stella whispered.

"Obviously."

"Oh. Please kill me."

I spotted Will through the crowd, flanked by Austin and Kyle. Kyle's eyes were practically glistening. I couldn't remember the last time I'd seen him like that.

He almost knocked my champagne out of my hand when he threw his arms around me.

"I thought for sure it was a guy," he whispered. "But, god, this is so much better."

"Thank you," I squeaked.

"You cut it close on purpose, right?"

"Um . . ."

"Never mind. Don't answer that." He put his hand on my shoulder. "Mom and Dad don't know yet, do they?"

I sighed. "Nope. Are you going to tell them?"

"Did you tell them about all the parties I threw when they were away? Or about the time Connor and I went to New York?"

"No."

"Well, there you go. But also, please don't die."

"'Kay."

"Was that story about our great-great-grandmother really true?"

I shrugged. "Could be."

"You're something else, Mattie."

"Thanks. I gotta pee. I'll be right back."

I weaved toward the restroom, stopping to tip the band along the way. The saxophone player winked at me, and I tipped my cloche hat. As I strolled down the dimly-lit hallway, I spotted our tour guide from Bristol. I had enough time to smile and wave before someone snagged my arm and pulled me toward the coatroom.

It was Connor.

"Hey," he said.

"Yeah. Hey."

He mumbled something, and then stopped and shook his head.

"Are you okay?"

He pursed his lips and stared at me in a way that made him look almost helpless. *Almost.* "Mattie, I . . . fuck, I don't even know what to say. I have a lot of things I want to say, and I just don't know how at the moment."

"Wow. Okay."

"I guess I always kinda knew you had something like that in you, but I'm still shocked. And I feel like an asshole for being shocked."

I wanted to look away, run back to the land of safe conversations with Stella and Miyu and Frankie, but Ginger demanded I stay the course. *I feel a real moment coming on*, she squeaked. *Milk it for all it's worth.*

"Your brother's my best friend in the whole world," Connor said. "But I don't think I can do this anymore. If I don't put some distance between myself and this place . . ." He let out a deep sigh. "I don't know if I'm even capable of something like what you just pulled off. But if I don't get the hell away from here, I'll probably never find out."

I consider myself an efficient escapologist, but not a graceful one. Akiko had a kind of easy, happy-go-lucky stage presence that I'll never be able to emulate. But Connor's perfectly imperfect words must have infused me with a fleeting note of grace. In one swift movement, I encircled his neck with my arms like a wreath and nestled the side of my face against his shoulder. He held me so close I could smell the fresh, soapy scent of his detergent and feel his heart beating through the veins in his neck. I don't know how long we stood there before he spoke again.

"I should've been nicer to you. And your first time should have been with—"

"Connor . . . don't," I pleaded.

He nodded as I let him go. "Enjoy your party," he said with a smile. "You deserve it."

After Will told his parents he was gay, they stopped objecting to co-ed sleepovers at his house. Stella and Frankie headed there shortly after the party wrapped up. Will told them we'd be right behind them, but we'd both had a tad too much bubbly. We sat in his car, parked on Knight Street, waiting for one of us to sober up enough to drive.

"We'll just tell them we hit traffic," Will said.

"At 2:00 a.m.?" I put my feet up on the dashboard and reclined the passenger seat.

He shrugged, his eyelids drooping, and we both giggled. His phone buzzed and a sloppy smile spread across his face as he pulled it out of his pocket.

"It was a good night," he said.

"Yeah, it really was."

He nodded as my phone began ringing.

"Probably Stella wondering where we are," I mumbled. But when I pulled my phone out of my bag, I didn't recognize the number. "Huh, weird. Should I answer?"

"I'll answer," he said as he plucked the phone from my hand. "This is the incomparable Ginger's personal assistant. What's shakin'?"

I laughed until the voice on the other end of the line frosted my veins.

Even with the phone pressed against Will's ear, I could hear her clear as a bell. "Will?" Meadow asked. "Will, is that you?"

His jaw dropped open.

"Hello?" Meadow said after a long, dread-filled pause.

I snatched the phone from him. "Hey."

"Mattie?"

"Yeah."

"So, your mom called Stella's house and found out you weren't there." *Oh fuck.* "I don't know why, but she called my house looking for you." *Oh fuck times two.* My go-to excuse for being out late had finally come back to bite me in the ass.

"I just called to give you a heads up," she said. "But I . . ." Her voice quivered as she trailed off. "I can't

ignore what I just heard. Betsy's my best friend. If
you found out Stella's boyfriend was hooking up with
someone else behind her back, you'd tell her, right?"

Double dammit. "Meadow, it's not like that."

"Mattie, I get it. He's a great guy. And things
have been weird between Betsy and him for a while.
Honestly, I'm glad it's you and not some awful bitch.
She'll take it better."

Will buried his face in the steering wheel.

"Uh . . . thanks?"

"Don't thank me. There's still gonna be fallout. See
you at school."

She hung up and I noticed the dozen or so calls I'd
missed from my parents, along with a string of increasingly desperate texts from my mom.

> ›Mattie, call me when you get a minute.
> ›Still haven't heard from you. Things
> okay?
> ›Got your phone on silent? Don't make me
> resort to calling Stella's landline.

I dropped the phone into my bag even though I
wanted to chuck it out the window and watch it smash
on the concrete.

"Will, you can tell Betsy whatever you want. If you
want to tell her we've been sneaking around, that's fine."

He shook his head. "Oh my god. I just . . . I can't
even think about it right now. Can we please just
pretend for the next few minutes that that didn't
happen?"

I reached for his hand and gave it a squeeze. I didn't
know how else to comfort him.

He rubbed his eyelids and started the car. "The good news is I now feel stone sober."

"Me too."

"Oh my heck," The Hummingbird's foster father said as he lugged her suitcase up the stairs to her new bedroom. "What do you have in here? Rocks?"

"Yes. I'm a collector."

I shimmered at the top of the stairs, giggling at her joke. But there was no sign of joy from The Hummingbird, not even the trademark smirk she'd inherited from her father.

"Is that right?" Mr. Butler said. "My father collected postage stamps. Not as heavy as rocks."

He and I looked to The Hummingbird for a reaction. Nothing.

I frowned by the window, but Mr. Butler looked unfazed as he continued up the stairs, dragging the suitcase behind him. He'd probably seen this sullen routine before from every other broken teenager he'd graciously taken into his home.

"He might seem dull compared to the bohemians you've grown up with, but people will always surprise you," I told The Hummingbird. "And he's perfectly nice. Nice is what you need right now."

She ignored me.

— *Akiko Miyake, Cranston, February 15, 2000*

Will With Two Ls Steals a Kiss

For the record, *oh fuck times two* doesn't even begin to cover it. But you can't blame Mattie. At that particular moment, she had no idea how high I'd been and thus, how far this turn of events caused me to fall. And I don't mean high on dope though I had a decent champagne buzz thrumming through my noggin. No, friends, I was high on a few fragrant whiffs of the ephemeral stuff that makes life worth living.

First, I watched Mattie wrap the crowd at Salone Postale around her unpolished little finger and then smirk right in death's cowed face. I didn't even care that the dress I'd spent weeks on now had an arrow-sized hole in it. In fact, the hole made it even snazzier, like a badge of courage or a Girl Scout patch awarded for engaging in death-defying art spectacles. As Mattie would say, the dress now had *history*.

Then, while sipping bubbly at the after-party, I met a boy.

Before you roll your eyes, you should know he was not the kind of boy I'd fantasize about for an hour or two and then forget. He wasn't a classic beefcake, or a prime cut, or a tall slice of red velvet slathered with cream cheese frosting, or any other creepy slang-isms that turn potential lovers into food. He was one of those quiet boys who's invisible to most folks. But not to me, maybe because I'm a fellow quiet boy at heart. I first noticed him at Mattie's house, leaning against the kitchen counter while Mattie's bro and his loudmouth friend yap-yap-yapped about I-don't-even-care. I could tell from the way his hazel eyes wandered around the kitchen that he was only half-listening to them. The other half of him was off in daydream land. I know because I'd worn that same look when I escaped to my imaginary speakeasies with my imaginary friends.

And at the after-party, he was the one who noticed me. The funny thing is, even as a fellow quiet boy at heart, I would've expected him to be all awkward shuffles and gawky limbs and self-conscious throat clearing to fill the silence between sentences. But he was none of that. When he sauntered up to me with bright eyes and rosy cheeks and said *Hey, you were great. Mattie is so cool. Isn't this place amazing?* I thought maybe he'd ducked into the bathroom to snort some blow. Then I realized, like me, he was just high as fuck on Mattie's act.

"Uh, yeah. Thanks?" I replied.

Turns out I was the awkward one. But I didn't regress into a fumbling, floundering train wreck for long because Austin is like a cup of chamomile tea. Chatting with him is like curling up with a good book on a rainy

Sunday afternoon. After a few stops, starts, and sputters, the words flowed from me. I took a moment to step outside myself and was flat-out shocked to find I didn't sound bored or antsy or like total palooka.

"How long has Mattie been doing this?" he asked. His eyes flooded my veins with warm fuzzies. I wanted to stare at them all day.

"The escape artist thing? About half a year, I think."

"Wow."

"Yeah. The first time I saw her, she escaped from an aquarium full of koi."

"An aquarium? They actually put an aquarium on the stage?"

"Yeah, it's on wheels. They keep it in one of the storage rooms backstage. Do you want to see it?"

He said yes before I even had time to realize I was about to be alone with a guy I kinda had a thing for.

Half a minute later, we found ourselves standing an inch shy of hip-to-hip, gazing at the aquarium. The koi stared back with glassy fish-eyes, their shadows dancing along the dusty floorboards. The buzz of the filter hummed pleasantly in the background.

When he reached up to touch the tank, one of his hands brushed mine in a way that didn't seen entirely unintentional. He ran a finger silently along the glass. One of the fish swam toward it and swished its nose against the side of the tank, almost like a playful dog who wanted to sniff us through the water. He chuckled softly and turned to smile at me. It could've been the bubbly percolating in my noggin, but I swear he winked.

I know this seems like nothing, but take a moment

to really marinate on it. When most people stand in front of an aquarium and want to get the attention of its colorful inhabitants, they don't run their fingers gently along the glass—they tap on it. They tap on it like obnoxious, gigantic toddlers with no regard for the fact that it clearly scares the goddamn daylights out of the fish. Imagine if God really were a big, bearded white dude and He showed up outside your house one day and started rattling your windows and shaking the foundation like, "Hey, anyone in there? Do something interesting. Entertain me!" Admit it. You'd think He was an asshole. And yet, I myself am guilty of occasionally tapping on aquarium glass and making silly faces at captive fish.

But not Austin. Austin's empathetic reflexes are posi-lute-ly catlike. He knew better than to act like a giant toddler-god. Instead, he used the simplest of gestures, like the physical equivalent of a whisper, to say, "Hi, fish friend. Just letting you know I'm here."

That simple gesture spoke volumes to me and made me want him more than I'd ever wanted anyone in all of my eighteen years. Even more than I wanted Gene Kelly after watching *Singin' In the Rain* in seventh grade, which brought on an obsession that rivaled Mattie's fangirl crush on Wil With One L.

I stared at Austin while he stared at the koi. The seconds passing felt palpable to me, like the ribs of a rope slipping through my hands. I told myself I hardly knew him. I told myself there would be plenty of opportunities, later, when I was ready.

But Will With Two Ls wasn't having any of it.

Maybe it was the champagne, or Mattie's act, or some combo of the two, but before I knew it my fingertips were grazing Austin's jaw line. He smiled again and leaned toward me, bracing one arm against the glass of the aquarium. I pulled him slowly into a kiss.

It wasn't a long kiss, and I certainly didn't shove my tongue down his throat. But it was assertive enough to send a clear and direct message.

I shook my head. "I'm sorry. That was really presumptuous of me."

"A little. But it's cool."

Then we kissed again. For almost a full minute. And there might have been a little tongue involved.

So there was that. And now, let's contrast that glorious moment with sitting in the driver's seat of my parents' Lincoln, knowing I was royally screwed in the Betsy department and everything was about to come crashing down. At first, it didn't even feel real. It felt like a cruel joke. And then my mind slipped into that same place it had the night I'd come out to Mattie. It flailed, grasping at every possible straw that might, someway somehow, turn back time. But deep in my solar plexus, I knew that wasn't possible.

Mattie squeezed my hand and, though I appreciated the gesture, nothing—not even Austin's warm hazel eyes and soft voice—would have soothed me.

I watched, shimmering by the window, as The Hummingbird marked another day off on her calendar with a big black slash in permanent marker.

"Why do you do that?" her foster sister asked. "You don't even know how good you have it here, do you? I've caught some really bad ones. Like, really bad. The Butlers are freaking saints. Don't be an ungrateful bitch."

The Hummingbird didn't respond. If she did, she'd probably end up in a fistfight she was bound to lose. Her foster sister had a good head on her shoulders, but the "bad ones" she spoke of had obviously toughened her like a callous. She kept her nails long and sharp and painted a steely blue. And she didn't lay her head down without a Swiss Army knife tucked safely under her pillow.

The Hummingbird climbed into bed and kept her mouth shut. She thought that once she turned eighteen, none of this would matter. She thought that once she earned the so-called freedoms of adulthood, this stranger's house and the strange girl she shared a room with would fade from memory like a fog evaporating in the heat of the morning sun.

I wasn't so sure. Even the slipperiest of escapologists can't escape the past once it's buried under her skin.

– Akiko Miyake, Cranston, September 30, 2000

Mattie on the Precipice

I decided facing the music would be better sooner rather than later and asked Will to drop me off at my house.

"When are you going to tell Betsy?" I asked as I unbuckled my seatbelt.

"Tonight," he said with a nod. "I'm still hoping I can get to her before Meadow does."

"Let me know how it goes."

"I will. Call you tomorrow, okay?"

"Okay."

The kitchen lights were blazing down when I walked in. My mom sat at the head of the kitchen table, flanked by my dad and my brother. I couldn't get a read on her through all that icy serenity, but the dark circles under her eyes scared me. My dad gave me a brief smile, but didn't say anything.

"Your Great Aunt Millie died," she said. "Funeral's on Wednesday. That's why we were trying to get ahold of you. At first, anyway. Then we were just terrified you were lying dead in a ditch somewhere."

"Oh my god, mom. I'm sorry."

She shook her head. "Have a seat."

I pulled out a chair, the legs squeaking against the linoleum like nails on a chalkboard.

"I don't want to be one of those willfully ignorant parents," my mom continued. "I won't pretend I have children who always do what they're told and never put themselves at risk. And if my older brother invited me to go out drinking in Providence with him and his friends when I was a teenager, I probably would have said yes."

I shot Kyle a glance. *I'm forever in your debt, big brother of the year.*

"But there's a happy medium, Mattie. You need to be honest with us. You need to be careful, and you need to tell us where you are."

"I know. I'm really sorry."

"I hope that's a sincere apology and not an empty attempt to placate us," she said.

My dad cracked a grin, but tried to hide it by turning to cough into his fist.

"It's a sincere apology," I said. "But, to be fair, if I'd told you what I was up to, you wouldn't have let me go."

"Not the point," she said sharply. "Now, if you have a fake ID, I want you to hand it over. Those things can get you into a lot of trouble."

"I don't have one, and that's the honest truth. They're pretty lax up in Federal Hill."

She scowled at me. "Second, I don't see any point in

grounding you now that you're eighteen years old. But you and your brother will make dinner for the family all this week to make up for scaring me and your father half to death."

"Fine," I sighed. "I can live with that."

"I'll be upstairs in a minute," my mom told my dad with a sigh. "I need to decompress in my office for a bit."

My dad remained at the table, thumbing his scruff as he eyed me and Kyle.

"I talked her out of calling the police," he said. "So, you're welcome."

"Thanks, Dad," we mumbled.

"For that, Mattie, you owe me a *Star Trek* marathon. I'm glad you've made some new friends, but you can't forget about your dear old dad."

I smiled at him. "Yeah, deal. Sorry I haven't been around a lot."

"No apologies needed, Mattie Ross. Just . . . use your head. Okay?"

I nodded and he headed off to bed.

At that point, my parental-emergency adrenaline was waning, but Kyle wanted nachos. He carefully layered a batch, and we sat in comfortable silence as it heated up in the toaster oven.

"That's a masterpiece," I said when he set a plate of cheesy goodness in front of me. "Also, thanks. And not just for the nachos."

"A small price to pay for a good night. I haven't seen Austin and Connor that happy in a while." He paused to shove another nacho in his mouth. "Are you ever going to tell them the truth?" he whispered.

"You mean Mom and Dad? Don't you think they'd, like, disown me?"

He laughed. "Uh, yeah. Probably. But they'd also probably dig your act. Especially mom."

I thought of all the times my mom had told me what it was like to play in a band. I pictured her onstage in a smoky bar, a guitar resting on her hip as her room-mate screamed her guts out into a shitty mic.

Clearly, that girl sporting a guitar—and her boyfriend who was addicted to Westerns and paying his way through trade school by delivering pizzas—would appreciate Salone Postale and my leap from consumption to creation. But they weren't just that punker girl and her goofy-smart boyfriend anymore. They were also my parents.

"They'd dig it if it wasn't me."

He nodded and swallowed a mouthful of nacho. "How did you do it?"

"I had a lot of help."

"Yeah, but how did you even know where to start?"

For the first time in probably ever, my brother was asking *me* for advice.

"You just start with something you love or, at least, really really like. Do you still like basketball?"

He shrugged.

"Does basketball make you want to spring out of bed in the morning?"

"No."

"Then it's not the right thing. When was the last time you were so absurdly happy you stopped thinking about everything except the thing you were doing?"

"Honestly, I don't even know. Most of the time, all I want to do is sit in my room and play video games."

"Hm. Maybe that's it then."

He squinted at me. "You think I should be a professional gamer?"

"Well, no. But someone has to make the games, Kyle."

He shook his head. "I don't know anything about programming."

"Not yet."

I hugged my brother, took one more nacho for the road and started to head upstairs. Something pulled me back down, and I found myself loitering in the doorway of the mom-cave.

"Can I help you, kiddo?" my mom asked from her armchair, her face half-obscured by an old issue of *Punk Planet*.

"Can I look through your old scrap books? I was just thinking about you and your days of Doc Martens and purple hair. I could use a good laugh."

She snorted. "Knock yourself out."

I scanned my mom's bookshelf and let my fingers brush the spines of her many photo albums. My finger stopped on a black leather spine labeled with Wite-Out pen—*Summer Tour - 1992*. I curled up on the sagging futon, hoping to find some comfort in those hilarious snippets of my parents' youth. As an admittedly lonely tween, I'd spent many a Sunday morning on that futon, giggling my little ass off as I pored over the photos, ticket stubs, guitar picks, and occasional love notes scribbled on the back of a set list or a grease-dotted receipt for fast food. My mom and her band had toured a few Midwestern cities and small towns after they graduated from Oberlin, playing sets in sweaty dive bars and decaying basement clubs. My dad had been their roadie that summer, though my mom always said he made a better electrician than an audio tech.

I paused to examine a candid Polaroid taken outside a frozen custard stand in St. Louis. My mom's purple hair stood out like a burst of Technicolor in the Polaroid's otherwise muted tones as she shoved a spoonful of custard into my dad's mouth. The band's lead singer laughed at the two of them, her toothy smile totally incongruous with the thick black liner rimming her eyes. The drummer, no doubt keenly aware of the importance of documenting the band's fleeting heyday, had taken the photo and left a small smudge on the upper right-hand corner of the lens, blurring the clouds in the background.

My mom and her bandmates gave themselves laughable pseudonyms like Cathy Crush and Ashley Asphalt. I'd always thought it was silly. As a smart-mouthed twelve-year-old, I remember asking if they'd lied about their real names because none of them really knew how to play their instruments. My mom just laughed it off, probably presuming that her preteen kid who liked Herbie Hancock more than Hüsker Dü couldn't possibly understand why she'd dyed her hair and picked up a guitar in the first place.

Turns out she was right. But almost half a year into my double life as a part-time escapologist, I finally got it. All that screechy noise and those larger-than-life stage names had given my mom and her friends license to transform themselves each night into the people they really wanted to be. Without Ginger the intrepid orphan standing like a smirking shadow between me and the crowd at Salone Postale, I wouldn't have been able to set foot on that stage for my first performance.

I glanced up from the photo at my mom. Though she didn't call herself Ashley Asphalt anymore, artifacts from her punk rock past filled her mom-cave. When she smiled at my dad, her face still held a glimmer of the wild-eyed grin she wore when the Polaroid was taken. And she didn't spend her nights filling a dive bar with feedback, but that kind of fuck-off brashness still popped up now and again, like when she chided my grandmother for her casual, old-person racism or rolled her eyes when people called her ma'am.

And yet, she wasn't some one-dimensional grownup version of a purple-haired stage persona. She was *my mom*.

My eyes fell back to the faded Polaroid, and I thought of all the gauzy, soft-focus photos of Akiko I'd stumbled on during my many feverish escapology research sessions. She never had a stage name, but with her neon wigs and her mysterious smile and her cryptic interviews, she'd obviously spent decades building a stage persona. The mythology surrounding her ran so deep it took on a life of its own, and fans like me were still clinging to it, almost sixteen years after her death.

But the Akiko in the journal wasn't just a plucky schoolgirl who talked her way into a magic show. She was also a scared-shitless kid who covered up her fear with snark and pulled out her own hair before every performance. And she wasn't just a demure but determined young lady who came to the U.S. on a visitor's visa and stayed to build an underground empire. She was also a hot-headed cynic with a soft-spot for bad boy clichés, and, let's face it, an occasionally neglectful parent who still really loved her accidentally-conceived daughter.

I pictured Miyu as a little sprite, swishing a foam samurai sword to get her mom's attention. How could a kid that young deal with having to share her mom with the world? Especially when the world only saw the neon-wigged Akiko who winked at the camera, not the patchy-haired Akiko who tucked Miyu in at night.

Now I felt like an ass for all the superfan questions I'd sprung on her. How was she even supposed to answer? The miary must have been her last-ditch attempt to stitch together the disparate pieces of life her mom left behind. To reverse engineer her mother's untouchable stage persona and turn her back into a flesh and blood human being.

"You look like you're thinking pretty hard over there," my mom said. "You're doing that same brow-furrowing thing your dad does when he watches Westerns."

"Huh? Oh, I guess. I might've just come up with a thesis for my history project."

"Hm."

She turned the page of her magazine and studied me over the rims of her glasses. I don't know how, but I felt it coming, like the way you can feel a sneeze brewing in your nose. "Mattie, is there something you want to tell me?"

There I was, standing right on the precipice. Not that arbitrary line I'd crossed when I turned eighteen, but a palpable line. On one side, I could remain a kid in my parents' eyes. On the other, I'd become something else. Some sort of quasi grown-up who risked her life to entertain and inspire a theater full of mostly-strangers.

Yes, mom. There are lots of things. But I can't. Not yet.

I'm sure it looks like this was all about me. But really, the poor woman had had enough for one night. The circles under her eyes looked as dark as newsprint smudges.

"You know," I coughed, "if you leave all your records stacked up like that, they'll warp."

"Though it pains me to take advice on vinyl from a millennial, you're right. Maybe tomorrow you can help me reorganize them."

"Yeah. Cool. Goodnight."

"Goodnight, Mattie."

I ran upstairs and checked LifeScape to make sure Meadow hadn't already spilled the misinformed beans about me and Will to the whole school. All was quiet on the digital front, but there was still time for the rumor mill to churn out something cringe-worthy.

"What were your parents like?" The Hummingbird's foster sister asked one night as the two of them were lying in their beds, both still awake and listening to the traffic outside.

"I've never met my dad. He was an art student."

"Yeah, that sounds about right."

"My mom was an escape artist."

"She took off a lot?"

"No, I mean she was literally an escape artist. She would get on stage and escape from straitjackets, chains, locks, handcuffs, aquariums . . .

The girl with the steely blue nails snorted. "You're full of shit, but you're funny, I'll give you that."

The Hummingbird and I both had a good laugh.

— *Akiko Miyake, Cranston, October 14, 2000*

Will With Two Ls Faces the Earsplitting Cacophony

After I dropped Mattie at her house so she could quell the impending 'rent-wrath, I figured I could spend the drive to Grayton contemplating how I could possibly explain what I'd done to the unsuspecting Bonnie to my Clyde.

But it was all for naught, because my phone rang before I'd even had a chance to drive ten blocks.

"Hey, babycakes," I purred, hoping against hope that she was calling for a little idle chitchat and still blissfully unaware of all the lies I'd ensnared her in.

"Don't you dare babycakes me, you dick," she screamed. "Are you fucking cheating on me?"

"Uhh . . ."

Two things should be noted at this point. One, even though Betsy had reinvented herself after junior high, for some reason I still expected her to react to the news from Meadow like a stereotypical tweenage drama queen. I had prepared myself for tearful hysterics, sniffly *woe-is-me*s, and long, cathartic love-hate notes penned in Betsy's loopy handwriting.

Instead, she let forth a string of curse words blue enough to make a sailor blush. I was so shocked I had to pull over my car or risk crashing into one of the little stone walls that run along the highway.

Two, for a moment, I actually considered telling Betsy I'd cheated on her with Mattie. I figured she'd hate me but she'd buy it, and I could go on keeping my secret from the populace.

But I owed Betsy (and Mattie) so much more than that.

"Can I come over?" I asked. The last thing I wanted to do was lay everything bare over the dry, icy landscape of a cell phone convo. Truly, that's not my style.

"You're joking, right? First off, it's two a.m. and my dad would have a shit fit. And if I see you in person right now I swear to god I will coldcock you."

"Fine," I sighed. "Where are you? Are you sitting down?"

"I'm in the basement so my dad can't hear me screaming my head off at you. And don't tell me to sit down. If I want to stand, then I'm gonna stand. Now stop stalling because I want all the shameful details. How did it start? Do you guys have a class together?"

"What? Who?"

"Mattie, you assface!"

"Oh. Jeezus, Bets, hold up a sec. Though I am indeed a two-faced, lying asshole, I'm not cheating on you with Mattie."

"Is it that twiggy smart-bitch, then? Stella?"

I had to bite my lip to keep from giggling at that one. *Focus, man. This is serious.*

"No. Good lord, Betsy, no." I exhaled a deep breath. "Okay, I need to tell you something. I know you're pissed, and you're probably going to be even pissier after I tell you, but I need you to just give me a minute so I can actually tell you."

"Great," she deadpanned. "Get on with it then."

"I love you Betsy, I really do. You're just . . . you're the cat's meow, and you've transformed yourself into such an amazing person."

"Stop buttering me up and get to the freaking point, Will."

"Sorry. I love you, but not the way you want me to. Because . . . I'm gay."

Silence. And not a small silence, but a deep, practically uncrossable chasm of silence.

"Hello?" I asked after almost thirty nerve-wracking seconds had passed.

There was more screaming and more cursing. And, because buried religious impulses tend to surface when folks are scared and angry, she told me I was going to hell. Then the distinct timbre of shattering glass echoed through the phone.

"Hello?" I asked again before realizing she'd hung up on me.

Honestly, I don't even remember driving home. But I must've because I opened the Lincoln's door to find Stella standing in my driveway.

"What happened to you guys?" she asked, though

she sounded more concerned than angry. "Where's Mattie?"

"Long story. Where's Frankie?"

She hooked her thumb toward her little jalopy. "Asleep in the back seat. Way past his bedtime. And my bedtime. I'm running on fumes. Everything okay?"

I realized the storm surge I'd felt the night I'd come out to Mattie had been a mere tempest in a teapot compared to the seismic tremor rumbling through me now. The tectonic plates of my life were buckling, slipping from their molten beds, free floating toward to-be-determined destinations. *Nothing is ever going to be the same.*

Stella has arms like a stick figure, but somehow she gives amazing hugs. Practically life-changing hugs. Before I could reply to her question, she saw the face of a boy confronted with a pile of crumbling lies and threw her arms around me.

There may have been some melodramatic sobbing and sniffling into Stella's cardigan sweater.

At some point, she coaxed me into the house, made me a cup of tea, and curled up on my parents' Italian leather sofa. By the grace of god, none of this woke my parents. If I'd had to face my mom at that point, I probably would have gone catatonic.

My phone rang as I took my first sip of Sleepytime Extra. I left Stella asleep on the couch and snuck out to the back deck before accepting the call.

"Hey," I answered with a shiver.

"I threw my phone through the basement window. Can you believe that? It woke my dad up so I had to come up with some story about how kids on bikes were throwing rocks at houses. Like some kind of preteen, gasoline-free biker gang."

I probably should have laughed at that, but given the circumstances it would have sounded so forced. "Betsy, I'm sorry. I don't know what else I can say."

She sighed. "What you did is beyond fucked up. You know that, right?"

"Yes."

"Did you know you were gay back when we first started dating?"

"Yes."

More silence. "Wow. Just, wow."

"I'm sorry."

"Why didn't you just tell me back in middle school? I probably would've been more than happy to be your beard back then. Secrets, lies, and drama. That was my bread and butter."

This time I did laugh. "I should've."

She sighed again. "I'm going to tell you two things, but they in no way excuse what you've done."

"Okay."

"I don't know if I could have gotten through my parents' divorce without you."

This brought on another bout of tears, though I managed to keep the sobbing inaudible.

"Also, and this is going to sound dumb, you probably saved me from four years of dating jerkweeds like Ryder."

This brought on more laughter and more tears and a little bonding over our mutual disdain for jovial, socially-oblivious cads who think they can do no wrong.

"Was it just awful for you when we fooled around?"

"No."

"Did you hook up with any guys while we were together? Wait, don't answer that."

But I did answer. And I answered a lot of other questions. Over the course of an hour, I came clean about everything I'd hidden from her. When we finally said goodbye, a few tentacles of early morning sunlight were poking through the trees behind the house, but I knew I wouldn't be able to sleep. Instead, I shivered in a deck chair and thought about what my life was going to look like from this pivotal moment on.

In the grand, relative scheme of things, Mattie and I are going to be okay. We're going to go to Bristol and get all liberal-artsy, and we're going to graduate even though Mattie will fail two required science courses, and my twentieth birthday will throw me into a raging quarter-life crisis. Stupid boys are going to break our hearts, and we're going to break the hearts of stupid boys. And we're going to stay friends even after rooming together for two years and then realizing we aren't built to fight with each other over stuff like laundry piling up on the floor and someone's initial-labeled yogurts mysteriously disappearing from the minifridge.

But in the wee hours of that morning, I couldn't see that far ahead. All I could think about was Meadow outing me on Monday morning.

"Hey." Frankie, all sleepy-tousled-hair and wrinkled clothes, climbed up the steps of the back deck and saved me from hours of wallowing in *shoulda-coulda-wouldas* and *what-ifs*.

"Hey."

"I fell asleep in the car."

"Yeah," I said with a laugh. "I know."

"I'm starving but all I could find in Stella's car was a few granola bars. You want one?"

"Sure."

The granola bars tasted like dry almonds and cardboard and had probably been sitting in Stella's glovebox for a year, but we enjoyed them anyway as we watched the sun come up and dry the dew on the grass.

The cab pulled up to my house in Grayton at ten a.m. The court-appointed trustees clearly had neglected to hire someone to mow the lawn for at least a month. Weeds climbed skyward out of the stone walkway and a pile of junk mail lay on the porch. I shuddered to think of the layers of dust that had probably collected inside, all over my antique dining room table and the crystal chandeliers I'd spent a small fortune on.

The Hummingbird stepped out of the cab and paid the driver before hoisting her suitcase out of the trunk. As the cab pulled away, she stood at the end of the stone walkway and smiled. It was the first genuine smile I'd seen from her in a long while. She didn't seem the least bit bothered by the tall grass.

She spoke aloud, though I wasn't sure if she was talking to me or to herself. "Now that I'm home, I'm never, ever leaving again."

– Akiko Miyake, Grayton, November 15, 2000

Mattie, Messages, and Microfiche

"Of all people, why Meadow?" Stella asked as we drove to school on Monday morning.

My hyperventilating lungs couldn't get a grip, and I could feel my heart rattling against my ribcage. The symptoms of my dread only served to remind me I had something to worry about, which made me worry even more, like a sick feedback loop I couldn't seem to disrupt.

"I don't know," I whined. "You were at St. Joe's and hers was the first name that came to mind. Did you get in trouble?"

Stella shook her head. "I told my mom I was sleeping at Will's house because that's what I was doing."

I wanted to slap the haughty pout right off her face. "Wow. Lucky you. Not all of us have such progressive parents."

"Ginge, I know you're not really upset with *me*."

I rolled down the squeaky window, hoping the fresh air would dry the sheen of sweat on my forehead. "Ugh, you're right."

My limbs stiffened as Stella parked the car. I buried my face in my hands, fighting off heart palpitations. I couldn't stop my mind from playing out every worst case scenario that might result from Meadow thinking Will had cheated on Betsy with me. *People will know who you are. They will be looking at you. And judging you.* I pictured myself holed up in a ladies' room stall, staring at all the nasty graffiti scribbled on the back of the door. I pictured roughly a gazillion snarky comments on LifeScape, all directed at me.

Stella reached over and unbuckled my seatbelt for me. "I know you're freaking out, but being late isn't going to make it better. And Meadow's more mature than she was in middle school. Maybe she'll surprise you. If you had a boyfriend and I mistakenly assumed he was cheating on you, I wouldn't start rumors."

"You are not Meadow, Stella. And she promised fallout."

She gripped the steering wheel with her bone-white fingers. "That's all the pep talk I've got in me this morning, Ginge. Please get out of the car."

I took a deep breath and opened the door. One foot at a time, I hoisted myself out of the safety of Stella's Volkswagen and shuffled up the steps and through the double doors. Those hallways lined with lockers wrapped around me tighter than a straitjacket, squeezing the sanity out of me, only I couldn't free myself with calculated shimmies and elbow grease. My back ached and I realized my shoulders had been stuck in tense little knots all morning. I tried to shake them loose as I opened my locker and pulled out my books for Liam's class.

"See?" Stella said. "No one's giving you the stink-eye. Even if Meadow told them, maybe they're just like, 'Who cares?'"

I slung my backpack over my shoulder and took a look around. The hallway full of students chatting, sipping coffee, typing on cell phones, and digging through lockers looked as it always did.

"Maybe you're right."

I closed my locker and turned around to find myself eye-to-eye with one of the basketball players who had a locker a few down from mine.

"Hey," he said with a smirk. "So . . . you and Will, huh? I have to admit I did *not* see that coming. I heard Betsy went pretty batshit. Are you guys gonna, like, have it out over him? You know, feline style?"

This was it. This was the moment I'd spent all morning dreading. The basketball player chewed on his upper lip, and I could only assume he was fantasizing about a Betsy vs. Mattie catfight that would never, ever happen. I waited for my adrenaline to surge and for my feet to carry me to the restroom on fear-based auto-pilot. But it didn't happen. A few butterflies flapped in circles around my stomach, but the paralyzing anguish I'd expected to engulf me never came.

The guy kept smirking at me, probably waiting for some kind of predictable, histrionic response.

"I'm sorry," I said. "I have literally nothing to say to you."

He squinted at me and then stalked off, muttering, "Bitches be trippin'."

Stella laughed, loud enough for the basketball player to hear. "Where did that come from?"

"No idea," I said.

Meadow gave me, Will, and even Stella the cold shoulder in homeroom, keeping her eyes and hands glued to her phone. No icy glance, no snort of derision, nothing. I couldn't blame her, really. I'd burn bridges to the ground if I thought someone hurt Stella. Hell, I'd do the same for Will, and probably Frankie, too.

Will and Stella chatted about Honors English, but Will gave an alarming number of one-word responses, like *yeah* and *nope*. And he kept gazing off into space, his face falling into a frown until Stella coaxed a fleeting smile out of him with a witty comment about Camus or Woolf. Saying the right thing in the right moment had never been my strong suit, and my mind drew a blank as I sat there, staring at the back of Meadow's head.

A discussion on wartime propaganda in my first period class with Liam succeeded in distracting me temporarily from Will's visible slide into mope-ville. The smelly kid and I were knee-deep in a heated argument about the significance of Rosie the Riveter when my phone buzzed in my pocket. And then buzzed again. And again.

As the conversation shifted to duck-and-cover cartoons, I slid my phone out and slipped it beneath a page in my notebook. Will had sent me a sob-fest.

> I'm a genuinely horrible person. First,
I screwed over Betsy. Now you've been

dragged into this whole mess.

>Stella told me Ryder came up to you and was like, "You and Will, huh?" If I wasn't such an inexcusable drip, I'd march into the locker room this afternoon and tell them what's what.

>But I am a drip.

Once again, I cursed the fact that I'd missed the era of innocent note passing by only a few decades. There was nothing I wanted to do more than pen a beautifully handwritten letter to Will full of inside jokes and quirky doodles and life-affirming words of encouragement. A lovingly crafted message in a bottle. Instead, I pulled my phone into my lap and settled for empty electrons.

>Oh my god, stop. Just stop. Yes, you lied. Yes, you made a mistake and Betsy got hurt. Everybody makes mistakes. And now you've come clean to her. You could have kept lying to her, but you didn't.

>And I don't care if people think the two of us are hooking up behind her back. You held my hand when I turned into a petrified, irrational mess. You protected my secret, I can protect yours.

I said I didn't care if people thought the two of us we're sneaking around because I thought it would make him feel better. But as I pressed send, I realized I kinda-sorta meant it. Maybe it was because I could see the light at the end of the tunnel. Maybe it was because I'd found a better version of high school at Salone Postale.

Cianci Regional just didn't carry the weight it used to.

Will perked up by lunch, or at least stopped frowning into space and sending me tortured text messages.

"Thanks for holding my hand," he said before shoving a tater tot into his mouth.

A few fellow students gawked at us as we ate our lunch, though none of them said anything, at least not to our faces. I shuddered to think of the snarky noise that was undoubtedly flying around LifeScape. *Empty electrons*, I reminded myself. *Just ones and zeroes.*

After lunch, I headed to the library for my fifth period study hall, hoping to get started on an outline for my history project. As I rounded a corner by the science wing, I spotted Betsy leaning against her locker. I kept my gaze straight ahead and hoped she'd ignore me like Meadow did.

"Hey."

Oh fuck.

I thought about nodding and continuing on my merry way, but I couldn't be that dismissive. "Hey."

"I gotta get out of here or I'm gonna lose it. Wanna come with me?" she asked. Her wispy blonde curls had lost some of their springiness, and the circles under her eyes looked darker than my mom's.

"Uhh . . ."

She snagged me by the elbow and dragged me toward a back exit. We cut across the courtyard to the parking lot. Sun glinted off the hood of her car as we piled in. She didn't bother to start it, so we just sat there, stewing in the heat. I cracked a window and surveyed the collection of beaded necklaces hanging from her rear view mirror. Each time a breeze snuck in through the cracked window, the beads would clack softly against each other. *Clack, clack. Clack, clack.*

Betsy cut the silence first. "I've never skipped class before."

"I did once, in middle school. I was supposed to give a presentation on Inuit tribes and panicked at the last minute. I took my sugar cube igloo and hid in a corner of the library, where the microfiche readers used to be."

"Sometimes I really miss microfiche. Using it always made me feel like a dogged reporter or something. Is that weird?"

"No."

Clack, clack. Clack, clack.

"I'm really sorry about what people are saying," she said.

I took a breath. *Empty electrons. Ones and zeros.* "It's not your fault Meadow's the vindictive master of the rumor mill."

She folded her hands in her lap, resting them on the dark denim of her jeans. "It wasn't Meadow. I asked Meadow not to say anything because I didn't want her to feel like an ass if the truth finally came out."

"So . . . it was you? Why?"

She chewed the pink gloss off her bottom lip. "I can't keep up the charade, and I knew people were going to ask questions. It was the only way I could think of to protect him."

"Oh." *Clack, clack. Clack, clack.*

"We talked for a long time last night. I knew he wasn't ready to come out. No one should be forced out of the closet. Meadow always told me I coddled him, giving him space when he needed it and never telling him how mad I was if he blew me off. I guess I'm still doing it." She laughed one of those pinched laughs that sticks in your throat when you're trying not to cry.

I recalled sitting in Stella's Bug with Will, thinking the little world I'd eked out for myself was about to fall apart. Cianci Regional might not carry the weight it once did, but if Will had exposed me then, I would have crumbled into jagged little pieces that refused to go back together.

"And, as we've discussed, my secret never threatened to knock me down the ladder of privilege."

"You did the right thing, Betsy."

"You really think so?" She fiddled with her keys, jingling them in the ignition. "Aren't you pissed I named you? I could have said it was anyone."

"Anyone else you named would have denied it. You know I won't."

She nodded. "I had a feeling."

"So . . . on a scale of one to nuclear, how mad are you about the whole thing?"

She coughed into her fist. "Nuclear would be a hideous understatement. I know this is sick, but I honestly wanted to strangle him through the phone. The last time I wanted to strangle someone through the phone was when my mom called from a motel to tell me she was leaving my dad for another man."

I smiled. "It's not sick, it's great. I can't tell you what a relief it is to know that nice people like you still get that pissed about stuff."

Betsy let out a weak laugh as she wiped her tears in that awkward, open-mouthed way girls do when they're trying not to smudge their mascara. "Isn't it awful that he's going to get less flak for cheating on me than he would for coming out?"

I sucked my lips into my mouth. "Yup. But I've known for a long time that good-looking boys who play sports and get good grades can get away with murder. You know, as long as no one knows they're gay."

"I still wonder if he'd be better off getting it over with." She sniffled and I wished I had a tissue to hand her. "Hiding a part of himself can't be easy, you know?"

Clack, clack. Clack, clack. "The night before our first day of freshman year, I was a wreck," I confessed. "Couldn't sleep. Kept getting up to pace around my room. My dad came in and said, 'Relax, Mattiekins. Just be yourself.' I love my dad, and he's a smart guy and always means well. But in that moment I . . . I just wanted to claw his eyes out. One, because he tried to comfort me with a pathetic platitude. And two, because it's so much more complicated than that."

Betsy laughed—a real laugh this time, not a precursor to crying—and tucked a wisp of blonde hair behind her ear. "I think I get it now."

"Get what?"

"Why Will could talk to you the way he did. I feel like I could tell you anything right now."

I smiled, and watched the breeze blow around a few pieces of litter that had escaped the trash bin.

"You can't stay in here forever," I told her.

But apparently that wasn't true. The wonders of the modern world, with email and online banking and groceries delivered to your door, made it possible to imprison yourself in your own home indefinitely.

There was an insidious side to it, too, like scaling a cliff. The farther up you went, the harder it was to climb back down without falling. Sometimes, I'd watch her stand on the threshold, trying to force her feet forward, stuck in some kind of emotional quicksand.

— *Akiko Miyake, Grayton, April 7, 2004*

Mattie in the City of Weird and Wonderful

It took roughly three days for the hoopla over me and Will to die down at Cianci Regional. Not that there was a whole lot of hoopla outside the basketball team and Betsy's little posse of pretty people, but after a big, old-fashioned fist fight broke out at a football game, and a bunch of people got suspended, Will and I were old news.

But that doesn't mean he was left unscathed. Each time we ran into Ryder, he very helpfully reminded Will that Betsy was a wreck. Then, because Ryder is gross, he would grin at Will and wink at me and go, "But it was worth it, right?"

Betsy maintained radio silence for almost a full month. Then she texted Will out of the blue the day after Thanksgiving to tell him she had some of his stuff and would toss it if he didn't want it. I rode over to her house with him, for moral support. They shared a silent hug, and he didn't even look through the box of stuff until we got back to my house. When he pulled out a copy of an old VHS tape, he burst into tears. The cover had David Bowie with some kind of fashion-mullet that defies explanation. But I didn't pry. Some things, like rock icons with terrifying hair, are best left between Will and Betsy.

When Stella came over later that weekend, she found Will lying facedown on my bed, groaning into a pillow.

"Will, you need to get back into a routine," she said. "What would you normally do on Sunday?"

"Go to brunch with Betsy," he said, though it came out all muffled by the pillow.

"Then let's go to brunch," I said.

So brunch became our Sunday thing. On the third Sunday, Will smiled at me from across a table that looked out over Wickenden Street.

"I have something to tell you, and I want to tell you before it turns into a thing."

"Please let it not be that you're actually straight and all of this was a clever ruse to become friends with me."

He laughed. "No, though that would've been impressive."

"Okay then, what?"

"I've been hanging out with a guy. And I don't mean shooting hoops and giving each other man-hugs. He's more than a friend. And you know him."

I almost choked on a home fry. "Really!? Who? Don't you dare hold out on me."

"Austin."

Who do we know named Austin? I know it sounds

ridiculous, but that actual thought ran through my head. "Oh. Is he that red-haired kid in your Honors English class?"

Will blinked at my ignorance and cracked up. "Mattie, no. Austin. As in your brother's friend, Austin."

"AUSTIN?" This simply did not compute. "But . . . that's . . . How did you two even meet?"

"At Salone Postale, obviously."

"Oh."

He exhaled a deep breath. "Are you mad?"

"Mad?"

Honestly, I was too shocked to feel anything. But then a bittersweet little memory from middle school swam up from the depths of my mind. I'd fallen off my bike and the concrete tore into my knees and right elbow, caking them with dirt and blood. I still remember how much it stung. My brother, who'd just gotten his driver's license, stopped only so he and Connor could laugh at me as I sat on the side of the road, choking back tears. Instead of joining them, Austin climbed out of the back seat and helped me up. When Kyle and Connor sped off, still laughing, he walked with me all the way back to my house.

"Of course I'm not mad. I mean, shocking, but kind of amazing."

"Phew," Will sighed.

"Does he make you happy?"

Will grinned as a blush crept into his cheeks. I don't want to take all the credit for this, but come on. If I hadn't taken a chance on myself, if I hadn't shown up on Miyu's porch that morning and refused to leave, Will and Austin probably never would've met.

"Does my brother know?" I asked.

"No. Not yet."

———

"Brilliant as always," Liam said as he handed back my history paper. "Dare I ask how you got ahold of your source material?"

For a second, I considered telling him about Miyu. But I figured one question would lead to another and soon enough I'd be lying to cover my tracks. "A lady historian never tells," I replied.

He shook his head. "I'm going to miss you next year, Mattie McKenna."

I glanced through Liam's notes on my paper as two of my classmates got into a politically charged discussion on the invisibility of women in American History textbooks.

"But they weren't doing anything important at the time," the smelly kid argued.

The girl with the earbuds and I both glared at him. "That depends on how you define important," I said. "They still have stories."

Earbud-girl, who'd been growing on me on a daily basis, laid into him with a surprisingly articulate diatribe on the power of patriarchy. My mom would have loved this conversation and that it was happening in a public high school. But as much as I wanted to participate, today happened to be December third, the anniversary of Akiko Miyake's death by plane crash, and I had important business to take care of.

I discreetly pulled out my phone and texted Frankie:

>Hi. I need your help with something today.

>Salutations. How can I be of service, m'lady?

>Sixteen years ago today, Miyu's mom died. I'd like to do something nice for her. I know she doesn't like to leave the house, but it might be good for her to visit her mom's grave, you know? Like, put some flowers on it or something. Does that sound weird?

>She'll never go for it.

>I know. Maybe we can talk her into getting coffee and then swing by Swan Point before she has a chance to argue about it.

>Swan Point? I have an idea.

>Thank god. I'll borrow Stella's Bug and we'll head there after school.

>Roger that.

After school, Frankie and I found Miyu sipping tea at the dining room table, wearing her forever-disgruntled expression like today was any other day. "You come in without knocking now?" she barked.

"Frankie's the one who opened the door," I argued.

"Cub Scout has privileges. I still expect you to knock. What do you want?"

"Ugh, whatever. So . . . we're here because . . . um . . ."

"We're going to pay our respects to H. P. Lovecraft's grave at Swan Point Cemetery," Frankie chimed in.

"You should join us."

Miyu stared out the window, tapping her fingers on the table. "I suppose I owe him that."

She got up and put on her coat, then, as usual, got stuck on the porch. "If you make it to the car in the next ten seconds, I'll stop at Greene Beans to pick up a latte for you," I said, trying to coax her onto the stone path.

"Fine," she barked. "But I want a shot of espresso, too."

"Done."

She scuffed her boots all the way to the passenger seat and called the drive-thru barista a useless clodpole when he got her order wrong. He flipped her the bird as we drove away, though she didn't seem to care now that she had the latte of her dreams.

A light snow began to fall as we drove into Swan Point Cemetery. I'd been expecting a hillside of tasteful plots. Swan Point was more like a silent city of the dead. Frankie pulled out the map he'd printed off, but we still got lost in the maze of winding roads and endless marble monuments.

Miyu huffed from the passenger seat. "For fuck's sake, Girl Scout. Take a right onto Pond Ave."

I hooked a right and parked the car by a stone fountain. Frankie led us to the Phillips family plot and the three of us huddled around H. P.'s modest headstone, shivering in the chilly twilight air.

"I AM PROVIDENCE," I said, reading aloud the quote on the headstone. "That's quite a proclamation."

"This city is full of weird," Frankie said.

Six months ago, I never would have even considered staying in Rhode Island for college. But now I knew the truth. Providence was full of weird. Weird and wonderful.

"Must be the johnnycakes," Miyu mumbled.

Just as Frankie and I had hoped, she shuffled away, but not back toward the car.

Frankie nodded at me, zipped his coat up over his face, and trailed after her.

A brisk wind swept over us, rattling the dead leaves and sending them swirling into the air. As we walked, a thirty-second news clip I'd watched at least a thousand times on YouTube sped through my mind. A dark haired thirty-something in a suit stood in front of Akiko's decaying lawn in Grayton. *We've just learned that Akiko Miyake, a resident of Grayton and a world-renowned escape artist, was among the victims of the December 3rd crash outside Houston, Texas* . . . I got antsy every time I watched it. His description of her— which included only her domicile and her occupation— seemed so reductive. *You don't even know her*, I wanted to scream. *She was so much more than that.*

I drew in a deep breath, letting the cool air chill my lungs. "I can't believe it worked."

He nodded and blew on his cold hands. "Sometimes you just need a detour."

Up ahead, Miyu took a left, weaving through a knot of headstones and stopping by a modest monument of pink granite.

"Should we give her a minute?"

Frankie nodded.

After a few minutes of respectful silence ticked by,

we made our way toward Akiko's final resting place.

Miyu blew her nose into a cotton hanky as we approached. "God dammit, Girl Scout."

Akiko's headstone bore her name, a small engraving of a hummingbird flapping its wings, and a single quote. *I love you, Hachidori.* No grand gesture, no pompous words of wisdom, just a simple and direct *I love you.* The unabashed lack of irony and artistic posturing took me aback. Miyu may have written the diary as a way to turn her oft-mythologized mom into something she could hold onto, but Akiko had used her final gesture to do the same thing. Like good old H. P., she could've turned her headstone into a soapbox to remind the world how larger-than-life she was. Instead, she used it to say something directly to the person she loved most in the world.

Frankie handed Miyu a fresh tissue.

"Thanks, Cub Scout."

Akiko may have reserved her last words solely for her daughter, but there were a lot of things I wanted to say to her. Saying them aloud didn't seem right, as if the sound itself would render them meaningless. I said them inside my head, kind of like the inverse of my desperate, drunken rooftop prayer.

Dear Akiko. There's no way I can possibly pay back the debt I owe to you and The Hummingbird. Thank you for allowing me to draw strength from your story, to use it as a platform from which to jump. If I ever have the opportunity to pay it forward, I'll do my best to see it through.

"I'm hungry," Miyu barked. "Let's get Thai food."

We returned to the lingering warmth of Stella's car, and drove through the cemetery gates as the first star of the night pierced the Rhode Island sky.

Acknowledgments

I've heard countless times that writing the acknowledgments is harder than writing the book. Turns out it's at least half true, if only because words alone don't seem like enough when you want to thank all the people who helped you turn a bunch of nutty ideas into a book. Pretty sure I owe everyone mentioned here a pizza party with bouncy houses at the very least.

Let's start with my agent and fellow recovering lawyer, Jennifer Chen Tran. Jen, thank you for seeing potential in Mattie and me. Thank you for taking a chance on me, and for not giving up on this book when the going got tough. Thank you for helping me turn this book into what it is. Thank you for always "getting it" and then telling me "it" could be even better. You are a rock star.

Thank you to the team at Amberjack Publishing, especially Dayna Anderson and Kayla Church for being the most important fangirls of all. I knew my book-baby would be in good hands with the two of you. Thank you to my fabulous editor, Jenny Miller, for all the spot-on editorial insights and for tolerating a few of my writer-diva moments. And for siding with me in the great "I heart you" vs. "I <3 you" debate (yes, I remember these things). To publicist extraordinaire Keara Donick, thank you for getting my name and my book in all the right places. I'm almost positive that, somewhere along the line, you promised someone your first born to make that happen.

To the illustrious Troy H. Gardner . . . there aren't really words, man. Thank you for being my longtime BFF, for being the first person ever to read this book, and for helping me make it better. Thank you for always being a kindred spirit and for sharing your awe-inspiring creativity with me. And thank you for keeping me on my toes with your ridiculous productivity.

To my very dear writer-buddy and critique partner TE Carter, thank you for being you. Thank you for helping me clean up this book when it was a big ol' mess and for also telling me it was a book that stuck with you. Thank you for the countless email and text chats and for being my sounding board through this whole process. Your talent is mind blowing. You are the bee's knees girl, and don't you forget it.

To Tracy Uhrin and Vinny Negron, I'm so glad I met you two weirdos. Thanks for making life fun and for NaNo-ing with me. Thanks for reading my book and telling me it didn't suck. I want you to know that, someday, when we're real grownups (like ninety or some-thing), I hope we're still hanging out in our NaNo-cabin, making snarky comments about New Adult books and listening to Vinny's typewriter go clack-clack-clack.

To Marlene Kaplan, thanks for being an amazing, supportive friend and for reading this mess when it was still just, like, 10k words in a Word doc. You've always had my back and I can't thank you enough for that. Here's to many more nights of chatting about writing and politics over craft beer.

To Roberta of Offbeat YA, my one-woman street

acknowledgments

team—I can't tell you how glad I am that I stumbled on your blog and emailed you. Your seemingly-limitless support for me and my writing is a treasure. So many times I've said, *Ugh, what am I doing? No one will read this...*, and then thought, *Oh, but Roberta will.* That alone gave me the strength to keep going. I know it's completely inappropriate to call a book blogger my friend but...yup, here I go. Thanks for being my friend. I hope we get to meet IRL someday.

Thank you to pro-editor Tanya Gold for all the encouragement and for the crucial insights that helped me see this book in a much-needed new light. Also, thank you for the kitty cat point marker stickies. You are adorable.

Many thanks to Steph and Danny at Amethyst Magic for responding to my random request on Twitter, for vetting a number of pivotal scenes in this book, and for clueing me in to things like suspension training and lung expanders. (Yes, that's right. Two actual escapologists helped out with this book. You should really go check out their website, amethystmagic.com.)

Many thanks to beta readers Scott Boyer, Erin Rhew, s.e. smith, and Josh Winning for giving me hope and, comment by comment, helping to shape this book.

Thank you to the many friends who have supported my writing and sad attempts at social media promotion since WAY back in the day, especially Mandy Christensen, Adria Brown King, Tyler King, Chuck Rissala, Malak Saddy, Alicia Thyne, and Dorothy Spencer.

Okay, family time. Thank you to the Tosh Clan, especially Helen, Laura, and Debbie for reading my writing and for telling me I could make this book thing happen. I never did mail my manuscript to Steven Spielberg but maybe someday.

To Marilyn, thank you for ALWAYS being my cheerleader, even before I picked up a laptop and started writing. And to Tim, thank you for your support and practical advice on writing professionally, including when it is appropriate to use "nauseated" instead of "nauseous."

To the Erkkila crew (Susie, Kris, Kath, Zola, and PJ), thanks for always being there and never asking for a big showy thank you. You guys are my rocks and you are all smart and hilarious. I probably don't tell you that often enough. And PJ, if I sell a gazillion copies of this book, I promise to always have a giant bowl of candy waiting for you.

To Linda "Aunt Lindy" Cutler, thank you for always being there and ensuring that I learned to love books at an early age. Your twin never throws anything away, so I still have all the Breakthrough and Mr. Men/Little Miss books, and will pass them on to The Goobess in the near future.

To my bro, thank you for being one of the coolest people I know and for never seeming to care that I'm not one of the cool kids. And thanks for all the podcast recs. Good stories help keep my writer-skills sharp.

To my parents, thank you for being awesome parents. There's a reason why all of the parents in this book are awesome—I don't really know how to write sucky ones. You are both amazing. Thank you for supporting me, no matter how weird my wants, needs, and dreams. You are two of the best people I know.

To Jerry and The Goobess, you are my two favorite people. Jerry, I couldn't ask for a better partner in life. Thank you for not just tolerating but actively supporting my hobby that is more than just a hobby. I absolutely could not have done this without you. Your love and patience are infinite. And RoRo—maybe when you are an angsty teen, this book will make sense to you. When that time comes, I promise to try and remember what it was like to be an angsty teen.

About the Author

Erin Callahan grew up by a small glacial lake in New Hampshire and, after brief stints in Colorado and Rhode Island, she settled back in the Granite State with her husband and daughter. As a small child, she told her mother she'd defaced a wall with crayons because she'd been possessed by an imp. She's convinced that same imp drives her to write. When she's not at her day job or cranking out novels on her laptop, you can find her soaking in the new golden era of television, stalking her favorite musicians on Twitter, and trying not to embarrass herself on the volleyball court. She loves giant squids and the color red, hates the phrase "no offense," and thinks birds are creepy.

Once upon a time, she was a lawyer but found herself unemployed at the height of the recession. For her own sanity she started writing, and to make ends meet she took a job at a residential program for teens. The kids she met there will forever serve as a well of inspiration for the contemporary YA she writes.